Mrs Bambi Knows

Mrs Bambi Knows

Chris Mason

Chapter One: Pigs Wings

From the Hood River [Oregon] Examiner
Friday, May 12, 1995

~~ Mrs. Bambi Knows ~~

Terrorized by generosity

Dear Mrs. Bambi:

I hate my husband. My soon-to-be ex-husband, I mean. I gave up a great career for this bozo, I moved all the way across the country to be with him, I left my family and my friends behind. What did he ever do for me?

Okay, he did give me this great house to live in, and a little red convertible to drive. He's sweet and kind and reasonably good looking. He makes enough money that I don't need to work. We have someone clean the house every week. And he does the grocery shopping and cooks all the meals. But what good is the lazy S.O.B.?

Just because I like to go shopping now and then, every other day or so, and I don't really see why I should go back to work, since he makes so much money, and I have to keep up with my seven favorite soap operas—he says I've changed. He says we're not compatible, and the marriage was a mistake, and I need to move out. How does he know we're not compatible? I've only been out here for two miserable years.

He offered me a big chunk of cash to get started again, but I say, the heck with that. I want more, mister. Give me half or I'll get nasty. My friends tell me I'm being stupid, I should just take what he's offering and run, but I think I've earned a lot more. What do you think?

—Exploited

1

Dear Pigface:

Oh no, by all means, take him for all he's got. After the huge sacrifices and hardships you've endured, my dear, you deserve everything you can get. No punishment is too severe for a monster like him.

Spurn his generous offer. Take him to court and charge him with brutal generosity and the emotional battery of kindness. And when the judge says you've already got more than you deserve and sends you off, penniless, with everyone in town laughing, just remember as you slink away that you could have been an adult about this and parted well off and friends.

By the way, what's this fiend's phone number?

Dear Mrs. Bambi:

What's the safest way to get a red wine stain out of a silk blouse? My boyfriend bought me this blouse and it means a lot to me.

—*Stained*

Dear Blotch:

Either dye it red or get him to buy you a new one. What do I know about silk? I'm a spandex and fleece kind of girl.

* * *

Richard Lantz picked up the first package of Twinkies he'd touched since childhood. Turned half away from the two women at the Quik Mart coffee machine, he pretended to read the ingredients.

'Can you believe that bitch?' the tall redhead demanded.

'Who?' Her companion was a thick-set brunette.

'Mrs. Bambi, who else? In today's paper? Elsie was so mad her eyeballs were steaming. I thought she'd have a stroke.'

'Was that really how it happened?'

'You're missing the point... Actually, I don't know if that's what happened, but that doesn't matter. She has no right.'

2

'I'm sorry? Who—' The brunette tore open a package of Sweet 'n Low and immediately dropped it on the floor. She looked around as if desperate for a Dustbuster.

'Someone ought to pull out her eyelashes with pliers. God knows, Elsie would volunteer after being Bambied like that.'

'Bambied?'

'You don't get it, do you?' Red said. 'Elsie didn't write that letter.'

'But...'

'No one writes the letters. Bambi eavesdrops on people having personal, private conversations and she writes the letters herself. She could be listening to us right now.'

'You mean she makes up the letters?'

'No, darling, she doesn't make them up.' Red set a plastic cover over her cup and whacked it tight. 'That would just be funny. You're not listening to me, are you? She's a vampire. She sucks our blood and uses it to write the letters we would write if we were crazy enough to ask advice from a harpy.'

'But her answers are funny.'

'Oh, grow up. I don't know why I bother talking to you.' Red flounced over to the counter, tossed some money down, and stormed through the door.

Richard grinned as he watched the confused brunette follow her outside. Bambied. He hadn't heard that one before.

He put the Twinkies back on the rack with the other poisons. The dark young girl behind the counter didn't so much as glance at him over her thick glasses as he paid for his gas. He was unexceptional, an average man in his mid-thirties, thin but not muscular. His receding hair was cut very short.

Once he had been annoyed that you couldn't pump your own gas in Oregon, but now he saw it as a blessing. The eavesdropping didn't get any better than this.

He got into his Subaru and headed into town. He had a date to meet A.M. at Pig's Wings.

*   *   *

The bar was a landmark in Hood River, an old house converted to a brewery and pub, perched like a cackling bird on a steep hillside looking down at the town. Stainless steel vats were visible through windows in the dark basement, gleaming ominously in the shadows.

Richard walked one flight up the outside steps, leaning on the rickety wooden railing, to the bar's entrance. The first floor had once been a restaurant but now seemed to be the employees' break room. Some of them were lounging in one of the wooden booths; they looked away as he came in as if afraid that he'd ask them for something. He trudged up another level and walked past stacked burlap bags of two-row malt into the pub.

There were still empty tables. When the live music started in an hour, it would get really crowded, but Richard expected to be gone by then. In a month or so the summer throng of windsurfers would make it impossible to find a place to stand, let alone sit, and he would be forced to go somewhere else for a drink.

His favorite table in the corner was empty, so he took a chair facing the entrance. Karen swung by, holding a tray of empties above her head, and he ordered a Boar's Rump Ale. Her ponytail swayed as she danced nimbly away toward the bar.

Pig's Wings was a small place, and he liked it that way. The bar area was tiled in white beehive hexagons, the words 'Pigs Wings' spelled out in black tiles just behind the stools. The rest of the loft was filled with small bistro tables like Richard's and longer ones that looked like workbenches, with raised sections in the center where people could put their food up out of the way of their drinks. Just to Richard's left, the elevated platform where the band would be playing was so high that tables were set below it. The musicians had to climb a wooden ladder to reach the stage, as if it were a huge bunk bed. Richard had yet to see how they managed to get their instruments up there.

Karen brought him his ale and vanished again. It was a dark Scottish brew; the first sip was reminiscent of coffee. One of the reasons Richard liked this place was that they only served what they brewed themselves, and their brew master was pretty good.

The bar began to fill up. There were a few locals and a lot of windsurfers, though the windsurfing season hadn't really started yet. Four young couples shared several pitchers of beer around one of the tables nearby. Most of them wore their fleece like a badge of rank: a vest or sweater, shorts or a headband. Two of the women on the far end of the table were trying to play

4

Scrabble while the short-haired men kibitzed, spilled beer, pounded the table in laughter, and ate burgers and fish-and-chips.

A.M. appeared at the far end of the bar. She waved at Richard and started weaving through the tables. Halfway across the floor she had to step over a child playing with Lion King plush toys in the aisle while its parents obliviously argued over their drinks.

Anamaria Mercado was short and dark, about ten years older than Richard, with an athletic but voluptuous figure. Her angular face might have been pretty if not for a prominent beak of a nose. Black hair in a loose braid hung so far down her back that she had to sweep it out of the way in order to sit down. She hung her purse on the back of the chair across from him and they grinned at each other for a moment.

'Beer!' she bellowed suddenly, startling him. Karen instantly appeared at her elbow. Gently: 'Beer, please.' Karen disappeared.

'You're looking good,' Richard said.

'Thanks.'

'Did you have to go to a funeral today?'

A.M. looked down at her clothes, black jeans and a deep blue sweater. 'What?'

'It's just so... somber. Compared to what you usually wear.'

'I was cold. Shut up.' Karen brought A.M.'s drink, a pale ale that was probably the Bristle Amber. A.M. raised her glass and they touched rims and sipped.

'New bracelet?' He leaned forward to study it. A stylized blunt-nosed crocodile, hand-worked in silver, wrapped around her right wrist.

'Yeah, I just got these in at the shop. Like it?'

'Is it Mayan?'

'Is the Pope white?'

Richard laughed and leaned in farther to see her earrings. They were done in the same style, loosely coiled golden serpents on a silver background, dangling from her lobes and brushing her shoulders. Each ear was pierced twice more, for a ruby stud and a diamond.

'Did you see the paper today?' A.M. said.

'Not yet.'

'Bambi Nose whacked someone I know.'

'Really?' Richard wasn't really in the mood to talk about Mrs. Bambi, but there was no way to stop A.M. once she got going.

'Yeah. Elsie Navarro, she's a customer.'

'You have customers?'

'Yes, smart guy, I have customers.' She sipped her ale. 'Just not very damned many of them. Now that I think of it, though, she never actually spent any money in the shop.'

'Then how can you call her a customer?'

'Her husband always paid.' Richard laughed. 'What's so funny?' A.M. said.

'If I could imagine anyone buying your clothes, A.M., it would have to be a guy buying it for a woman.'

'Why?'

Richard imagined the extremely short dresses, the revealing blouses, the unbuttonable vests. 'Forget it,' he said. 'How's the shop doing, anyway?'

'Financially or aesthetically?'

'Oh... Never mind.'

'Yeah. Anyway, Elsie came in this afternoon to see if I knew anything. She seemed to think that if anyone knew who Bambi Nose was, I would.'

'I heard a new one at the gas station,' Richard said. 'When Mrs. Bambi writes a column about you, you've been Bambied.'

'I've heard that one. You know, someday someone's going to figure out who she is. They'll find her naked body crucified on the clock tower. The police will be powerless in the face of overwhelming public satisfaction. It'll be the major unsolved case of the nineties.'

Time for a new subject. Before he could think of one, Karen came back and asked if they wanted refills. Both of them did. A.M. caught Richard watching Karen walk away, and turned to watch as well. The waitress's slim hips slung from side to side as she negotiated the obstacle course back to the bar.

'She's got a nice ass,' A.M. said. 'You should ask her out.'

'She's gay, dummy. You ask her out.'

'I know she's gay. And I can't ask her out, Sylvia would kill me.'

'How is Sylvia?'

'Horny all the time.'

6

'I don't want to hear it.' Richard fiddled nervously with his empty beer glass.

'Fine. You don't know what you're missing, though. Guys pay good money for smut that's a lot less exciting than my life.'

'I don't like smut,' Richard said.

'So why don't you ask her out?'

'Because she's gay.'

'So what? Just because you're an arrow and she's polar doesn't mean you can't have a good time.'

'Right. I'd just go home alone and horny. That would be a lot of fun.'

'You go home alone anyway,' she said, 'so what's the big deal?'

'What makes you think she'd go out with me, anyway?'

'I don't know, let's ask her.' Karen popped up with their beers.

'Wait a minute—'

'Hey, Karen,' A.M. said. 'Do you think Richard is good looking?'

Karen set the glasses down and stood back, cocking her head and examining Richard as if he were a new species of bug she was about to crush.

'Not especially,' she said. 'But I like him anyway. He's got the coolest daughter.'

'True. So, would you do him if you were straight?'

'Sure. If I weren't celibate.' Karen walked away and this time Richard didn't watch.

'She's celibate?' he said.

'Nah, she's just really, really picky.' A.M. sipped her beer and looked into the glass for a moment. 'You haven't heard anything about Bambi Nose, have you?'

'Me?' Richard said with more calm than he felt. 'Why would I hear anything?' She shrugged. 'A.M., you know I'm the least wired person in the whole damn valley. Teenagers become grandparents while I wait for anyone to tell me anything.'

'It was just a thought.'

He took a drink and noticed that his hand was steady. He knew that someday he would tell A.M. the truth about himself; he just hadn't found the right moment yet.

She said, 'What're you doing on your night off? Want to watch some videos with me and Sylvia?'

'Thanks, but I can't. Clarence asked me up to dinner. He's finally finished remodeling the living room.'

'You can't be serious. You're going to spend Friday night with a guy? A straight guy?'

'How is that worse than spending it drinking with you and your lesbian friends?' Actually, it probably would be a lot more interesting to watch videos with her and Sylvia. A.M. loved to rent weird movies and talk back to all the idiots in them.

'Because,' she said, 'we're a hell of a lot sexier than that scruffy Edison-wannabe.'

'Don't knock Edison. You wouldn't have a vibrator if it wasn't for him.'

'You don't know anything about my vibrator. Maybe it's AC.'

'Maybe you're not.'

'That was low. Shut up.' She sipped her ale. 'Where's Miriam?'

'Tiffannee's. Hey, you'll love this. This morning she said maybe I need two nights off every weekend so she can stay at Tiff's on Saturday too.'

'What'd you say?'

'I said I didn't deserve that much fun.'

'Ordinarily I'd agree with you. But even you could get lucky in here tonight. Come on, I'll pimp for you.'

'Jesus, A.M.!'

'Look around. Come on, pick yourself out a wench and I'll tell you if she's available.'

'Not interested,' he said. This was worse than hearing about her sex life.

'When was the last time you got laid, Richard?'

'None of your fucking business.'

'Oh, a pun. Ha ha.' A.M. leaned across the table. 'I've known you for seven years, Richard. I've seen you puke your liver out a dozen times, but I've never seen you take a woman home. It's time to let her go.'

'A.M....'

Rosalind wasn't the problem; he'd come to terms with her death years ago. Maybe he'd just lost the knack of talking to straight women. Something must have shown on his face, though, because her expression softened.

'Hey, Richard,' she said, 'I'm sorry. I shouldn't have said that.'

'It's okay.' He thought for a moment. 'Oh, what the hell. Go ahead.'

They looked around the bar together.

* * *

All the tables were full now and people—couples and hopeful singles—were crowding around the wainscoted edges of the room. It was a non-smoking bar, but the air wafting up to the cedar-ribbed, vaulted ceiling looked dense, like the air in the Gorge when the humidity was high: nearly opaque.

At the bar a dozen young jocks stood in a bellowing, shoving mass, blocking the waitresses and pissing off the bartender, a thick-necked man who glared at them and turned away in disgust. The kids at the group's periphery tried to elbow their way farther in, without success. For a fraction of a second the ebb and surge of the windsurfers gave Richard a peek into the center of the knot, and he saw his friend, Valerie Ridenour, grinning with her eyes half-closed, basking in testosterone as if it were sunshine.

A.M. said, 'I suppose you could give Val a try.'

'I'd have to get in line. She'll probably take three of those wind junkies home with her tonight.'

'I doubt it. I have it on good authority that she likes even numbers.'

'Yuck. That's an image I could've lived without.'

'Oh, just deal with it. Now let's see, who else is here?' She turned in her seat to look around the crowd. 'You know, there is too damned much marriage going on these days. Most of these women are hitched or bitched.'

'What do you mean, bitched?'

'Gay and involved, dummy.'

After a moment of searching faces, A.M. turned back in her seat and lifted her glass to drink.

'What,' Richard said, 'you're giving up?'

'It's hopeless. You're just going to have to let 'em hang tight.'

Richard felt irritated. For a moment he had hoped that A.M. could really introduce him to someone. He pointed at a very short woman with very large breasts standing by herself under the bandstand, beer in hand.

'What about her?'

'She's seeing a guy in Mosier, and those tits are fake.'

Richard looked around and spotted a cute, dark-skinned girl with tattooed arms and a stud in her nose, sitting alone at a small table. 'Her?'

'Dating a banker from Portland. Wait till he takes her home to mommy.'

9

A very tall woman standing aloof at the bar. She had a gaunt face and muscles: she looked as if she could lift the bar.

'Married,' A.M. said. 'Two kids. Can you believe that?'

'What about her?' Another solitary drinker, medium height, red hair, and a face that was all freckles.

'She's gay.'

'You know everyone in town and their entire sexual history, don't you?'

'Yeah. It's a hobby.'

'Okay, what about those three who just came in?'

A.M. turned to look. The women stood near the entrance to the loft with their heads together, probably discussing whether to fight the crowd or go somewhere else. The other two were cute, but the tall one caught his eye right away: she was unusually pretty, with long, tightly-curled brown hair.

'The one on the left is straight. I think she's screwing the mayor, but his wife hasn't found out yet. The one on the right is probably gay, but she hasn't come out. The middle one...' She turned back and picked up her glass again.

'What?' he said.

'She's single, and I think she's straight, but I've never heard of her dating around.'

'Wait a minute. You think? I thought you knew everything about everyone.'

'I know everything there is to know. If there's nothing to know, I don't know it.'

'Okay,' he said. 'What's her name?'

'Pamela Castle. She's a realtor.'

'Here in Hood River?'

'Yeah. And she's a true freak. Windsurfing, snowboarding, mountain biking, skiing, hiking, rock climbing, kayaking, the whole damn package.'

Richard felt his interest droop. Not another sporthead.

'What?' she said. 'You don't like sportos?' She turned back to look again. The three newcomers had decided to stay and were fighting their way toward the bar, where they eventually piled up at the logjam of Val's admirers. A few of the unsuccessful outer suitors turned toward the women and after a moment of conversation bought them drinks. Richard found the spectacle mildly depressing. How could he even imagine competing against these jocks?

10

'What's the difference?' he said.

'You worried about those wind-addict poster boys at the bar? Fuck them. If she wanted that she could have it any time, and like I told you, she doesn't date.'

'Right, she doesn't date, so she wouldn't date me.'

'She hasn't met you yet. Maybe you'll charm her right off her feet, if you know what I mean.'

Richard finished his beer and tossed some money on the table.

'You're not even going to try?' she said.

'Not tonight.'

'What a wuss. What a computer geek wimp. What a–'

'See you, A.M.,' he said, and stood up.

'That's it? You're leaving?'

'I'm going to be late for dinner with Clarence. I'll drop by the shop this week and you can call me some more names.'

'Okay, you coward.'

'Bye.'

He was halfway to the loft stairs when A.M. shouted after him, 'Hey, Richard, does Miriam know that her father is a total loser?' The bar was utterly silent for a moment. Then A.M.'s laughter kicked-started the hubbub again and Richard walked out, half-amused, half-embarrassed, with all eyes—especially, he feared, Pamela Castle's—watching him.

Chapter 2: Running Dogs

Row harder, eat your sprouts

Dear Mrs. Bambi:

I don't understand children these days. My grandson is so ungrateful, it just rubs me raw, after all I've done for him.

My daughter works two or three days a week and always has trouble finding a steady sitter, not to mention the cost, so I often watch her son for her. He's only four, but already I've taught him to weed the garden, scrub the floors, sweep out the garage, clean out the litter box, and many other useful life skills.

The other day his mom called him from work at her lunch break, as she often does, and I overheard the little ingrate saying that he doesn't want to stay with me any more. He said I'm mean, that I make him work all day long and force him to eat celery and Brussels sprouts.

Well, I never! All I'm trying to do is teach him the joy of hard work and a job well done, and to give him the nutrition that I know my daughter isn't providing.

Have you ever heard of such a spiteful child?

—Aghast

Dear Ghastly:

What an arrogant, ungrateful slave. Why don't you sell him?

Or, and this is just a wild thought, maybe you could mix in a little love and kindness, playfulness and fun in between the chores and the drudgery and the vegetables. What is this, Victorian England? Let him have a childhood.

Dear Mrs. Bambi:

You think you know everything, right? Try this.

If a spaceship travels away from Earth at 50% of the speed of light for one year of ship time, and then immediately returns at the same speed, how long has the ship been gone?

—Mr. Einstein

Dear Frizzy:

Do you think I don't know the Lorentz transformation? By ship's time, your travelers have been gone for two years. By our time, they've been gone 2.3094 years, or about two years and four months.

Don't mess with me, bub. I do know everything.

* * *

Clarence lived in Trout Lake, a farming hamlet about half an hour's drive into Washington. The center of town, little more than a crossroads, huddled at the foot of Mt. Adams, a volcano thirty-five miles away from Mt. St. Helens and a twin to her before she lost her temper in 1980. Despite its beauty and ample opportunities for outdoor fun, few people from Oregon ever visited the area; Hood River had its own volcano, Mt. Hood, and you didn't have to pay the bridge toll to get there.

Richard grudgingly paid his fifty-cent fare and drove across the grated bridge deck. A few windsurfers were out on the Columbia River below him, despite the cool weather and sporadic wind. He pulled off the bridge on the Washington side and drove along the river. The setting sun shining through the haze lit the stepped-back cliffs of the Gorge like a Chinese painting. Clusters of golden poppies and nameless blue wildflowers crowded the bluff to his right. A huge barge plowed up the dirty brown river to his left.

Following the White Salmon River away from the Gorge, Richard drove a winding road, past steep hillsides draped in chain mail to keep the glacier-rounded boulders from raining down and killing the tourists. When he reached the plateau above the Columbia he was in farmland. Cows and occasional sheep dotted the hills that rimmed the White Salmon's valley. The lowlands here were all in hay and orchards, greening in mid-spring, the hills covered in fir and pine except for ugly, bare grayish areas where the trees had been clear-cut.

After passing through several small towns that were worthy of notice only because the speed limit dropped below fifty-five, Richard drove into Douglas fir forest. A few minutes later the farms reasserted themselves, with llamas and bison and cattle. He turned off the main road and drove down a freshly-oiled side street, past vast fields of herbs with views of both Mt. Adams and Mt. Hood, over the White Salmon River again, and soon pulled into the driveway of Clarence's house.

The small, pale yellow farmhouse had once presided over hundreds of acres of dairy farm. Over the last century pieces of pasture had been broken off, bequeathed to children or sold to settle debts, eighty acres here, forty there, until all that was left was a few buildings and four acres of weeds. Richard parked in front of the pole barn that protected Clarence's vintage tractors. The house was dark so he walked toward the big cattle barn.

The cattle were decades gone. Clarence ran his mail-order company out of the old milking room, a corrugated steel addition to the original wooden structure. Richard pushed open the door, with its peeling white paint and windows opaque with dirt, and ducked below the metal-shaded light bulb that hung over the entrance.

'Clarence?'

The office was small, nearly filled by a desk, a bookshelf, and a work table. Clarence's new computer sat on the desk, surrounded by a temporary clearing that would soon be buried under catalogs, books, and papers, just like the rest of the room. Richard walked through a door into the older section of the barn.

The next room was somewhat larger than the office, dominated by a stained and burned workbench covered with machine parts, storage tins, and unfamiliar tools that looked like mutant wrenches. Everything was smothered in dust and cobwebs. Mysterious farm implements cluttered the rest of the space: an old compressor, an evil-looking contraption with long tines.

14

Richard stooped to pass through a low doorway into the stables. Only a dozen or so stalls survived. They must have been used for calves, or perhaps horses, because they were too small to hold full-grown cattle. The packed-earth floor was covered with dusty straw and mouse dung. He passed through a very large, open door into the main space of the barn.

His footsteps echoed in the cavernous space that was only partially filled by Clarence's inventory, most of which was stored in long rows of metal shelving and cabinets. The rough plank floor, sprinkler system, and bright lights were all new. The cleanliness and order made a bizarre contrast to the dirt and disuse of the rest of the barn, as if the portal from the stables led not just to another room but another time.

Clarence appeared from behind a tall cabinet, carrying an armful of stuff. He glanced up and spotted Richard walking toward him.

'You're late,' Clarence said. He set his load down on a low workbench.

'It was A.M.'s fault.' Richard watched as Clarence packed shrink-wrapped note pads, bookmarks, and a small desk lamp into a cardboard box, then stuffed the box with heavy-weight wrapping paper, tossed in an invoice, and efficiently taped it shut.

Clarence Hoskins was a few months past his fiftieth birthday. He looked older. His shoulders were stooped, his face lined and weathered, and his long, shaggy hair had gone completely gray. Dark-rimmed glasses slid down his nose. His gaunt body in blue jeans and an untucked flannel shirt would have made a fine scarecrow.

'How is the old dyke, anyway?' Clarence said.

'Same as always.'

'You hungry?'

'Uh huh.'

Richard followed Clarence back the way he'd come. When they got to the office, Clarence paused.

'You notice the new computer?' he said.

'Yeah. How's it working?'

'It's not. The damn printer won't print. You know what's going to happen now? I won't be able to do my invoices, I'll go out of business, and I'll starve.'

'Maybe I could take a look at it.'

Clarence blinked as if this were a radical idea. 'Thanks. I'll go start dinner.'

Richard sat down in front of the computer and started it up. While he waited for the stupid thing to boot, he said to himself, 'What do we do with Windows? Throw rocks through them, of course.'

It only took a few minutes to determine that Clarence had installed the wrong printer driver. Richard printed a test page and checked out the rest of the system; it looked fine. He shut it off and went outside. The sun had set below the hills to the west, but the sky was not yet dark. He joined Clarence on the deck and took the Corona he offered him.

'You find the problem?' Clarence said.

'Sure.' Richard swallowed some beer. 'The problem is you didn't buy a Macintosh.'

'Shit.' Clarence tossed a couple of marinated chicken breasts onto the grill. He must have started the charcoal before Richard arrived, because they sizzled immediately. 'I was sure I ordered a Mac.'

* * *

When they were almost done eating, Richard suddenly realized he hadn't seen Clarence's dog. 'Hey, where's Joe?'

Clarence avoided his eyes. 'He ran away.'

'You're kidding me. When?'

'Today.'

'What the hell happened?'

'I finished my dog wash last night.'

'Well, that's great.' Clarence didn't look very happy about it. 'Isn't it?'

'I tried it out this morning. It worked fine. Joe came out cleaner than, than...' Clarence set his plate down on the deck. 'Well. I let him out at lunchtime and he lit off down the road like he smelled one of his porcupines. And he never came back.'

'Aw, shit,' Richard said. 'You want to go drive around and look for him?'

'There's no point. He'll come back if he wants to. And anyway, I already did that. All afternoon long.'

* * *

Richard tried hard to like what Clarence had done to the living room, but he just couldn't. Room by room, Clarence had been going through the house,

16

restoring the old woodwork, replacing the windows and the peeling wallpaper, and buying new furniture. The result was charming, but to Richard's eye the place was slowly losing its soul. He looked around the room, with its floral walls, refinished hardwood floors, clear-stained trim, and elegant sofa and easy chair, and knew he was going to miss the ratty old, beat-up place where he and Clarence had spent so many evenings arguing, playing chess, and watching the scratchy picture on Clarence's battered old TV.

'Have a seat,' Clarence said, but Richard would rather have gone back outside, despite the deepening gloom and chill.

'It looks great,' he said. He sat on the couch. It wasn't as comfortable as it looked.

'I read your column,' Clarence said.

Richard sighed. 'Go ahead.'

'You are one mean bitch.'

'She deserved it. Everyone knows she's been spending his money like—
,

'I meant about the wine stain.'

'Oh.'

'Everyone knows you use white wine to get out red wine stains, dummy. You know what you need?'

'No.'

'You need a woman.'

'That's what A.M. was just telling me.'

Clarence nodded. 'She's a smart broad. How long has it been since your wife died?'

Richard hesitated. He knew to the day. 'Almost ten years.'

'That's too long to be alone.'

'You're alone.' Richard instantly felt like an ass.

Clarence stood up and looked out the window. Mt. Adams floated above the ridge like the ghost of a whale, lit by the moon. With his back to Richard, he said, 'How long can you keep this up?'

'What? Oh, you mean Mrs. Bambi?' Richard shrugged. Clarence couldn't have seen it, but he took it as an answer.

'You've been writing that column for what, three years?' He turned back to face him. 'What are your friends going to say when they find out the

17

nastiest bitch in town is their friend Richard? How's A.M. going to handle that, or Nadine, or Karen?'

'It didn't upset you when you figured it out.'

'I'm not a woman, Richard. The only people who know that you're Mrs. Bambi are me and that asshole Frank. You don't know how the women'll take it. But I can guarantee you—at the very least they'll be pissed.'

Richard leaned back and tried to get comfortable. The couch fabric was stiff and slightly scratchy. 'You're saying I should shut it down.'

'Yeah.'

'You know, there are days that I want to. I get tired of following people around Wal-Mart trying to stay in earshot. But sometimes the spy stuff is fun. And I don't mind writing the letters.'

'Not to mention answering the letters you just wrote.'

Richard grinned. 'That's the best part.'

Clarence leaned back against the window frame. 'What does Frank say?'

'He wants me to use real letters.'

'Well, why the hell don't you, then?'

'Because there are no real letters. All we get are anonymous obscene rants and Hints From Heloise questions.'

'That's because you're an obnoxious shrew. Who wants advice from the Wicked Witch?'

'I just tell them what they need to know.'

'Bullshit,' Clarence said. 'You've got a chip on your shoulder bigger than a block of granite. Someday someone's going to mistake it for your head and lop it off.'

Richard spread his hands in resignation.

Clarence shook his head. 'The hell with it. Chess or Gin?'

* * *

Richard was walking out to his car when he noticed a silvery box outside the mud room door. 'Is that the dog wash?'

'Yep. Let me show you how it works.'

The machine was constructed of galvanized ducting. You shoved the dog into the box and an automatic wash and rinse cycle—just like a drive-through car wash—took care of the rest. The machine nudged the victim into the

18

blow-drying module, and when the dog was dry it got a treat and the door into the house would open.

Richard had once made his living as an inventor, so he was impressed by the simplicity of the mechanism and the care that had gone into ensuring that the sprays didn't drown or blind the animal. What he couldn't figure out was why Joe hadn't bitten Clarence before he ran away.

'I just wanted to keep my new carpets clean,' Clarence said. 'You know how he loved playing in the irrigation ditch.'

Richard nodded. They said goodbye and he got into his car. As he drove back to the highway, he kept an eye out, trying to spot Clarence's dog. But he knew the truth. By now Joe was probably miles away, sitting at some kind stranger's feet with a full belly and his head on his paws as he watched TV. After one trip through the dog wash, Joe was never coming back.

Chapter 3: Seize the Cow

Love is worth the risk, dude

Dear Mrs. Bambi:

I have a big problem. I really like this girl, but she's a windsurfer, she only lives here in the summers. I've seen her around for the last three years, and I think she is the hottest chick that ever wiggled out of a wet suit. I mean, she melts the sidewalk when she struts by in her little shorts, T-shirt, and Birkenstocks.

The problem is, I live here, and she goes wherever for the rest of the year. I think I love this babe, but I can't just pack up and follow her like a little doggie, you know? I mean, I like to windsurf now and then, but she lives the life, and I don't know if I could hack that. And even if I could, I don't have the bucks to do the sail-and-ski circuit.

So, here's my question. She's leaving in a few weeks, and I've decided that this year I'm either going to bag her heart or erase my hard drive. But I don't know which. If I ask her out, she could blow me off, right? Or say we really hit it off, and she wants me as her main dude, it's still only going to be for the summer. Then she goes off to Vail or wherever and all these other sport-heads will be hitting on her. I don't know if I can handle that.

So, is the hassle worth it? I mean, is love worth the risk?
—Daredevil

Dear Gutless:

Don't be such a feeb. Love is always worth the risk. If you were a chick I'd say seize the bull by the horns—but forget carpe diem, dude, carpe vacca: seize the cow. Seize the cow by the udders! (That's just a figure of speech—don't go molesting the poor girl.)

Take a chance. If she says no, at least you'll be free of your doubts. But she may say yes, and even if you only have summers together, that's infinitely better than what you've had the last three years. You could have been melting the sidewalks together if only you'd written me sooner, you lunkhead.

Dear Mrs. Bambi:

I'm going away to college soon, and I was wondering: which dictionary is the best?

—*Studious*

Dear Bookworm:

'Best' is subjective. It's purely a matter of taste and what you're accustomed to.

Go to the reference section of a good bookstore. In each college dictionary they have, look up the definition of 'clueless.' Whichever one sounds the most like you, buy it.

* * *

It was refreshing to step outside on a sunny Saturday morning without the hangover that was always the price of evenings spent with A.M. Richard closed his front door behind him and, as usual, did not lock it.

The first half mile of his weekly walk to the grocery store was the only enjoyable part. The houses here had been built in the early part of the twentieth century, and most, like Richard's, had been renovated in the last decade. This part of Oak Street, unlike the commercial center of town four blocks away, still had many oak trees standing in the deep front yards. The young leaves seemed to glow of their own shimmering light as Richard walked west, away from downtown.

Thirteenth Street was the dividing line between the genteel old houses and a modern shopping district. This was the newest concentration of shops in Hood River, a mile-long row of Wal-Mart, Safeway, Payless, car and tire dealers, fast food places, and struggling, mostly awful local restaurants. There was an older strip on the Heights, the bluff above town, that had hoped in the sixties to become the new economic center of town. Richard believed that downtown Hood River would continue the economic renaissance begun a decade ago when the windsurfers had arrived, and that the future of this mass of concrete and junk food joints could be read in the run-down, low-rent Heights. But his friends just laughed, called him a curmudgeon, and continued driving to MacDonald's.

The Safeway had once been located downtown. The newer store here on the west end of town was bigger but it had no soul. It didn't even have a face. Richard walked through the automatic doors, grabbed a cart, and headed for the produce.

And stopped. The tall woman from the bar—Pamela Castle—was standing in a checkout lane halfway across the store. This was his chance. She was alone; he should introduce himself.

And say what? I saw you at the bar yesterday? How original.

No one was in line behind her. Richard felt an unusual surge of resolve. The hell with it: carpe vacca. He would just go up to her and say whatever came to mind. If it turned out to be something stupid, he could slink away to the ice cream aisle. He abandoned his cart and started walking toward her, but a young couple, pushing their cart together shoulder to shoulder with their arms intertwined, got in line behind Pamela and started unloading their groceries.

Now what? He could circle around to where the bagger was loading her stuff into paper bags. No, there was too much activity there—checker and bagger and cash register—it would be too distracting. Or he could wait by the exit and say hello as she walked by. No, he might look like a stalker, or even worse, a salesman. At best she'd just pass by with an aloof greeting.

While he dithered, Pamela gathered her bags and walked out the door.

Great. Terrific. Suave. Shit.

Richard recovered his cart and pushed it into the produce section. The Hood River daily circus was often on parade here in Safeway. He glanced at the other shoppers as he wandered up and down the rows of bins between the vegetable cooler and the fruit.

A skinny young woman leaned over the tomatillos, her long blonde hair sweeping the papery husks; the Calvin Klein logo on her boxer shorts was visible where her shirt had pulled up and her sweat pants drooped. Three Mexican men in dirty T-shirts and extremely worn, ripped jeans argued in Spanish about the bananas. A woman in late middle age pulled an empty cart past him without even glancing at the produce; her face was gaunt from dieting or illness. A boy of about four, no parent in sight, dodged through the bins to the candy display in the back corner and stood before it with one finger in his mouth, enraptured.

Richard never used a shopping list. He preferred to make meals based on the contents of his refrigerator instead of planning them ahead of time. So he wandered among the displays, choosing lemons, lettuce, carrots, eggplant, onions, shallots, and whatever else caught his eye. He left the produce area and was passing the fish counter when he heard a snippet of interesting conversation. He parked his cart and stood nearby, examining the sausages. Two women were huddled in front of the salmon steaks.

'They stole what?' one of them said. She was in her mid-fifties, with thick glasses and silvery hair tied back in a ponytail.

'The neighbor's pig,' said the other woman, a plump bleached blonde wearing brand-new red Keds. 'One of those midget Vietnamese pigs with the fat belly.'

'Why would they steal the neighbor's pig?'

'How should I know?' Keds said. 'First they stole the pig, then they took my car. I was at the chiropractor's, Robin Cordell, you know I've been having these strange pains in my lower   back. They walked the pig over to Robin's office —'

'How?'

'What do you mean how? On a leash! Suzie had my spare keys and they just drove away, Suzie and that boy and the pig.'

'Hmm,' Ponytail said. 'Is this the one with the spiky green hair?'

'No, that was the last one. This one has a buzzed top, long in the back. Where was I? Oh, after I came out of Robin's, I was feeling splendid until I saw that my car was gone. Just gone. That ruined my whole day. At first I thought I'd forgotten where I parked it, but then I remembered parking right across the street. I know because I stopped to look at the stupid wildflowers those idiots planted on the hill by the new parking lot.'

'Was that when you called the police?'

'Yes! They asked me a lot of questions, then they talked to the people who work at that surfboard shop next to Robin's. Hmmph. No one had seen a thing, of course. I swear those people are all on another planet half the time.'

'It's the drugs,' Ponytail said.

'Of course it's the drugs. Everyone knows that. So. Robin suggested I walk home. He said the exercise would be good for me, but after I did I felt worse. It's all uphill to my house, you know.'

'So what happened?'

'I ate a quart of ice— Oh, you mean... Well, the sheriff called that afternoon, and said they'd found my car. They caught Suzie and that horrid boy racing up and down country roads in Parkdale. He's been a terrible influence on Suzie. I'm very worried.'

'What were they doing in Parkdale?'

'They said the pig needed fresh air.'

A convulsive laugh exploded out of Richard's chest. He coughed several times and picked up a package of breakfast sausages to read the label. He was afraid to look to see if the women were staring at him.

'Did the sheriff throw him in jail?' Ponytail said.

'No, he let them go with a warning. He marched Suzie right up to my front door and handed me her keys. I was so embarrassed. I grounded her for a month, but she just laughed in my face and said she was eighteen, if I grounded her she would move out and go live with Phillip.'

'That's so cold. What makes children so hateful?'

'I don't know,' Keds said. 'I really can't imagine.'

*　*　*

At this time of year, Richard's yard looked different every morning. The crocuses were long gone, the daffodils were beginning their fade from butter to brown, the annuals were just starting to bloom, and the new oak leaves shivering in the breeze looked larger each day.

Richard's house was over eighty years old. It retained an air of dignity that newer houses could never quite manage, even though it had been remodeled twice before he gutted and rebuilt it ten years ago. White clapboards with gray trim framed an elegant façade, with a large front porch below a balcony off the turreted master bedroom. A garage had been added

24

decades after the house was built. Perhaps the owners of that time had been embarrassed about it; the garage was off at an angle, and a connecting breezeway kept it at a distance.

Juggling the grocery sacks he carried in his arms, Richard managed to prop open the screen door with one hip and fumble the door open. He carried the bags into the kitchen and didn't notice until he set them down that his daughter was sitting at the small table there, drawing with her colored pencils. She couldn't have been there long; her Friday night sitters all knew that Richard went shopping every Saturday morning, so they usually dropped her off right around the time he returned.

'Hey, thanks for helping with the door,' he said.

Miriam looked up at him with an innocent expression. A month shy of her tenth birthday, she was so thin she was nearly two-dimensional. Her wire-rim glasses had slipped down on her nubbin nose, making her look like an unwrinkled granny. Long hair, so black it had blue highlights, was tied back in a French braid fastened with a yellow ribbon. The braid was neat and tight; Tiff's mom must have done it.

'It's obvious you didn't need help, Dad,' she said.

'What?'

'Well, you managed, didn't you?'

He couldn't let her get away with that. 'Wait a minute. Suppose you were hiking in the mountains and you came to a cliff where a man was hanging by his fingertips. Would you stand by watching while he struggled, until he finally managed to find a handhold and pull himself up, and then say he obviously didn't need your help because he could save himself?'

Miriam had gone back to her drawing as he spoke. She continued coloring as she considered the problem for a moment. 'No,' she said.

'Okay. Lesson learned?'

'Sure, Dad.' She looked up again. 'If you're hanging from a cliff holding the groceries, I'll be sure to open the door.'

He grabbed the nearest vegetable, a zucchini, and tossed it at her. She bobbled but caught it and nonchalantly set it down beside her sketch pad.

'That's your lunch,' Richard said. 'I suppose you and Tiff had the usual orgy of junk food and cable TV?'

'No, we rented some videos.' She looked up again and smiled. 'And ate a lot of junk food.'

'That's it. Nothing but vegetables for you all week. Let's see here, I have cauliflower, eggplant, green beans, radishes, ouch.' He rubbed his head where her eraser had bounced off it. 'Nice throw.'

'Thank you.'

He started putting away the groceries. 'What are you working on?'

'Frogs.'

'Frogs?' He shut the refrigerator door and went to look at her drawing. She had covered several sheets with meticulous, colorful and childish but recognizable pictures of frogs, using a volume of his encyclopedia as reference. Tree frogs, poison dart frogs, bullfrogs, common frogs—one pair seemed to be copulating. 'What's this?' he said, pointing to the libertines.

'Leapfrog, Dad.'

'Oh.'

'What did you think it was?'

Think fast. 'Square dancing.'

'Frogs can't dance, you know.'

'Really? I didn't know that.' He went back to his groceries. 'What got you started on frogs?' Last week it had been kittens.

'Tiff was talking about the princess who kissed a frog. You know the one who was really a prince?' How could he possibly forget? It had been Miriam's favorite story when she was five. He'd had to read it to her every night, sometimes twice, before she would go to sleep.

'So,' Miriam said, 'I said ponds usually have lots of frogs, not just one. Did she kiss every one of them? Did all of them turn into princes? Maybe some of the real frogs just wanted kisses and pretended they were princes too, so she'd kiss them. Maybe by the time she found the real frog prince, she'd be all covered in slime and he wouldn't want her any more. Maybe she'd just decide the whole thing was too gross and go home and watch TV.'

She delivered this monologue while continuing her coloring. Richard shook his head. Where did she get this stuff?

'Dad,' she said, 'why don't we have a TV?'

'You know why.'

'If we had a TV, Tiff could sleep over here sometimes.'

'That's a good enough reason right there.'

'Dad!'

26

'Miriam, we're not getting a TV. Anyway, we don't need one. You get all the schlock you need over at Tiff's, and A.M.'s, and Nadine's.'

'But we could get one of those new satellite dishes, the small ones? Then we could get fifty channels of movies. Wouldn't that be cool?'

'Nope.'

'Dad!'

'Do you want to go to the park today?'

She glared at him for a moment before resuming her drawing. 'No,' she said in a hurt, childish voice that he knew was feigned. 'I need to go to the library. I'm running out of frogs.'

* * *

The moment they stepped inside the library door, Miriam ran off to find her frog books. Hood River's library was a small one, with several online catalogue terminals and a few computers hooked up to the Internet. The stacks ran around the edges of the main room, leaving the center to the computers and a few study tables. Richard browsed the biography section for a few minutes, chose three books about people he'd never heard of, and headed for a table to wait for Miriam.

Pamela Castle was sitting there with a yellow legal pad in front of her, surrounded by thick, open volumes. Her long, curly hair was tied back today. She was dressed up for work in a lacy white blouse.

A.M. had said she was a realtor. What could he think of to say to a realtor? Ah, nuts. Richard walked to her table and took the chair at the opposite corner. Pamela looked up at him briefly, smiled politely, and went back to her work. She was wearing a red skirt. He liked red. He opened one of his books and stared at it without reading.

He wasn't very good at this. A.M. was right, it was time for him to start dating again, but he didn't know how. He wasn't even sure how to start a conversation with Pamela, let alone ask her out. The last woman he'd asked out was Rosalind, and that was thirteen years ago. Unlucky number; maybe he should wait another year.

He knew some straight, single women, but not many. Most of his friends were women, but almost all of them were gay. That was A.M.'s fault: she kept introducing him at her parties as her linear but warped buddy, which seemed to amuse her lesbian guests. And, to be honest, all of his friends—including A.M. and Clarence—were people he'd met from his little consulting business, or people that those people had introduced him to. His acquaintances were also customers, or else parents of Miriam's friends.

He'd never once become friends with, let alone dated, someone he met at, say, a bar, or the checkout line at Safeway.

Miriam squeaked to a stop at his elbow. 'Hey, Dad, look what I found!' She dropped a thin book on the table in front of him. Glossy pages showed closeups of tropical rain forest frogs. One of them had skin the same shade as Pamela's skirt.

'Cool. Are you going to take it home?'

'Yeah, but I'm not done yet.' She bounced away.

'How old is she?' Pamela said.

He blinked at her in surprise. 'Nine. She'll be ten next month.'

'She has a lot of energy.'

'You should see her after she eats chocolate.' Pamela smiled and started to reach for one of the books in front of her. In desperation, he said, 'Do you have any kids?'

'Not yet. Maybe someday.'

'They're not as much trouble as people say. You just have to paper train them early on, give them treats when they roll over, and keep a short leash. You know.'

She frowned. 'Are you talking about kids or dogs?'

'One little critter is a lot like another.'

She laughed, confused. 'Well, you and your wife must be very proud. She seems like a very nice little girl.'

'Oh, um, thanks.'

She must have heard something in his voice. 'I'm sorry. Are you divorced?'

'No, um, her mother died. In childbirth.'

Pamela's face contorted in embarrassment and polite sympathy. 'I'm really sorry.'

'That's okay.'

'So... Then you've raised your daughter all by yourself?'

'Sort of. My friends help out a lot. They take her one evening every week to give me a night off. I spend the rest of the week undoing the spoiling she gets on Friday nights.'

'How do they spoil her?'

'Junk food. TV. Horseback rides.'

'But horseback rides aren't bad for her, are they?'

Richard got up and moved to the chair directly across the table from her. 'They are when she comes home wanting me to buy her a horse.'

'So how do you undo that?'

'I take her for long drives in the city.'

Pamela laughed loudly, but stopped abruptly. Both of them looked around to see if anyone was staring. Two volunteers were shelving books and the full-time librarians were both behind the checkout desk at the opposite end of the room. No one had noticed.

Richard held out his hand and said, 'My name is—'

'Richard Lantz.' She shook his hand. Her skin was cool. 'I'm Pam Castle. I've seen you around. You live on Oak Street at Ninth, right?'

She knew who he was? He felt his heart racing. 'How did you know that?'

'I'm in real estate. It's my job to know everybody and where they live.'

'What else do you know about me?'

'You do computers, right?'

'Yeah.'

'Well, that's it. I don't even know your daughter's name.'

'It's Miriam.'

'That's an unusual name.'

Richard gathered his courage. 'Do you believe in harmonic convergence?'

'What is it?'

'I'm not sure exactly. But I believe in it.'

She laughed, more quietly this time. 'How can you believe in something when you don't know what it is?'

'Ask a Catholic.'

'I'm Catholic.'

'Oops. Sorry. But then you know what I'm talking about.'

'No, I don't.' Her eyes were twinkling. He thought that might be a good sign.

'It wasn't an accident that I sat at this table,' he said.

'You mean a Higher Power made you sit here so we could have this silly conversation?'

'No, I mean I saw you at Pig's Wings last night.'

'Really.'

That sounded bad. He hurried on. 'Then I saw you again at Safeway this morning.'

'Are you following me?' Decidedly cool.

'No, no, that's what I mean by harmonic convergence. Before yesterday I'd never seen you before. I brought Miriam to find frog books, and here you were. That's the third time I've seen you in twenty-four hours. It must mean something.'

'Yeah, it means we live in a really small town.'

'No, I think it means something more than that.'

'Like what?'

He took a deep breath. 'I think it means I'm supposed to ask you out.'

She was silent for a moment, watching him. He suddenly realized that she was smiling faintly.

'Is that what you're doing?' she said.

'Not yet.'

She leaned back and waved her hand at him. 'Go on, then.'

'Okay.' He took another deep breath, then had a thought. 'Wait a second. Do you go by Pamela? Pam? Pammie?'

'If you call me Pammie I'll bop you with this book. Call me Pam.'

'Pam. Okay. Pam, would you like to go out to dinner with me next Friday?'

'Sure,' she said, smiling.

* * *

Richard finished tucking Miriam into bed. She grabbed the new stuffed frog he'd bought for her that afternoon in the stationery store after they left the library. It was orange.

'Dad,' she said, 'how did you and Mom meet?'

He thought for a moment as he brushed strands of hair out of her face. 'We were trapeze artists in a traveling circus. I had just been hired to replace

30

the guy that used to jump into the glass of water. He missed. They promised me I could work up to the glass of water by jumping into a bowl first. They showed me the bowl. It looked pretty good, so I said okay. Meanwhile I was supposed to swing on the trapeze and then let go. This sweet young thing was supposed to catch me. She had thin wrists and little arms. I didn't think she could hold a rag doll, but she sure was pretty, so I did it. I swung out, way up in the air, and let go. She caught me and held me and never let me go. I was scared, but while we were swinging up there she whispered in my ear that her name was Rosalind, and that she would never drop me. Then she set me down on the platform and I was okay. And I decided right then I was going to marry her.'

Richard looked down at Miriam. She was asleep. He smiled and turned off the light.

Chapter 4: Free Advice

Nosy Parkers and tiny barkers

Dear Mrs. Bambi:

Why are the private lives of women somehow public property? I've just started going out with a wonderful man, and my friends are all elbowing each other out of the way to give me advice.

One says he dates a new woman every week. (We've been together for a month, so I doubt that.) Another felt compelled to tell me every detail of his messy divorce three years ago. Half a dozen other people have given me simpleminded recipes for making it work, or for getting everything I can out of it for myself since it's doomed in the end anyway.

Have you ever noticed how pregnant women's bellies are owned by the community? Everyone wants to rub them. And everybody feels entitled to play with babies in strollers whether their moms want them to or not.

Now my love life has become part of the co-op. I want my privacy back. How can I get them to leave me alone? What's wrong with people?

—Meddlophobe

Dear Prissy:

People are morons, that's what's wrong with them. Some people are congenitally compulsive about giving unwanted advice. You can't shut them up.

If some biddy asks how your love life is going, tell her that your lover's into whips and you're getting to like it. Or grab your man and move out of this nosy town. Or you could marry him. If you've only been together a month, that would stop them from talking to you, if you're willing to have everyone in town talking about you instead.

32

Dear Mrs. Bambi:

I rented 'The Wizard of Oz' last night, and I don't believe that Toto is really a dog. He looks a lot more like a big, hairy gerbil to me. My girlfriend has a weird gerbil and it looks just like Toto. So why does Dorothy call him a dog?

—*Ozzie*

Dear Little Man Behind the Curtain:

Who cares? What I want to know is, have you ever seen a more obnoxious little punt dog than Toto?

Tiny, ugly dogs are not gerbils. Gerbils are honest, lovable rodents, and puny dogs are way, way below rodents on the evolutionary scale. They've regressed past their insectivorous ancestors right back to pond scum. Their yapping gives me a headache.

Take my advice, kid. When you grow up, get a real dog, a Lab or a Shepherd. Stay away from animals that, when they squeak, are saying, 'My ancestors were wolves. Look what you did to me!'

* * *

When Miriam left for school Monday morning, Richard stepped outside to get the mail from the box hanging by his front door. The sky was overcast, the air cool. It felt more like April than mid-May. He shut the door on the grumpy weather.

There was a slim manila envelope from the Hood River Examiner, just as there had been every Monday for the last three years. Richard tossed the rest of the mail on the kitchen counter and tore open the envelope. It contained four notes, all of them hand-written. He laughed at the first one, a stupid letter that would do just fine for the second half of his column. The next two were more interesting.

33

Dear Mrs. Bambi,

You've slandered the wrong person this time, you bitch. I'm going to find you and cut your heart out with a dull letter opener. You'd better watch your big ass, because it's only a matter of time before I figure out who you are, and then you're dead.

By the way, I'm suing you and your stupid paper. The editor and publisher will be receiving a subpoena requiring them to reveal your real name. If I were you, I'd leave the country now.

Elsie Navarro

The second one wasn't signed. The handwriting was crabbed and jerky.

To Mrs. Bambi,

I hope you roast in hell for what you said about my friend. I pray at night that the devil will baste you in hot lava every half hour. You're a God damned turkey, ready for stuffing. I hope you die real soon so the pain can start right away.

The fourth page was from his editor, Frank.

Hey shithead:

Looks like you Bambied the wrong woman. She hand-delivered this note on Friday just before lunch. I spent the rest of the day in a conference call with her lawyer and mine. We finally convinced them that they couldn't possibly win, so they dropped the suit. Thanks a lot.

You're selling a lot of papers, but the heat is getting pretty intense. I'm going to have to start explaining why I don't cover the controversy as a story, and that will make me look like an ass. Cut out the fake letters. I mean it.

The anonymous letter was dropped in the mail slot Saturday. Your fan club just keeps growing, doesn't it? And you are a turkey.

Frank

Richard carried the pages upstairs to his office. He threw Frank's note in the trash and stuck the two nasty letters in his hate mail file. The first time he got a vicious note, over a year ago, he'd felt sick for days. Now if they affected him at all, it was only when he laughed at the illiterate ravings. This week's batch was typical, and he felt nothing at all in reaction. Apparently you could get used to anything, even death threats.

He sat down at his desk with the fourth page, the silly letter, and turned on his Macintosh. The deadline for his columns was Wednesday, but he liked to get them out of the way as early in the week as possible. While the computer started up, he looked out the window toward the river, thinking about Vietnamese pigs, unruly daughters, and Wile E. Coyote.

* * *

A.M.'s shop, Mayatek, was located a block off Oak Street on Third. That meant that she got almost no tourist traffic, because visitors seemed unable to find their way off Oak, Hood River's main street. It didn't really matter. If they had found her shop, they wouldn't have bought anything anyway.

Richard paused to examine the window display before going in. A.M. dressed the windows as well as designing and sewing all the clothes in her shop, so there was a consistent Mayan weirdness to all of it that Richard found disturbing. The gray, glitter-shot mannequins posed in the windows didn't seem intended to represent human bodies; the abstract planes of their faces, obscenely glossed with carmine lipstick, suggested praying mantises. Their limbs were splayed as if they were having epileptic seizures.

The clothes themselves were surely drug-induced. One mannequin's chest was sheathed in electric blue cloth, perversely showing erect nipples on an otherwise insectile body. Long, flaring trains of striped earth tones hung between its legs to the floor, one in front and one behind. The tops of these tails were twisted into a tiny breechcloth that barely covered the crotch. The second doll's otherwise naked torso was barely covered by an open, buttonless vest. The tails on the back of the vest wrapped around to become an extremely short, pleated skirt, under which bright pink bikini bottoms were easily visible.

It was impossible to imagine anyone in Hood River actually wearing these monstrosities, or avoiding arrest for indecent exposure if they did. Not even A.M. wore her own designs on the street. Richard wouldn't mind seeing someone model them, just for the voyeuristic thrill of it, but he couldn't say

35

he liked them. After years of trying to admire her clothes out of friendship, Richard had given up and slumped into awed disgust.

The shop itself was like a fever dream. Pinpoint spotlights lit racks of weird clothes and yet more grotesque mannequins. Somehow no matter where he looked a light was always shining blindingly in his eyes, but much of the shop seemed to be in utter darkness. Richard always found it difficult to breathe in here, as if by stepping across the threshold he was transported to a mountaintop in the Yucatán.

A.M. came out of the back of the shop and smiled at him. She was wearing her normal work clothes—a jaguar-print vest buttoned only halfway up, and a bizarre white skirt. The skirt was very short in front, leaving her tanned legs completely bare, with a big, complex knot covering her abdomen. The back of the skirt was long, trailing down to end in a fringe at her ankles. He didn't see how she could sit down, and if she leaned over she might as well be topless.

'What do you think?' A.M. said.

'About what? Your tits or the clothes?'

'The new line, dummy.'

Richard glanced around again but the shop looked pretty much the same as always. Exotic clothes like the ones in the window and on A.M.: sack dresses that would have been normal if they hadn't been gigantically oversized, wrapped skirts like saris that completely exposed the groin, a dress that flared from the bust like a lamp shade and ended at the hips.

'What's different?' he said, giving up.

She pointed. 'Hats and shoes.'

A ceiling-high wire frame against one wall was hung with several different styles of... he supposed he'd call them sandals. One had a normal sole, but the uppers were constructed of a series of independent leather bracelets that ran up the calf, held together with thin garters. Another looked like knee-socks with leather soles.

On an adjoining rack, mannequin heads were impaled like the heads of Scottish rebels on the London bridge, but as a further humiliation they wore ridiculous hats. Some of these were made of little stuffed animals—pigs, llamas, snakes—suspended above stiff brims. There were tight-fitting caps with bulbous hanging extensions on the back, feathered bonnets, and a helmet constructed from a flaring cascade of copper plates that overlapped like a crab's legs.

'Um,' he said.

'Thanks.' She smiled as if he'd given her a sincere compliment. 'Come on back.'

The back room was where she made her clothes. A long table used for cutting and piecing cloth dominated the center of the room. An expensive sewing machine stood out from the wall nearby. In one corner a small, round dining table was burdened with books, most of them references on Mayan art and civilization that A.M. used as her inspiration—if that wasn't too strong a term—but a few contemporary novels, Smiley and Tyler, peeked out from the mess.

'Coffee?' A.M. said.

'Sure.' It was the only thing Richard liked about her shop: she always had great coffee. She poured him a mug and another for herself. They tore open little paper packets of sweetener, sugar for him and Sweet 'n Low for her.

'What's going on?' she said as she sat down across from him.

'You remember that woman we saw in Pig's Wings Friday?'

'Sure. Pamela Castle. The one you wimped out with.' She looked at his face for a moment and burst out laughing. 'Don't tell me you asked her out!'

'Yes, I did.'

'What did she say? Please tell me she said she was gay. Please, please, please?'

He folded his arms and glared at her.

'Oh well,' A.M. said, 'too bad for me. So what did she say?'

'What do you think she said?'

'I think she said, 'Get away from me, you weirdo.''

'Try again.' A.M. shook her head, refusing but smiling, and raised her coffee mug. He said, 'We're going out Friday night.'

'Yeah, right.'

'We are.'

'Really?' She looked impressed. 'Well kiss my chilly crevasse. Where?'

'What do you mean, where?'

'This is a special occasion, bozo, your first date since... ever, I guess. You can't just take her to MacDonald's or the no-name Chinese place. Let's see...'

'Will you get serious?'

'I am serious... I know. Take her to the Columbia Gorge Hotel.'

'Jesus! Way too expensive.'

'You're right. It's too much for a first date, she'll expect you to fly her to Cancún next time. Okay, Vito's maybe. No; the food's mediocre and you never know what kind of service you'll get. Well, maybe you should just take her to Portland. Hey, that's a good idea, then you can pre-book a hotel room.'

'A.M., it's just a first date. We're not going to... you know.'

'Why not?'

He never really wanted to hear about her sex life, and he was definitely not going to talk about his own. Especially since he didn't have one yet.

'I'm not looking for a one-night stand, A.M. I'd be happy with someone who'd let me hold her hand in the movies.'

She studied his face for a moment. 'You really like her.'

'Yes, I do. She's pretty and she seems really nice. She smiles a lot.'

'Okay. I'll see what I can dig up on her.'

'Thanks,' he said. He finished his coffee. 'Miriam's birthday is next month. Are you going to help me and Nadine plan her party?'

'How is Miriam?'

'She's great. Looking forward to getting out of school.'

'Do you have anything special planned this summer?'

'Yeah, I thought we'd spend a couple of months in Italy. Sicily, Naples, Rome, Venice, Florence. Kind of eat our way up the boot.'

'You can start by licking my boot, funny boy. You've never been out of the country in your life.'

'Will you help with the party?'

'Sure,' she said. 'I'll call Nadine. By the way, you need to go up there.'

'Why?'

'She's got a new accounting package and she wants you to install it for her.'

Richard sighed. 'Why won't she call me?'

'She won't call anyone. You know that.'

'Then why does she bother having a phone?'

'So you can call her, stupid.'

That made a twisted kind of sense. 'When does she want me?'

'She doesn't want you — you've got the wrong equipment. Oh, you mean for her accounting stuff. Tomorrow or Wednesday, in the afternoon.'

'Okay.' He stood up and carried his mug to the little sink by the coffee maker. 'I've got to go.'

'All right,' she pouted. 'Go ahead. Leave me alone with my boring work and my empty shop.'

'I hate to say this A.M., but maybe the reason your shop is empty has something to do with the way you dress.'

'What's wrong with the way I dress?' She stood up to give him a hug. He tried not to look down her vest, but he couldn't help himself. It hung wide open.

'Well,' he said, 'maybe you could actually wear some clothes. Then you might not scare off the customers.'

She laughed heartily. 'What damned customers?'

Chapter 5: Two Pear

Mrs. Bambi Knows (Archive)

Bust no excuse for busting her

Dear Mrs. Bambi:

I have a little problem with my love life. My guy is a good man, but he drinks a bit too much sometimes. He has a lot of stress with his job, you know, his boss is kind of a creep. And money is short most times, and he really had a horrible family life growing up. And I know I'm hard to live with, I can see that.

I just wish he wouldn't hit me so much.

I have an idea how to fix it, though. Do you think if I got breast implants he'd be happy?

—*Small Chest, Big Heart*

Dear Microprocessor:

You have a big heart but it's your brain that needs implants, not your boobs.

Leave this worthless creep now before he kills you. Don't stop to pack. Walk out the door right now and never go back.

If you don't have a friend who can take you in, go to the women's shelter in Bingen. They'll help you start over. And get some therapy, before you find yourself starting over with another monster like this one. Don't you understand that when someone's beating you, IT'S NOT YOUR FAULT!

Dear Mrs. Bambi:

Should I transplant oak trees now or wait until fall? I've been raising pin oaks from acorns, and I'm worried about how to keep them going.

—*Oak Grover*

Dear Pinhead:

Most trees prefer to be transplanted in the spring, but oaks are unusual in that they prefer to be planted and transplanted in the fall. They need the entire winter to soak up water for their growth spurt when the snow thaws.

Where did you get pin oak acorns, anyway? They live in the Northeast. What do you want to grow them for? What's wrong with our native Oregonian oaks, like the Californian black oak—not good enough for you? What kind of nut are you, anyway?

* * *

Richard picked Miriam up after school on Wednesday and drove out into the country to Nadine's farm. Parkdale was another farming hamlet like Trout Lake, but the farms in Parkdale were orchards instead of dairy, and it seemed farther away, even though it was in Oregon and actually ten miles closer to Hood River.

Perhaps it was the numbing sameness of the terrain. Unlike the diversity of the climb away from the Gorge in Washington, here all he could see was Mt. Hood looming over the vast acres of pear and apple trees. The blossoms were gone now, leaving only the budding leaves. Trees grew almost up to the edge of the highway, marching away in all directions in neat rows until they broke like a wave near the crests of the hills that loomed over the Hood River valley. Above the orchards the sere hilltops were covered with native vegetation, much of it already brown. It was still spring, but Hood River was near the edge of the desert.

If any proof was necessary that the area lay within the Cascade Range, the numerous cinder cones provided it. Each of these perfectly conical hills— failed volcanoes, small mountain-sized mole hills—was covered with trees, either orchards or pines, and many had homes perched on their summits.

After passing through several towns, some so small that not even a flashing yellow light marked them, Richard turned off the highway onto a two-lane road. They went by one orchard after another, with nothing but

41

gravel driveways between adjacent fields. He pulled into one of these, past Nadine's smallest field planted with young pear trees, and stopped in front of the tractor shed. Before the car came to a complete stop, Miriam flung open her door and bolted off into one of the fields, squealing with delight. In a moment she had disappeared into the orderly grid of trees.

Richard smiled ruefully as he reached over and pulled her door shut. He grabbed the shoulder bag he used for a briefcase from the back seat. As he got out of the car he saw Nadine strolling out of the field that had just swallowed his daughter, pulling off her elk hide gloves.

Nadine Szabo was in her mid-twenties, strong but not stocky, with big shoulders and wiry arms. She looked tall until she got closer, when it surprised him as always that she was on the short side of average. She stuffed her gloves in the back pocket of her jeans and brushed loose strands of blonde hair out of her broad face. As she reached him, she pulled a pack of cigarettes out of the pocket of her white T-shirt, shook one out, and lit up. They stood facing each other for a moment; she smoked, smiling faintly, and Richard just waited patiently.

'So, Richard,' she said at last, 'you've come to rescue me.'

'From what? The ferocious accounting program?'

'You know I hate computers. They're monsters.'

'It's just a Mac.'

'No it's not, it's a ravenous beast. It eats my time like a child eats potato chips.'

'It's just a tool, Nadine. Like a tractor. Or a telephone.'

'Yah, a tool. A tool of the devil, I think. You go exorcise it for me, okay?'

'If you can fix a frost fan,' he said, 'you can learn to use a computer.'

'Yah, maybe someday. Then I control it instead of the other way round.'

'What about right now? Come on inside and I'll teach you.'

She frowned at him and shook her head. 'I still have some sprinkler lines to move.' She ground out the cigarette under her boot and pulled out her gloves. 'You go make the evil thing work. I'll come in later and you can show me.' She walked back toward the field she'd just come from.

Richard headed for the house. It was large and old, but well-maintained, with white clapboards and black shutters, and a tidy flower bed beside the concrete steps. Inside, the rooms were dark and small, but there were a lot of them. He had once counted seven rooms being used as bedrooms.

42

The computer sat on a battered wooden desk in the living room. The rest of the furniture was just as old and worn, but the room was very clean. There was no dust on the tables, no dirt on the hardwood floors, and the wallpaper was faded but not peeling. Richard hit the power button and picked up the shrink-wrapped program he'd recommended that she buy. It took almost two hours to install the program and convert her old data. By the time he finished, Nadine had come to sit beside him and watch, her hair still wet from a shower. They spent some time together going over the new program, until he was sure she could run it as well as the old one—she didn't really understand it, but she knew the procedures to do her work.

When they finished it was dinner time and Richard realized he had been hungry for a while. Delicious smells and clattering noises were coming from the kitchen. Nadine stood up and stretched. When she looked at his face, she burst into a laugh.

'You want to stay for dinner?' she said.

'Um... It's not going to be anything weird, is it?'

'Yah, vegetarian, if that's what you mean.'

'I'm just worried that Consuela might have made that eggplant casserole again. I thought Miriam was going to throw up halfway through dinner.'

Nadine snorted. 'Your memory has gopher holes I could lose a tractor in. Miriam loved it. You were the one turning green. But don't worry, I asked Consuela not to make that one when you're around.'

'Well then, thanks, I'd love to stay. I'm starving.'

They went into the kitchen together. Nadine's partner, Consuela, was stirring a pot of something on the stove. The smells were enticing and very Mexican: peppers, onions, cumin, cilantro. Consuela smiled at them and sat down at the table to continue chopping tomatoes. Miriam was sitting beside her, separating cilantro leaves from the stems. Richard was surprised; he'd expected to have to haul her in out of the fields. She glanced up at him and raised her eyebrows, grinning.

'Fifteen minutes,' Consuela said over her shoulder.

'Let's go for a walk,' Nadine said to Richard, and led him outside.

Several women were working around the tractor shed as they walked outside, cleaning tools and storing equipment. Richard recognized none of them, but that wasn't unusual. Every time he visited Nadine there were new women working or staying with her. She led him to the small field beside the driveway.

Like many other farmers in the valley, Nadine had given up on apples and was concentrating on pears. Red Delicious apples, for decades the prime cash crop of the Hood River valley, were so glutted on the market that some years the farmers left fruit hanging on the tree—the low price wouldn't pay for the picking and packing. Field after field of Pippins and Delicious was being bulldozed and replanted in pears. It broke Richard's heart to see thousands of sixty-year old trees being knocked down, but there was less poetry than economics in a farmer's heart. And why not? They had to eat.

It had been four years since Nadine replaced her small apple orchard with these young Bartlett trees. A few Anjous were scattered among them for pollination. The trees were spindly-looking and shorter than he was.

'When will they bear fruit?' he asked her.

'We should get the first usable crop this year.'

'You're kidding. They don't look strong enough to grow grapes.'

'Grapes grow on vines, city boy, not trees.'

'Oh really? I didn't know that.' Sarcasm, as usual, had no effect on her.

'They'll come into full bearing in another four years.' She stopped at a tree with wilted leaves that was smaller than the others. It looked like it needed a good watering. 'You see this?' She grabbed the thin trunk and pulled it effortlessly out of the ground. The roots were gone; only a thin horizontal tuber with one feathery rootlet remained. Nadine threw it to the ground. 'Damned gophers. I'll lose a quarter of these trees to the bastards before they reach maturity. Miriam was out here hunting for the damned rats this afternoon, but we didn't find any.'

The sun was below the western hills and the air was getting cooler, but they walked on until someone rang the dinner bell. When they got back to the house, Nadine went to wash her hands and Richard walked on alone into the dining room. Seven other people were already sitting there. Other than Miriam and a young boy, the rest were all women, and all strangers to him except for Consuela. She pointed to an empty seat near Nadine's place at the head of the table. In a moment Nadine came in and Consuela started passing dishes around the table.

'Ladies,' Nadine said, 'this gentleman is Richard Lantz, a good friend of mine. That little sweetheart over there is his daughter, Miriam. Now sitting beside Miriam is young Matthew, and that's his mother, Pru.' Matthew was a nervous boy of about six. He waved jerkily when his name was mentioned. His mother was in her mid-twenties, either excessively shy or embarrassed; she didn't even glance up as she was introduced, but kept her eyes on her plate and her hands in her lap except to serve herself or her son.

'That handsome young woman over there,' Nadine said, 'is my cousin Becky.' They looked enough alike to be sisters: they had the same Slavic features, the same fine blonde hair, and the same smirk. 'And next to her is her partner, Jane.' Richard nodded hello and did a double-take. Jane wasn't merely pretty, she was remarkably beautiful, with very short brown hair, a small nose, and full lips. 'Jane and Becky have been helping out for the last few months.' That was odd. Richard had been out to the farm recently and had never seen them before. 'They'll be staying on at least until harvest, but if I had my way they'd live here permanent.

'Next to Jane is Roberta. She's new to the valley, just come up from California. She's thinking about maybe moving here, and I'd appreciate it if you'd help me talk her into it.' Roberta had a quick smile and long dark hair. Nadine ran a sort of underground railroad for lesbians and abused women, which was one of the reasons she had so many bedrooms. Richard guessed that Roberta would be finding an apartment in town soon. 'And you all know Consuela.'

With the introductions done, Nadine shut up and concentrated on the food. There was a casserole of corn tortillas layered with vegetables and cheese, rice and steamed vegetables with an astonishingly tasty white sauce, a black bean and chili dish that was unlike anything Richard had ever eaten before, and two kinds of fresh salsa.

When everyone was digging in, Richard asked Nadine, 'How does the crop look this year?'

'Really good,' she said. 'This might be one of the best years in a long time. If we can stay on top of the fireblight, I think we'll have a record crop.'

'Yah,' Becky said, 'fireblight and gophers.' She sounded just like Nadine too. If it weren't for the obvious five years that Becky had on Nadine, Richard would have guessed they were twins.

Miriam was bouncing on her chair. She nudged Jane, who elbowed Becky.

'Oh, right,' Becky said. 'Um, Richard? Miriam wants to know if she can help us nuke gophers after dinner.'

Richard looked at Nadine. 'Nuke gophers? What does that mean?'

'They're going to drop poison pellets in the gopher runs,' Nadine said.

'Poison?' He thought he knew what a gopher run was, but what the hell were they doing with poison?

'It's perfectly safe, Richard,' Becky said. 'We dig out the run a bit, drop in a pellet, and cover up the hole. The gas doesn't start right away, so unless you're careless or stupid, you don't even get a whiff of it.'

'Gas?' What were they talking about?

'Richard, you're turning green,' Nadine said. 'Calm down. The pellets release a toxic, biodegradable gas when they're exposed to moisture in the soil. The gophers become fertilizer, then the gas breaks down safely. Like Becky said, you can't get hurt from it unless you try, and believe me, Becky is very careful.'

Richard thought about it for a moment. If she said it was safe... 'Okay,' he said reluctantly.

Miriam was bouncing again, smiling hugely and squeaking a bit. Matthew leaned over to his mother and whispered up at her. Pru shook her head, but he whispered loudly enough for everyone to hear, 'Please, mom?'

Pru looked across the table at Becky. 'He'd like to come along,' she said quietly. 'Is that okay?'

'Sure,' Becky said, and Matthew squirmed on his chair with pleasure. Miriam looked disappointed, but after a moment she went back to her food with a tiny smile.

* * *

'So, Richard,' Nadine said over ice cream, 'I hear you've got a date on Friday.'

All conversation stopped. Richard sighed and set his spoon down. Everyone was looking at him, but even worse, Miriam looked as if she might cry.

'Do we have to do this?'

'With Pamela Castle, right?'

'You have a date, Dad?' Miriam said. 'A real date?'

She was sitting diagonally across the table from him. He ignored everyone else and locked eyes with his daughter.

46

'Yes, sweetie, I do.'

'You didn't tell me.'

'I was going to,' he said. 'I just haven't figured out how.'

Miriam continued to look upset for a few seconds, but it didn't last. A sly look crept over her face. 'Who is she?'

'Her name is Pam Castle. You saw her at the library on Saturday.'

She twisted her face to try to dial up the memory. 'I did?'

'Yes, when you were showing me your frog book.'

'Frog book?' Nadine said.

'I don't remember,' Miriam said.

'I'll tell you about her later, okay?'

'How much do you know about her?' Nadine said.

'Not a lot. A.M. said she's a realtor and a sports nut.'

'A.M. also said you nearly fainted when you first saw her.'

'That's a lie,' Richard said. 'A.M. was the one who got excited.'

He suddenly realized that Becky, Jane, and Roberta were leaning in, grinning. Pru was staring at her lap, Consuela was eating her ice cream as if nothing was going on, and Nadine was wearing an infuriatingly insolent smile.

'Okay, okay,' Richard said. 'We were having a drink at Pig's Wings. Pam walked in with some friends and was immediately mobbed by windsurfers. I had to leave for a dinner engagement. And that's all.' Miriam was looking around the table, happily watching the adults watch him.

'That's all?' Nadine said. 'A.M. said you were going to ask her out, but you grew feathers.'

'No, no, no. First A.M. wanted her for herself. Then she wanted me to ask her out, but I didn't want to.'

'Why not?' Becky asked just as Nadine said, 'But you did.'

'That was later. Look, she had ten guys hanging on her at the bar. I would have had to fight them off just to say hello. Then I saw her the next day at Safeway—'

'What?'

'Never mind. When I saw her again at the library, we got to talking, I asked her out, she said yes. That's it.'

There was a moment of silent scepticism. Then Nadine said, 'I know her.'

'What?'

'I know her. In grade school, I was best friends with her little sister Rhonda. Pam was in high school then and already a jock. Track, volleyball, basketball, tennis, all of it.'

'Did you know her very well?'

'Not really. But she was real nice to us. We used to follow her around, and she let us. Sometimes she'd play with us. A couple years ago, she dropped in and asked if I wanted to sell the farm. She had a buyer who was looking for a place just like this, but I wasn't interested and that was the end of it.'

Nadine put her hand on his arm. 'She's a nice lady, Richard. She keeps to herself, likes her privacy. She doesn't date around. I'm sure those guys at the bar put some gawky moves on her, but I don't even have to guess if she went home alone. She's just what you need, my friend.'

Richard felt relieved but confused. 'You know a lot for a farmer who lives up-valley.'

Nadine smiled and went back to her ice cream. 'A.M.'s been asking around.'

* * *

Becky, Jane, and the kids went out to ambush gophers while there was still light. Richard tried to help clean up, but Consuela shoved him out of the kitchen and he found himself sitting in the living room with Nadine and a cup of coffee. The other women had vanished.

'Is Pru an out-placement?' he asked Nadine.

'Yah. Sad story, but they're all sad stories, aren't they?'

'What's happening with the shelter, anyway?'

'You were there. That idiotic city council meeting. The morons won't let them rebuild.' The women's shelter in Bingen had burned down over a year ago, and the city council, under pressure from the shelter's neighbors, had used a technicality to deny them a permit to rebuild. Because there were rumors that one of the children staying at the shelter had set the house on fire, most of the neighbors were afraid to have the shelter next door any more. Richard had always wondered why there had been no arson investigation to settle the question.

'So what happens now?' he said.

'They're out of business. Their federal and state funds were tied to that address. If they move, they lose all their funding.'

'So that's it?'

'They're still doing what they can. I take some in. A few other people do. They're running out of time.'

Before the shelter had burned down, Nadine had usually housed only women who were being stalked by their abusers. Now it seemed she always had at least one battered spouse staying with her.

'The worst part about that meeting,' Nadine said, 'was the Washington people whining about Oregon. 'If those Oregon people want a shelter so much, why don't they put it over there?' Bullshit. Most of the abused women were from Washington. They think only Oregon has shitheads?'

Oregon? Richard was suddenly struck by a brilliant idea. He had been a supporter of the women's shelter, helping them with painting parties and contributing money occasionally. He saw a way that he could help them again—and at the same time help Pam, and maybe himself, too.

'What?' Nadine said.

'Huh? Oh, nothing. I was just thinking that maybe it would be better if they found themselves a new place. Someplace better.'

'I told you, they'd lose their funds. They're going to lose them anyway if they don't do something fast.'

'Yeah.' He looked at his watch. 'I'd better be going.'

'How much I owe you for the work?'

'Forty bucks.'

'You liar. How much?'

'Forty bucks.'

'What are you charging, minimum wage? It took you three hours.'

'Forty bucks.'

Grumbling, she wrote him a check and threw it at him. He caught it deftly out of the air and put it in his pocket.

'Thanks for dinner, Nadine,' he said.

'Yah, you patronize me and then thank me for dinner. Go home, city boy.'

They walked outside together and Richard shouted for Miriam. A few minutes later, she ran out of one of the fields hand in hand with Matthew, grinning and barely breathing hard. Matthew ran off toward the house and

Miriam hugged Nadine before getting in the car. Richard waved goodbye and got in too.

* * *

Miriam was obviously exhausted, but she started grilling him as soon as they left Nadine's driveway.

'Daddy, why didn't you tell me about...' She stopped, unable to remember the name.

'Pam.'

'Uh huh. How come?'

'Sweetie,' he said, 'I only asked her out a few days ago. I was going to tell you, I promise. I've just been worried that you would be upset, and I wasn't sure how to go about, um, breaking the news. I'm really sorry you found out this way. It never occurred to me that Nadine might know about it, or that she would mention it if she did.'

Miriam was quiet for a moment. In the dim light of the car's instruments, Richard could see her frowning.

'So, is she nice?' she said.

'Yes, she seems very nice. We're going to go out for dinner on Friday. I'll tell you all about it when you get back from Tiff's on Saturday morning.'

They drove on in silence for a while. It was getting late, and the traffic heading up-valley was light. When the occasional oncoming headlights lit up their car's interior, Richard could see that she was still awake, and though her frown was gone she seemed to be thinking hard about something.

Finally, she said, 'Do you think she'll like me?'

He stifled a laugh. So that's what all the worry was about.

'She's going to love you,' he said. 'She already told me she thought you were nice.'

'She did? When?'

'When she saw you at the library. She said you had a lot of energy and you looked like a very nice girl.'

'Oh.' Miriam thought about that for a second. 'Do you think you might marry her?'

Richard laughed. 'We haven't even gone out on our first date yet, munchkin!'

50

'But someday?'

'Who knows? Maybe. But not until you've gotten to know her, and I promise I'll talk to you about it first.'

'Okay.' The single word carried the simple finality of youth: as far as Miriam was concerned, the issue was settled. She put her feet up on the dashboard. Richard decided not to make an issue of it.

Marriage? At this point, he'd settle for a chaste good-night kiss.

Chapter 6: Fresh Air

From the Hood River Examiner
Friday, May 19, 1995

Mrs. Bambi Knows

Pig thieves need love, too

Dear Mrs. Bambi:

I'm going out of my mind. My daughter just turned eighteen and she's running around with a truly horrid boy. He's shaved most of his head, except for a long strip down the middle that he's moussed up into awful green spikes. I just don't understand these revolting haircuts.

Last week the two of them stole the neighbor's Vietnamese pot-bellied pig, then they stole my car from outside the chiropractor's office and took the pig for a joy ride in the country. They said the pig needed fresh air! The police caught them and brought them home, but I can't discipline her, she'll just run off with this nasty boy, who's really been a terrible influence on my sweet, innocent daughter.

She's going to graduate next month, and I'm afraid of what will happen then. Please, what can I do to save my poor baby?

—Distraught Mom

Dear Ditz:

You are wrong, wrong, wrong.

Pigs do need fresh air. All living things do, especially rebellious daughters.

Why are you assuming your daughter is innocent? The pig prank may have been her idea. And what exactly do you mean by sweet and innocent—virginal? Dream on, girl.

52

Why do you think her boyfriend is horrid? Because of his haircut? That sounds a lot like your parents, doesn't it?

Here are some suggestions to help you straighten up.

1. Get your daughter her own pot-bellied pig. Then she won't have to borrow the neighbor's.

2. Ask her boyfriend over for dinner and be nice to him. Get to know him. Don't give them anything to rebel against.

3. She didn't really steal your car, she just borrowed it without your permission, right? Why don't you take away her car keys?

4. Don't just wring your hands worrying about your daughter—talk to her. I'll bet it's been a really long time since you just sat down and listened to what she has to say. You might be surprised.

5. Her boyfriend's haircut sounds kind of cute. Why don't you get one just like it and give them something to complain about?

Dear Mrs. Bambi:

Why doesn't anyone ever feel sorry for Wile E. Coyote? Why does everyone take the Roadrunner's side? Coyotes have to make a living, too. That Roadrunner is nothing but a smart aleck, and if you ask me he deserves to be somebody's lunch. And it's just not funny the way the coyote always falls off a cliff and there's a little puff of dust where he hits. That must hurt.

—*Coyoteus Sympatheticus*

Dear Supergenius:

This is Hollywood's fault. It's the Roadrunner Show, not the Coyote Show. When the coyote has some solid hits under his belt—maybe an action movie or two—and gets his own show, he can be the hero. Then he can snack all he wants to on cute, defenseless birds that are just trying to mind their own business.

Until then, the coyote is going to have to put up with being the fall guy, and Prozac might do you a world of good.

* * *

Richard was beginning to regret his agreement with Pam to meet her at the restaurant. He'd been standing here on the porch of the converted house for fifteen minutes, dodging the waitresses scurrying by with platters of food for the stubborn idiots eating on the patio. It was chilly and getting colder as the sky darkened, but some of the young people out here were wearing shorts. The rule among the windsurfers seemed to be: if the temperature is above freezing, wear shorts; sandals optional.

When he'd lived in Seattle, Richard had seen couples walking downtown in the winter, wearing matching Patagonia shorts, heavy sweaters, and hiking boots, clutching their steaming Starbucks cups in both hands to stay warm. Some of that same hardy Northwest frontier lunacy lived on in Hood River.

In five minutes she was going be late.

It would have been better to pick her up at her house—at least then he could wait in the car or her living room—but she'd suggested meeting here. She had given a reason, but he couldn't remember what it was. He knew the real reason: first date jitters. She didn't want to be dependent on him to get home, and maybe she was uncomfortable with him knowing where she lived, even though he'd already looked her up in the phone book and driven by the small bungalow on May Street.

He checked his watch again. In three minutes she was going to be late.

Then he saw her strolling up the street. She spotted him and waved. Richard felt a ridiculous sense of relief, as if he'd expected her to stand him up. She smiled as she came up the stairs to the porch where he'd been waiting.

'Been here long?' she said.

'Not too long. Why, are my lips blue?'

'No, but I could see your goose bumps from a block away. Let's go in.'

Cosmocafe had once been a small farmhouse. Now it was a cramped and dark restaurant, the first floor rooms all crammed with tables nearly on top of one another, lit poorly by sconces and votive candles flickering on the tables. A few rubber trees and other tall potted plants were placed randomly in an attempt to provide some privacy, but it didn't work; in most cases if your table was missing a salt shaker, you could grab one from the next table without getting up. It wasn't clear how the plants survived, because even in daytime the rooms were dim.

The conventional wisdom for building homes in the gray Northwest was to use light-colored woods in rooms with high ceilings and large windows. Cosmocafe had low, dark rafters and high, small windows. It should have been called Cosmocave. As a starched, stiff-faced young woman led them to their table, Richard expected a bear to come charging out of the kitchen.

Because it was so cramped and dark, and the service so strange, and the menu so eclectic, this was Richard's favorite restaurant in Hood River.

They were seated at a bistro table just large enough to hold two plates. Richard hung his coat on the back of his chair and Pam took off the short jacket she wore over her dress. The dress was cream colored, blousy on top with a pleated skirt, embroidered with small flowers that might have been blue if there were any light. He suddenly realized he was staring and looked up to find her grinning at him.

'Sorry,' he said.

'I was just wondering if you know the difference between punctual and early.'

'Sure. Punctual means half an hour early, and early means an hour early.'

'That's what I thought.'

'Well, you were right on time.'

'So I was late?'

'Yeah,' he said, 'that's what I said. Did you walk all the way from work?'

'No, I parked around the corner. You?'

'Two miles is a bit too much of a hike for me.'

'So what do you drive?' she said.

'The Pacific Northwest hiker's vehicle of choice.'

'Oh, a Subaru station wagon, huh? What color?'

'White.'

'Oh, Richard! Living right out on the edge, aren't you?'

Their waiter suddenly appeared at her elbow and dropped their water glasses on the table. Richard looked up—and up—into his stern, disapproving face. The boy was in his early twenties, lanky, and so tall that his knotted hair brushed the ceiling. He handed over the menus and sullenly waited for their drink orders. Pam ordered a glass of Sauvignon Blanc and Richard asked for a Corona.

55

'So,' she said, 'you drive the hiker's favorite car. Are you a hiker?'

'Not at all. I'm an anti-hiker. Whenever a hiker and I collide, we annihilate each other in a flash of light.' She laughed and he sipped his water. 'What do you drive?'

'Guess.'

'Well, a realtor needs to haul clients around. Now if we lived in a city—'

'What do you call this, the wilderness?'

'No, I call this the toolies. One rarely finds orchards inside a city. Now in a city, I'd guess you drive a Cadillac.' She grimaced. 'Okay, wrong generation. A Lexus.' She smiled. 'Out here, half your work is probably selling farms or driving to farms, or houses perched on the edge of a cliff. And I heard that you're a big jock. So I'm going to guess that you drive an Explorer with a bike rack on the back and a board rack on the roof.'

'What color is it?'

'Um...' Actually, he'd seen her car parked in the driveway of her house. He'd already memorized the license plate number, but there was no reason to mention that. 'Red.'

'Ha! That shows how much you know. It's black.'

The stork waiter returned with their drinks. After he set them down the table was completely full; something would have to go to make room for a bottle of ketchup. He stood with a pencil poised over his order pad. They hadn't even glanced at the menus yet, but both of them were familiar with the place, so they chose swiftly. The stork stalked off without a word.

'How do you like to be called?' Pam asked. 'Richard? Rich, Rick, Rickie, Dick, or Dickie?'

'Just Richard.'

'Good. It's very classy. I don't think I could call you Dick. How did you—'

The stork flapped by and without even slowing down hurled a salad plate on top of Richard's dinner plate and dropped a small basket of bread in front of Pam. She opened the paper napkin cautiously.

'Oh, good,' she said, showing him the bread inside.

'What?'

'I thought there might be a baby in there.' He choked on his salad but recovered. 'I don't think I've ever seen a Caesar salad with mushrooms.'

'Well, they have their own way of doing things here. It's a fungal kind of place.'

'That explains the darkness.'

Actually, his eyes were adjusting to the gloom. He could actually differentiate the mushrooms from the croutons on his salad.

'So,' she said, 'how did you know I was a real estate agent?'

'Well, you had that big billboard on State Street, and all those ads in the paper.'

'No, I didn't. You're thinking of Jennie Lancelot.'

'Oh. Um... I saw your face on For Sale signs?'

'You drive around studying For Sale signs?'

'Well... No.' She was so cute nibbling on a piece of bread, no butter, that he decided to give in. 'Okay, I have some friends, well, one friend in particular, whose hobby is being nosy. She checked you out for me?'

'Really? I've never been investigated before. What did she find out?'

'Apparently you're married to a truck driver. He's been cheating on you with your sister. You have six children, and you nearly didn't finish high school because of the first one, who is eight years old and not your husband's. Your highest ambition in life is to meet Billy Graham and kiss his naked feet.'

Pam closed her eyes, threw back her head, and laughed like a donkey. Richard dropped his fork in surprise and chuckled weakly in response. He'd never heard anyone make a sound like that before. The other diners were all staring. The stork materialized, grabbed Richard's salad even though he wasn't finished yet, and glared at Pam before vanishing again.

'That's an amazing laugh you've got,' he said when she was done.

She waved her hand at him, wiped her eyes, and took a sip of wine. 'Your friend is incredible. Can she do this for anyone?'

'Oh, yes.' He drank some beer and idly wished they would serve it with lime. He'd ask for some but they'd probably bring him a lemon. 'Okay, really? She said you were a nice lady, never married, you keep to yourself, and you're one hell of an athlete. And straight.'

'Straight? Why would she say that?'

'Oh, she's gay. She was threatening to ask you out herself if it turned out you were the same. But then her partner would have shaved her head and painted it orange, so it's just as well for everyone's sake you're linear.'

'Linear?'

'That's what A.M. calls straight people.'

'A.M.?'

'Anamaria Mercado. Everybody calls her A.M.'

'Wait a minute, I think I've heard of her. Doesn't she own that clinky shop on Third Street?'

'Right,' Richard said. 'Mayatek.'

'Yeah, that's it. I've walked by there, but the window displays are so weird it never occurred to me to go in.'

'The people who do go in usually regret it.'

'What do you mean? Isn't the shop doing well?'

'It's doing great. Unless you mean making money. By that standard they've unplugged the respirator and they're waiting for the wheezing to stop.'

'That's too bad. Do you know her well?'

'She's my best friend.'

'Really?' Pam said. 'Do you have a lot of gay friends?'

'No. Yes. I guess so. Let me think...' It was hard to do that when she was smiling at him that way. 'Okay, two of my friends are straight. The rest are lesbians.'

'I didn't realize there was such a large gay community in Hood River.'

'There's not. I don't have many friends.'

She had just begun another laugh when the stork flapped in to fling them their dinners and glare down his beak; then he flew off. Richard watched her twirl some vegetarian Phad Thai onto her fork and take a bite. He tried his crab enchiladas. They were good but there was something weird in the spices. Anise, maybe. Nothing was ever quite what you expected at this place.

'I met A.M. when I set up the computer for her shop,' Richard said. 'She invites me to her weird parties and introduces me to her friends. Most of them seem to find me amusing.'

'Hmm. I thought most lesbians were, you know, anti-male.'

'No, most of them aren't. A few are corkscrewed, but I get along fine with the rest. I have another good friend I met at one of A.M.'s parties, she's an orchardist in Parkdale.'

'Huh.'

Richard paused to admire her dexterity with the noodles. Another forkful disappeared behind her lips.

'Actually,' he said, 'she and I have a mutual friend who's looking for a house in Hood River.'

Pam froze. 'This isn't a business meeting, is it?'

'No! No! This came up since I asked you out. But I thought, someone's going to sell this woman a house, why can't it be you?'

'Okay, then.' She picked up her fork again.

'Do you like your job?'

'It's okay. I like working with lots of different people, and I get to set my own hours. On nice days I can usually take time out to go windsurfing. But I've been working a lot lately. I'm worried about making the desk fee this year.'

'What's a desk fee?'

'It's... Well, it's like rent. Where I used to work the broker took most of the commission. I worked my tail shiny and he got rich. So I went to work for a different kind of broker. Now I get to keep all my commissions, but I have to rent my office from her and buy my own office supplies and ads. To make a living I have to sell about a million dollars a year, and there's a lot of competition in the Gorge.'

'Maybe we can help each other out, then.' He finished the last bite of his dinner and set his fork down.

'Do you want me to call your friend?'

'Um... Not quite. I'm going to find a house for her. She doesn't live in town.'

'You're going to pick it out?'

'Right.'

'Okay. That's kind of strange, but I've seen a lot of strange things in this job. What's she looking for?'

'Something roomy, four bedrooms at least, and in reasonably good shape. A big yard, preferably fenced in. It would be nice if it's close to the hospital.'

'That's my neighborhood.'

'Really?' he said innocently.

'I know the area really well. There are a couple of houses for sale right now that might work. How about if I call you in a few days and we can go look at them?'

'That sounds great,' Richard said. Now he knew for sure that he'd see her again.

59

* * *

'Do you know Frank Morris?' she asked him over coffee.

'Um...' Why was she bringing him up?

'He's the editor of the Examiner.'

'Oh, yeah, I thought the name sounded familiar.' I'm going to roast in hell.

'He's an old friend of mine. I was talking to him today about the Mrs. Bambi controversy.'

'Oh, really?' Oh shit.

'You know what I'm talking about, right? The advice column in the Examiner?'

'Sure.'

'Have you read today's column yet?'

'Not yet. It usually takes me a few days to get to the paper.' That was true, anyway.

'It was about someone's daughter who borrowed the neighbor's pig to take it for a ride in the country.'

He tried to look surprised and amused. 'Ha!' That sounded forced.

'I heard about the pignapping, actually. It really happened. The mother is the sister of a woman that works in my office.'

'Huh. Small towns.'

'Yeah. Well, my colleague asked me to see if I could find out anything about this Bambi woman. The Examiner's offices are right next to ours, so I dropped by this afternoon to see if Frank would tell me anything.'

'What did he say?' Richard tried to think of what to do with his hands. The palms were sweating. He dropped them in his lap. He should give up the damned column. Mrs. Bambi was going to ruin his life.

'He wouldn't say anything. He just smiled that shark smile of his and put his feet up on his desk. I said, 'Frank, everyone knows the little witch makes up the letters herself. No one would actually ask Satan's love slave for advice.''

'And?'

'He said, 'That's not true. We get a couple of letters every week.' So I said, 'Right, it's probably all hate mail and questions about the Roadrunner.''

She had that right. 'Then what did he say?'

60

'He asked me if I'd been out sailing yet.'

'Have you?' he said.

'What?'

'Been out sailing yet?'

She looked at him silently for a few seconds, befuddled. 'Yeah, a couple of times. Don't change the subject, I'm not done with my story yet. I said, 'Frank, you have to know who she is. Just tell me, I swear I won't pass it on to more than a dozen people. We'll have a nice, quiet lynching and no one will ever know that you tipped us off.' You know what he said?'

'I have no idea,' Richard said, bracing himself.

'He said, 'Pam, not even Mrs. Bambi knows who she is. Believe me, if I told you it wouldn't do you any good, and I'm not going to tell you.' Pretty bizarre, huh? It's like Rosebud.'

'Maybe. But Frank Morris is no Orson Welles.'

'You're right. Frank is only about half of an Orson Welles. But what do you think that means, 'Not even Mrs. Bambi knows who she is?' Is someone writing the columns in her sleep? Is it multiple personality disorder? This is so cool. I love a mystery. I'm thinking about tracking Bambi down myself, just for the fun of it.'

'That sounds like a bad idea.'

'Why?'

Good question. Uh... 'She seems like a pretty twisted woman. Maybe she'd get violent.'

'I can take care of myself.'

She probably could beat him up, if it came to that. 'Don't you think some mysteries are better left unsolved? I mean, the solutions to mystery novels never really live up to the suspense. It's like opening up a beautiful Christmas package and finding wool socks.'

'So you could just let it go, and never know who the sick tramp really is?'

'Why is she a sick tramp?' he said. 'Because she writes letters for people who won't ask for help themselves?'

'What? Do you think it's okay for someone to eavesdrop on private conversations and print them in the paper? And then, to squeeze lemons on the wound, give sarcastic advice completely unasked? Is that what you'd call civilized behavior?'

61

She had a point. 'Maybe not. But let me ask you something. Do you think she's funny?'

Pam's face twisted as she struggled with a response. She finally admitted, 'Yeah, okay, she always makes me laugh.'

'And do you think her advice is ever worthwhile? Does she actually help anyone?'

'Yes, sometimes her advice makes sense. But that doesn't—'

'I agree,' he said, 'what she's doing is bad. But maybe it's also good.'

Pam considered him, until the stork swooped down with their check.

'Do you know who she is?' she said. 'Why are you defending her?'

'Because no one else will.'

She looked at him for another moment and let it go. Richard paid the check and they walked outside. There were no streetlights and it was very dark. Overhead a few stars were shining through holes in the muddy gray clouds.

'I had a great time, Richard,' Pam said.

'Really?'

'Yeah, really. I don't get to talk to people, really talk to them, very often.'

'Then maybe we can do this again soon,' he said.

'I'd like that.' She leaned in a little and he took a half-step forward and kissed her, awkwardly and briefly. She was grinning when he pulled away. 'So I'll call you this week about houses for your friend.'

'Okay, I'll look forward to it.'

She turned away and started walking down the block, then stopped and turned back.

'There's something I should tell you,' Pam said.

'Okay.'

'I love hiking. I do it all the time, year-round. So if you and I collide, there's a chance we'll annihilate each other in a flash of light.'

'I'll take that chance,' Richard said without hesitation, and she laughed. He watched her walk around the corner and out of sight.

* * *

Richard woke up to the bedside phone ringing. He glanced at the clock with bleary eyes: 7:02 in the damned morning—Saturday damned morning.

Miriam wouldn't be back for several hours. He didn't usually get up until after eight. He considered ignoring it, but then it occurred to him that maybe Tiff's parents were calling about Miriam—she could be ill, or injured. He snatched the phone off the hook.

'What is it?' he croaked.

'Richard!'

'A.M.?'

'How did it go with Pam? Did you sleep with her? How was it? Is she kinky? Is she still there? What's going on?'

'Fuck you, A.M.,' he said, and hung up the phone.

Chapter 7: Lunch Crowd

Mrs. Bambi Knows (Archive)

Perfect girl in a jealous world

Dear Mrs. Bambi:

I was born with a slender build and big boobs. (To be accurate, the boobs came later.) I have a pretty face and long blonde hair. All it takes to stay trim is to watch what I eat and exercise every now and then.

Naturally, women hate me and men love me too much. When girlfriends ask me my secret and I tell them the truth—that I'm 100% natural, no artificial colors and no silicone, I don't have any special diet, and I get most of my exercise in bed—they practically spit in my face.

Men, on the other hand, don't seem to care if it's real, they just want it. They want it right now and all the time. I like sex as much as the next girl, but it would sure be okay with me if a guy wanted to talk first. I have a master's degree in political science, but no one wants to discuss the continuing repercussions of Watergate on our perception of the political process, or the growing and perhaps unconstitutional role of the chief of staff in the executive branch of government. They just want to see what's behind my 36D bra.

How can I get people to look past my appearance and see the real me?

—Unappreciated

Dear Female Pooch:

You need to change your habits. Have you considered a convent?

No, really, I know it's not your fault you were born perfect, you filthy slut. But if you were really concerned about being appreciated for your mind and not your body, you'd behave differently, wouldn't you?

64

Do you spend a lot of time and money getting that blonde hair shining and manageable? Do you wear tight, sexy clothes? Do you flirt with every guy you meet? Do you find yourself smirking at women with imperfect bodies or strict diet and exercise regimes?

No, don't answer. You've got it, so you flaunt it. But if you're going to flaunt it, don't complain about the results. The wind from your boobs flapping around is going to stir up some dead leaves of resentment and lust.

Dear Mrs. Bambi:

I just built a new house. The bonehead plumber was so galactically incompetent that we need a new word for it.

I'm talking leaking faucets, reversed hot and cold water taps, toilets that don't work, pipes that freeze every time the sun goes down, and backward plumbing on the hot water tank.

The moron has come back a dozen times to attempt to 'fix' things. At best he leaves things as bad as he found them, but usually they get worse, so there's really no point in having him come back again.

I'm thinking about a lawsuit. And maybe I should take out a full-page ad in the paper to warn other poor saps away from this idiot. Any other ideas?
—*Plumb Tired*

Dear Sleepy:

I wish I could tell you that a pipe bomb would be poetic justice for this simpleton, but I can't do that—not in print, anyway.

There must be a state licensing board for plumbers. Start a letter-writing campaign and put him out of business. Hire someone else to come fix the problems and stick Dopey with the bill. Keep on telling everyone what a half-wit he is. With some luck, in time evolution will simply erase him.

* * *

Richard waited for Pam to arrive, half-hidden behind the bushy potted junipers that separated the tables from the Oak Street sidewalk. For the last quarter-hour he'd been trying not to look at his watch. This isn't a date, it's a business meeting. So calm down.

She appeared suddenly and he realized that he was full of it. This was a date—to him, anyway.

Pam peered through the foliage for a moment before she spotted Richard. She flounced down into the seat next to him. 'I'm starving,' she said.

'We'd better leave then. I don't think they have any food here.'

'Really? What do you call that stuff on those peoples' plates?'

Richard looked. The sunburned young man was slurping up angel hair pasta that was garnished with a tiny dab of pesto. How did he get a sunburn in May? He must have been up snowboarding on Mt. Hood. The lean young woman was picking at a salad.

'I'd call that swill. Have you had the pesto here?'

'No. All right then, what do you say we just graze on these flowers here?' The large planters between their table and the sidewalk were fringed with alyssum and white-and-purple dianthus. They probably weren't edible.

'Nah. Then I'd have to watch you chew your cud all afternoon.'

'Are you calling me a cow?' She didn't seem offended. A.M. had said she had a sense of humor, and their first date had proved it.

'I wouldn't do that,' Richard said.

'Moo.' Approvingly.

A waitress pushed through the door from the main dining room and told them about the specials. She stood with pen poised over her pad, cheeks pink and shirt white like fresh mountain powder in the sun. The waitresses at Vito's always looked as if they'd just stepped out of the shower. Or as if they'd been smooching the cook and had just stopped to come and take his drink order.

Richard asked for a Caesar salad and the tomato bisque. Pam ordered a small salad, the tortellini with marinara sauce, and a glass of white wine. The clean or possibly dirty waitress took their menus and went back inside.

'You drink on duty?' he said.

'Only when I want to get drunk.'

'Why do you want to get drunk?'

'Because I have three houses to show you this afternoon. Two of them are vacant.'

'Um...'

66

She laughed at his face. 'I'm kidding. Not about the houses, though. How much time do you have?'

'As much as it takes.'

'Oh, right, rub it in. Mr. Man of Leisure.'

'That's me. Mr. Man.'

The waitress pushed the door open with her hip and carried out a tray with their salads and a plate of bread and butter.

'The bread here is pathetic,' Richard said after she left.

'What do you mean?'

'Look at this.' He held up one small white oval and waved his hand. The bread wiggled. 'No body, no crust. It's like Italian Wonder Bread. A good Italian bread should be crusty, with a light center that has a lot of air holes. And a little flavor would be nice.'

Pam set down her fork and leaned her chin on the back of her hand. 'You're some kind of food snob, aren't you?'

'Sure,' Richard said. He bit off half the sorry piece of bread in one bite. 'But so are you. Vegetarian, right?'

'Yeah. I eat seafood occasionally, but otherwise yes.'

'Now I'm an omnivore. I like everything: seafood, land food, and air food. All I ask is that it be good.'

'Oh. So you're not picky about what you eat, just about how it's prepared.'

'Um...'

'You don't care what your food went through, how miserable its life was, or how painful its death, as long as it's cooked properly and served in a tasty sauce.'

'You're right,' Richard said. He held up a forkful of Romaine. 'I will torment the lettuce no more, forever.' He set it down, uneaten. 'Aw, the hell with it.' He picked it up again, stuffed it in his mouth, and chewed noisily. When it was gone, he said, 'Are you going to try to convert me to tofu?'

'No. I'm not an evangelist.'

'Good. You are kind of a pain in the ass, though.'

'Ha,' she said. The door opened and the waitress came out with their main courses. 'You haven't even seen my steel-toed boots, yet.'

* * *

67

They had barely started in on their food when Richard saw A.M. walk by, grinning and waving boldly. She was wearing normal street clothes, so she'd either changed just for this appearance or hadn't opened her shop yet.

Richard rolled his eyes at her. Instead of continuing her stroll, A.M. decided to interpret his expression as an invitation. Pam looked up from her food as A.M. pulled out a chair from their table and dropped into it.

'Hi, Richard,' she said.

'A.M., slide off, will you?'

'Oh,' Pam said, 'you're Richard's friend A.M. He told me all about you.' She held out her hand. 'My name's Pam.'

A.M. shook it. 'He must like you more than he does me, then, honey, because he never tells me dick.'

'About what?'

Richard said, 'She thinks it's my responsibility to tell her every detail of my life.'

'Nonsense,' A.M. said. 'I only want to hear the juicy parts.'

'There aren't any juicy parts.'

'Well, that's the whole problem, isn't it?'

'She called me,' Richard told Pam, 'at seven in the morning after our d— dinner the other night.'

'That's sweet,' Pam said. 'She wanted to make sure you got home all right?'

'She wanted to find out if I went home alone. She's an incurable busybody.'

'Oh, swallow it,' A.M. said. 'After all the steamy stuff I feed you, the least you can do is live an outrageous life and tell me all about it.'

'She tells me every detail of her life,' Richard said, 'including her sex life.'

A.M. had been slouching in her chair. In the silence that followed that, she reached over and grabbed a piece of bread and started nibbling it. After a moment she tossed the slice down and started getting up.

'Sorry to interrupt,' she said. 'I was just walking by and thought I'd say hello.'

'You don't need to go,' Pam said.

'Yes she does,' Richard said. 'Who's minding the shop?'

68

'That's right, Richard told me about your shop. I'm sorry I've never stopped in.'

'Don't worry about it, sweetie. The only ones who do come in are people who need a laugh.'

'I don't understand.'

Richard said, 'A.M.'s shop is a little... um... sophisticated for Hood River.'

'Oh, it's not doing well?'

'If it was doing any worse,' A.M. said, 'I'd be paying people to stay away.'

'Well, I'd like to see it some time.'

'Stop by any time. I'm never busy.'

'See you later, A.M.,' Richard said.

'Okay, soup and salad tough guy, I'm leaving. Nice to meet you, Pam.'

'Same here,' Pam said. A.M. carefully pushed her chair back in and walked away. 'She seems like an interesting person.'

'You have no idea. She didn't just happen by.'

'What do you mean?' Pam went back to eating her pasta.

'After her wake-up call Saturday, I stopped by her shop to have a fight and then make up. I mentioned that we were having lunch here today and she said she might stroll by. I thought it was one of her jokey threats. I didn't think she'd actually do it.'

'I don't mind.'

'Really?'

'Why should I mind? Don't you want me to meet your friends?'

The idea was startling. He hadn't had time to get used to the fact that he was dating someone, even if they'd really only gone out once. He was going to have to tell all his friends about her.

'Well?' she said.

'Sure. I mean, I want you to meet my friends. If you're serious, I have the perfect opportunity.'

'What's that?'

'Monday's Memorial Day. I know someone in Trout Lake who throws a big party every year. Including fireworks. Pretty much everyone I know goes to it. Do you want to come?'

'Fireworks on Memorial Day?'

'It's a tradition.'

'Well,' Pam said, lifting a forkful of tortellini. 'I can never resist fireworks.'

Really? That sounded promising. Richard ate some of his soup. It had gone cold.

*   *   *

Pam had nearly finished her pasta when Richard heard a girlish squeal and felt the bisque churn in his stomach. Was everyone he knew going to stop by their table before they finished lunch?

An anorexic woman bulled through the planters and squealed again. Her age was impossible to determine: her skin had become finely creased leather from too much tanning and at least one face lift, and her hair was coarse and crudely dyed blonde. Skeletal hands fluttered at the ends of bony wrists.

'Richard!' she shrieked.

'Connie.'

'I'm so happy I spotted you! I was just crossing the street—' There was no way she could have seen him from over there. She must have sniffed him out. '—said to Millie the other day I was going to have to come and find you— Who's this?' She stood above them with her maned head tilted to one side like a cockatoo.

'Connie Tamblyn, Pam Castle.'

'Uh huh.' She hadn't unglued her eyes from Richard's face. He could see her forget in a split second that Pam was there. 'Richard, I have a question for you do you mind if I sit down.' She pulled out a wrought-iron chair, the feet screeching on the concrete, and collapsed into it. 'That computer you installed for me a little while ago—' Two years ago. Why had he agreed to help her? She'd paid him what he asked—not enough, two million dollars wouldn't have been enough—and then tried to drag him into her bedroom. And she'd hounded him ever since. '—no matter what I try to do, the silly thing crashes.'

Tuning her out wasn't going to be enough. Killing her was probably out of the question. He didn't have a knife sharp enough to saw through that turkey vulture neck. He didn't think he had the strength to strangle her; she could talk for minutes without taking a breath. There was no obvious bludgeon within reach. So murder was out. If he just walked away, she'd

70

follow him. Even into the men's room, he had no doubt, and there was no telling what she might try to do to him in there. He had tried ignoring her before, but she refused to be snubbed.

The pain in his stomach told him that she wouldn't go away unless he actually helped her.

While Pam watched, smiling in pitiless amusement, Richard began the tedious process of diagnosing a problem he hadn't seen and which Connie couldn't describe. She didn't know the difference between the computer and the software it ran, between memory and hard disk, between application and operating system. The only reason he could imagine why she even owned a computer was to torment him with it.

After five minutes he concluded that her computer crashed every time she ran a particular program that someone had given her. He put his hand on hers where it lay on the table. It was like grabbing a bag of chicken bones.

'I want you to listen to me,' Richard said.

'I am listening, I always listen to you, you know—'

'Connie!' She shut up for a second, then twisted her wrist so that they were holding hands. Pam snickered and he glared at her. 'Listen to me. Are you listening?' She nodded. 'Pay attention, now. Are you paying attention?'

'Yes, Richard,' she said meekly.

'Go home right now. Throw that program in the trash and never use it again. And never use any other program that anyone gives you free. Free programs eat your machine. They rot the circuits, melt your hard drive, poison your dog, and burn your house down. Do you understand?'

'Yes, Richard.'

'What are you going to do?'

'I'm going to go home, throw the program away, and never use free programs again.'

'Good. Go on, now.'

'Okay. But what are you doing this afternoon, Richard? Maybe you could come delete that bad program for me and check out the rest of my—' What was he going to have to do to get rid of her? Pam was being no help at all. She was lounging back in her chair, the sun on her face, her eyes half-closed, a small grin on her lips. She looked like a cat enjoying a spring sunbeam after eating a mole. '—could relax until dinner I could show you around the house you've never seen the upstairs you know—'

He knew what she was after, but the thought made him ill. Even if he wasn't dating Pam—he actually was dating her, wasn't he? — he couldn't imagine sleeping with Connie. It would be like humping a dinosaur skeleton.

He needed to get away. How was he going to shut her up?

'Sorry, Connie,' Richard said, 'but I have to go now. I have a chemotherapy appointment.'

Connie's mouth snapped shut like a refrigerator door. 'Chemo?' she said, barely moving her lips. He had guessed right. To anyone so obsessed with staying young, even the mention of cancer would be terrifying.

'Yes.' The waitress must have brought the check while he was ignoring Connie. He reached for it but Pam grabbed it away, tore off the receipt, set some cash down, and weighted it down with the salt shaker. 'It's bone cancer. Pretty bad. I only have a few weeks left to live. So I'm sure you'll understand that I have a lot to do.'

He stood up. Pam came around the table and joined him.

'Oh, Richard,' Connie whispered. 'Cancer?'

She didn't look up as they walked away. Before they'd walked half a block Pam had to stop to double over laughing.

'That was cruel,' she said when she got her breath. 'But I'm so glad you did it. Is she a friend of yours?'

'Not at all.' He felt shaky. Maybe he did need to see a doctor.

'There is something wrong with you,' she said as if she'd heard his thought, 'but it's not in your bones. Come on.' She took his arm. 'I have some houses to show you.'

* * *

They walked through three houses, two of which were empty, without a single opportunity for Richard to touch her. No chance to take her arm and help her up a steep stairway; no mud puddle to throw his cape over. But he paid attention to the houses, so when she asked him what he thought, he was able to give a coherent answer.

'The first one was too small,' he said. 'Either of the others would probably do, but the second one was perfect. It has four bedrooms, three other rooms that could be converted to bedrooms, a big yard, and it's only a block from the hospital.'

'Do you think your friend would like it?'

'I'm sure of that.'

'She'll want to have a look at it before she makes an offer.'

'Um...'

They were sitting in Pam's Explorer, parked in the driveway of the last house. Pam set down her clipboard and turned in her seat to face him.

'What's going on, Richard? There is no 'friend,' is there?'

'Oh, she's real. She just doesn't know I'm buying her a house.'

Pam's face grew pinched. 'Give me the condensed version. What is this, a gift for a mistress? A kinky sex getaway? Is that why it has to be near the hospital, in case things get too rough?'

'No! Jesus, where did that come from? It's nothing like that.'

'Then what is it like?'

'It's for the shelter.'

'Huh?'

He took a deep breath and let it out. 'You know that women's shelter that burned down in Bingen?'

'I read something about it. They're having trouble rebuilding.'

'Right. The city wouldn't renew their conditional use permit, so they can't rebuild the house. They're pretty much out of business. So I thought I'd buy them a new place.'

'You're going to give them a new house?'

'Yes.'

She stared at him for a long moment. 'Why? I mean, why you?'

'I've always been a supporter. Since before they opened, actually. Do you have any idea how many abused women need help in the Gorge every year? It's over—'

'I know, Richard. But why you?'

'That's the ancient question, isn't it?' He shrugged. There was only one answer. 'Why not me?'

After another silence, she started the car. 'Okay. But don't you think you ought to check whether they want to move to Oregon first?'

'I already did. One of my friends takes in women from the shelter. She said that Gail would be willing to move here but she can't afford to lose her grants. I figure if she didn't have to pay rent, she'd have time to reapply.'

Pam shook her head. 'Okay, then. Let's go to my office and we can start the paperwork.'

'No,' he said. 'Let's go to my house.'

'Okay.' She looked over her shoulder and backed into the street. 'If you're doing this to impress me, you son of a bitch, it's working.'

* * *

They walked up the flagstones from the driveway to the front door. Richard pulled back the screen and opened the front door for her.

'You don't lock your house?' Pam said.

'Never.'

'I've heard that a lot of people in town still don't. Aren't you afraid you'll be robbed?'

'Not really.'

'There's been some gang activity around here lately, you know.'

'I've heard that,' Richard said. 'But I'm not going to barricade myself in. I moved here to get away from that. Anyway, what are they going to steal?'

They were standing in his living room. Replete bookshelves, lamps, a couch and a few chairs, pictures on the fireplace mantel.

'No TV,' she said.

'Nope.'

'Can I see the rest?'

'Sure.'

He led her through the dining room, which was nearly filled by an ornately-carved antique table that he and Miriam rarely used, into the kitchen. It was bright and well-organized but not very large. A bay that was all windows held a small, round breakfast table. A dozen well-used cookbooks stood on a wall shelf near the stove.

'Do you cook?'

'Miriam and I cook together,' he said. 'When she was little I could sometimes remember how to make toast. As she grew up she got tired of burnt toast, so we sort of taught each other.'

Pam smiled. He led her upstairs to Miriam's room.

'Did you say she was ten?' Pam said.

'Next month.'

'Well, this looks like a ten-year old's room.'

There was almost no visible floor. Heaps of clothes, toys, and books lay scattered around. A corkboard displayed multiple layers of Miriam's drawings. The rest of the walls were papered over with posters: horses, fairy tale scenes, movie posters, and Einstein.

'Is she a fan of Albert?'

'She just brought that home a few months ago and tacked it up. I think they were talking about him in science class. Her top career choices right now are physicist, artist, and rock star.'

'Who does she like to listen to?'

'Sarah McLachlan, night and day.'

'It could be a lot worse,' Pam said.

'Oh, yeah, I know. Come on, I'll show you the rest.'

The next room down the hall was Richard's office. His computer and printer stood on a small desk near the window. A larger desk, massive and dark with age, hunched down under its load of papers and books. A comfortable reading chair sat beside the antique desk. Bookshelves walled the rest of the room.

At the end of the hallway, Richard paused with his hand on his bedroom door. He wasn't sure if he would be implying some lewd intent by admitting Pam to his room. But it would be strange to stop here, so he opened the door and led her in. She didn't seem uncomfortable: she peeked into the bathroom, glanced at his sleigh bed and dresser, and headed right for the balcony that looked out on Oak Street.

'Nice view,' she said. Through the trees, houses, and power lines, they could see the Columbia River and the white shoulder of Mt. Adams up the White Salmon River valley. Two Adirondack chairs and a small table took up about half the little deck. 'Has anyone ever serenaded you up here?'

'What, like Romeo and Juliet?'

'Well, you'd have to play the part of Juliet, wouldn't you? I was thinking of that woman at lunch: 'Connie, oh Connie, wherefore art thou Connie?''

'Baying at the moon is more her style.'

'Haven't you ever howled at the moon?'

'Sure,' he said. 'Every month, at the full, just before my haircut.'

'Ah ha. I knew you had a deep, dark secret.'

Shit. 'What do you mean?'

'I can tell when someone's hiding something.'

'Um...'

'And your secret is that you're a werelamb.' He laughed. 'Come on, let's go write up your offer.'

They went back to the dining room and took adjacent chairs. After discussing what a fair offer price would be, she pulled a staggering mass of paper out of her oversized purse and started feeding him forms to initial and sign. She asked him about financing.

'I'll pay it in cash,' he said.

She blinked at him. 'All right. That'll simplify things. So the only contingency will be getting a conditional use permit to allow the house to be used as a shelter.'

'Do you think that'll be a problem?'

'I doubt it. There's a lot of businesses in that area, and being near the hospital should help. I'll get that started right away.'

'Great. I don't have a clue how you'd go about getting one.'

She smiled at him. 'You talk to your realtor, of course.'

When it was all done, his hand was cramped. Pam gave him his copy of all the forms and packed the rest away in her bottomless purse.

'I'll present this today and call you as soon as I hear anything back,' she said. 'We'll probably get a response tonight.'

'That's fast.'

'Not as fast as you. Do you always jump right in like this?'

He leaned back in his chair and looked at her face, the tied-back curls with escaped strands framing her cheeks, deep brown eyes, and lightly swarthy, smooth skin.

'No,' he said, thinking of the first time he'd seen her, at Pig's Wings. 'Not always.'

'Okay. I'd better get going.'

She started toward the front door and he almost bumped into her as she stopped in front of the fireplace. She touched a framed eight-by-ten photograph. In it, a younger Richard with quite a bit more hair stood stiffly in a black tuxedo. A tall, smiling young woman in a formal wedding dress stood beside him, one hand clutching his elbow, the other at her side holding a bouquet. They were outside in front of a stone church, and Richard was squinting just a bit in the sunshine. Pam leaned in closer and barked a laugh.

'Is that a knife she's holding in her hand?'

Richard took the picture down and looked for the millionth time at the familiar couple. Half-hidden behind her bouquet of daisies, baby's breath, and roses, Rosalind was holding a large silver knife.

'We were just about to cut the cake when the sun came out for the first time that day,' Richard said. 'The photographer rushed us outside and then we realized she still had the knife.'

'She could have just tossed it on the ground.'

'I suggested that. She said she didn't want to get it dirty, and anyway it might come in handy if I didn't behave.'

'She was beautiful.' She was. Beneath her veil a fountain of jet-black hair welled up. Her face was British, aristocratic, with a dark Mediterranean tint to her skin. Richard put the picture back on the mantel and they walked outside.

Miriam was rushing up the stairs from the street, carrying her backpack slung over one shoulder. He coat was unzipped, her hair was loose and swatting her in the face, and one of her shoes was untied.

'Hi, Dad,' she said breathlessly as she raced past them and into the house.

'I'll call you,' Pam said. They stood still for a moment, then she leaned in and kissed him briefly on the lips. Before he had registered what was happening, she was getting into her car. He watched her drive away.

'Miriam,' he called as he stepped inside, intending a lecture on manners and attire.

She was kneeling on the couch, smiling at him. She had obviously been spying on them.

'Geez, Dad,' she said. 'You're a little ahead of schedule, aren't you?'

Chapter 8: Pyrotechniques

From the Hood River Examiner
Friday, May 26, 1995

Mrs. Bambi Knows

Mother's ailment slays son

Dear Mrs. Bambi:

My mother is sick, but not as sick as she thinks she is. She's an incurable hypochondriac, and I think it's going to kill me.

Last week her vision went blurry. She called me at one in the morning, hours after I'd gone to bed, to tell me she had an eye tumor. I drove over and cleaned her glasses for her.

The week before it was bone cancer, because her hip joint was hurting. She's had that problem ever since a skiing accident forty years ago. A while ago it was lung cancer. She has never smoked. Last Thanksgiving she thought she had prostate cancer. I had to explain to her that she doesn't have a prostate.

She's 64, she can out-hike both me and my children, she has strong bones and she's going to live to be 99. I doubt if I'm going to make it to 40 if this keeps up. How can I make her stop complaining about her health?

—Fed Up

Dear Grouchy:

Get sick.

Dear Mrs. Bambi:

I've read about a new migraine pill that has almost no side-effects. I get migraine headaches once or twice a month, so I looked up the information on this stuff. It's pretty scary. When they gave extremely high doses to pregnant rats, the rat pups tended to die within the first four days.

Now I'm confused. Is this drug safe or not?

—*Head Pained*

Dear Pain In The Neck:

The answer is simple. Don't take this medicine if you're pregnant and the father is a rat.

* * *

'Honk the horn,' Miriam said.

'That's not polite. Wait here.'

Richard was halfway to Pam's front door when Miriam honked the horn for him. He turned back and she smiled and waved at him. He wondered why he bothered telling her anything; she just did what she wanted anyway. By the time he reached the foot of the concrete steps leading up to her front door, Pam had it open and was standing there watching him.

'Don't you know it's not polite to honk your horn?' she said. He spluttered and she smiled. 'Give me a minute, I'm almost ready.'

She hadn't asked him in, so he waited outside. Pam's house was a pleasant little yellow-painted cottage located several blocks away from downtown Hood River. Neatly trimmed yews stood at attention like sentinels, guarding the house. The tidy lawn needed to be reseeded, but the pansies planted among the shrubs that marched along the walkway to the front door made up for that. It looked like a realtor's house: cozy, cute, ready to sell at a moment's notice.

It took Pam three minutes, not one, but that was close enough. She came out wearing jeans and a white blouse, carrying a sweater and a baking pan. Miriam climbed into the back seat when she saw them coming.

When they were on their way, Richard said, 'Everything okay with the house?' His offer to buy the house for the shelter had been accepted the day before with only one round of counter-offers.

'Just fine. We should close sometime in June.'

'Good.' Richard stopped at the only traffic signal downtown—a blinking red light. 'That's a nice little house you have.'

'Thanks. My mom left it to me.'

'Oh. So she's—'

'About five years ago. Breast cancer.'

'Sorry,' he said.

'It's okay. How about your parents?'

'My mom lives in Seattle. My dad died a couple of years ago.'

'I'm sorry to hear that,' Pam said. 'Do you see your mom much?'

'Not since I moved to Hood River.'

'I've never met her,' Miriam said.

Richard pulled up to the booth at the Hood River bridge and handed a dollar to the toll troll. The wizened, scowling man gave him back two quarters.

Pam turned around to look at Miriam as they drove onto the bridge. 'You've never met your grandmother?'

'Sure she has,' Richard said. 'She just doesn't remember.'

'That's because I was only three months old, Dad.'

'You don't remember being a baby?' he said. 'What's wrong with you?'

Miriam sat back and pretended to sulk.

'Any brothers or sisters?' Pam asked Richard.

'One of each. I don't see them either.'

'Why not?'

'My brother ran away when he was sixteen and no one's heard from him since. My sister is a lot like my mom. Neither of them will leave Seattle. They hate traveling.'

'Do you talk to them very often?'

'No.' He concentrated on his driving for a moment; the road curved sharply at the end of the bridge and he was driving too fast. 'Hood River might as well be Pluto to them. They gave us a goodbye party when I moved and that was pretty much it. Sometimes I get a card at Christmas.' He glanced over at her. 'How about you?'

'I have a younger sister. She got married and moved to Canada. I don't see her very often but we talk on the phone at least once a week.'

They climbed out of the Gorge and reached the rolling farmland. The sky was clear, washed-out blue. It was a perfect afternoon for a picnic. The silence lasted a few miles, then Pam turned in her seat to look back at Miriam.

'What did your dad do on his night off?'

'He got drunk with A.M.'

'I did not!' Richard said.

'Yes, you did.'

'No, I didn't.'

'You went out drinking with A.M.,' Miriam said patiently.

'That's true.'

'You came home really late.'

'So?'

'You had a hangover on Saturday morning.'

'No, I didn't!'

'Yes you did, yes you did, yes you did,' she chanted.

'Did you?' Pam said.

'I had a few beers with A.M. I didn't really get drunk, and I didn't have a hangover. I would have been fine if Miss Priss hadn't come home early and pushed me out of bed.'

'It was nine o'clock, Dad.'

'Oh, it was not.'

'Yes, it was. You were up until the a.m. with A.M.,' Miriam sang.

Pam laughed. 'So what were you and A.M. talking about all night?'

'You, of course.'

'Really? What about me?'

'She wanted to know why I was drinking with her and her pals instead of b— being out with you.'

'Goo-oo-oo-ood question,' Miriam said.

'Mind your own business,' Richard said.

'Hey, Pam?'

'Yes, dear.'

'Do you like my dad?'

Pam looked at him for a moment and couldn't keep the grin off her face. 'I haven't decided yet. Why?'

'I just wanted to let you know that he's available.'

'Hey,' Richard protested. There was no other traffic visible before or behind them so he swerved over into the oncoming lane and then back, then over again. Pam and Miriam were thrown from side to side. Miriam squeaked and Pam punched him in the arm.

'Cut it out,' she said.

Richard moved back into the right lane, smiling. They drove between the greening trees to Clarence's house.

* * *

Miriam had her door open before Richard stopped the car. By the time he pulled the parking brake, she had vanished into the big barn, leaving her door wide open.

Half a dozen other cars were parked in front of the pole barn. Clarence's baby, a red 1954 International tractor, had been pulled out into the small front field and was hitched to a wagon, ready for hay rides.

Richard retrieved his bowl of marinated vegetables from the back seat. Pam had baked caramel brownies. When told that this was a pot luck, she had insisted on making something even though he assured her that one dish per carload of people was sufficient. They set their food with the rest of it, on a round table in the middle of the deck. Its threadbare linen tablecloth fluttered in the cool breeze. The table was loaded with baked beans, corn casserole, several salads, fried chicken, loaves of bread, and a tall white-frosted cake under a glass dome.

'It looks like we'll have enough to eat,' Richard said.

'Where is everyone?'

The shouts of children came from behind the barn. Miriam must have found some playmates.

'The kids are back there, so I guess the adults are in the house.' They both looked at the screen door for a moment without moving. Richard wasn't sure he was quite ready for this yet. 'Come on, let me show you something.'

He led her across the back lawn beside the pole barn to a small pond. An irrigation ditch, running high with clear water on its way to the hay fields and herb farms, divided Clarence's property from the neighboring farm to the east. A small water wheel rotated slowly in the current, picking up little buckets of water and dumping them into a narrow wooden trough that ran into the pond.

Completely surrounding the pond was a garden, six to eight feet deep, that was so densely packed with flowers that no dirt was visible. Many of the plants had yet to bloom, but what was blooming was enough to take their breath away. Deep purple dwarf iris, fading daffodils, dusty blue and white bachelor's buttons, ferns like magnified insect's antennae, buttery California poppies, petunias of every color, golden marigolds, coreopsis, and a dozen things for which Richard knew no name.

The water trickling into the pond made a soft, soothing sound. Pam smiled faintly. 'Did your friend Clarence do this?' Richard nodded. 'It's magnificent.'

They had another minute for quiet contemplation before the screen door slammed open and a crowd of people jostled out onto the deck.

'Richard,' Clarence bellowed. 'You're late.'

Richard was halfway to the group before he was close enough to get a good look at Clarence, and it stopped him cold. He'd last seen Clarence about two weeks ago, on the day that his dog ran away—which was also the day that he'd seen Pam for the first time. Clarence had been sad and a little thin but basically fine. Now he looked ten years older and ill. His face had become gaunt, almost skeletal, with dark smudges under the eyes. The jeans and work shirt that ordinarily hung loosely on his bony frame were now simply too big. His skin looked ashen, and his shoulder-length gray hair had taken on a yellowish tint.

'What's wrong?' Pam said. 'You look like you've seen a ghost.'

Richard shook his head. 'Nothing. He's just—'

'Who's this?' Clarence said. His voice, at least, was as strong as ever.

'Pam Castle, this is Clarence Hoskins.'

'So this is your new girlfriend, huh?'

'No,' Pam said. 'He's my new boyfriend.'

Clarence laughed. 'Come on and get yourself a beer.' He took Pam by the arm and led her toward the deck.

'Clarence—' Richard said. His voice must have conveyed his concern, but Clarence gave him a dark look and a shake of the head and Richard let it go.

'Got to go perform some alchemy in the kitchen,' Clarence said. 'You two mingle. Pam, get Richard a Corona before he has a coronary.'

When he was gone, Richard said, 'He looks awful. I saw him a few weeks ago and he was basically—'

Someone grabbed his arm and yanked him away from Pam.

'Honey,' A.M.'s rough voice said, 'haven't you got anything better to do than talk to this out-of-shape chiphead?'

'A.M.,' Pam said, smiling. 'Nice to see you again.'

'Introduce me, boardbrain,' another voice said. Richard turned to see Sylvia standing behind him.

'Pam,' A.M. said, 'this is my partner, Sylvia Ferguson.'

Sylvia was a bit taller than Richard, at least nine inches taller than A.M. Her blond hair was cut very short, leaving her long, thin face unsoftened. She was just as fit as A.M., but her height made her look gangly instead of athletic.

'Excuse my rude roommate,' Sylvia said. Her voice was soft and melodic, a pleasant contrast to A.M.'s rasp. 'She's flirting again.'

'I never flirt.'

'You never stop flirting,' Richard said.

'Then you can't say I flirt at all,' A.M. said.

'What?'

'If I'm flirtatious by nature, then I never flirt. It's like saying a fish is going for a swim. It's nothing special, just its nature.'

'I need a beer,' Richard said.

'Good idea,' A.M. said. 'You go get drunk. Then I can flirt at will with Pam.'

'Like hell,' Sylvia said. 'Nice to meet you, Pam. We're leaving.'

'No we're not,' A.M. said, but she let Sylvia lead her away.

There were over a dozen adults milling around the deck and the lawn. Richard knew about half of them.

'Do you recognize anyone you know?' he said.

'A few. Let's see. Oh, there's Frank Morris over there, by the pond.'

Terrific. His editor. That's all Richard needed was for Frank to start harassing him in front of Pam. 'And there's Ralf Doppman.'

'Where?'

'By the tractor.'

'You know Ralf?' Richard said.

'Not very well. He asked me out a few times.'

'Really?'

'No, not really. I think it was more like twenty times, actually.'

'And...'

'What? You want to know if I went out with him? Is that any of your business?'

'Um...'

Pam laughed at his expression. 'No, I never went out with him. The guy's a scumbag.'

There was a persistent rumor that Ralf had made his sizable fortune selling drugs to children in New York City. He had retired to spend his time windsurfing, skiing, and chasing women. Richard didn't believe that Ralf had been a sleazy drug dealer. He knew for a fact that Ralf had been a sleazy junk bond salesman.

'Look,' he said, 'there's Karen.'

'Karen?'

He pointed her out: a cute woman in her late twenties, with medium-length brown hair, wearing a blue corduroy dress. 'The nicest waitress at Pig's Wings. I thought you might have met her.'

'Sorry.'

'I don't know how Clarence knows these people. He really doesn't get out much.'

'Hey,' Pam whispered. 'Isn't that the town tramp?

'That's not very nice,' Richard said. 'She happens to be a friend of mine.'

'Oh? A close friend?'

'Is that any of your business?' He wasn't sure whether to laugh or frown. 'I've never slept with her, if that's what you mean.'

'Then you're just about the only guy in the Gorge who hasn't.'

'That doesn't make her a bad person, you know.'

'No, it just makes her a tramp. I thought you only liked lesbians?'

'I like you.'

'Does that mean I have to become a lesbian?'

He snorted. 'Come on, I'll introduce you.'

Val was standing at the food table, inspecting the dishes with a critical frown. For once she was not surrounded by men, but that was probably because the only unattached men here were Frank the curmudgeon, Ralf the playboy, and Clarence.

'Richard,' Val said as they walked up.

'Val, I'd like you to meet a friend of mine, Pam Castle.'

'Val Ridenour,' Val said, offering her hand. Her voice was smooth and deep. She was dressed in jeans and a man's work shirt, but she looked like a queen doing the Prince and the Pauper routine. Her hair was shoulder length, very glossy brown, framing a handsome but not beautiful face. He didn't really find her attractive, but everyone else seemed to. She was thin, sexy, intelligent, extremely rich, and confusing: he liked her anyway.

'So you're Richard's new lady,' Val said. 'I'm happy for you both. It's about time Richard found someone.'

'Thanks,' Pam said. 'But we've just started dating.'

'No, you guys will make it. I can tell.'

'Right,' Richard said, 'like you're some kind of expert on relationships. Have you ever spent more than six hours in a row with the same guy?'

'Forty-eight once, if you must know. So Pam, what do you do when you're not putting up with Mr. Personality, here?'

'I'm a realtor.'

'Real estate, huh? But that's just your day job. What do you do for fun?'

'Sports,' Pam said. 'Windsurfing, biking, snowboarding.'

'Really. Me too. I'm surprised I haven't seen you on the river or up on the slopes.'

Richard wasn't surprised. Females were utterly transparent to Val.

'Maybe we could go sailing some time,' Pam said.

'That would be fun.'

That would be the day. 'Val has some unusual hobbies,' Richard said. 'What is it this month, Val, differential equations?'

'Partial differential equations.' Pam blinked. 'I was a math major,' Val explained.

'Harvard,' Richard said.

'You have to keep up with it. Math is like muscles. If you don't use them, you wake up one morning flabby and old.'

'You can see her in the coffee shop sometimes, drinking her non-fat lattés and filling pads of paper with gibberish.'

'Richard wants us to think that he's just a normal, beer-drinking, fun-loving guy,' Val said. 'But he's not. Are you, Richard?' She touched Pam on the arm. 'Nice to meet you.' She walked off toward the barn.

'What did she mean by that?' Pam said.

Good question. Did she know about Mrs. Bambi?

'I used to be an engineer,' Richard said. 'And I know the difference between differential equations and partial differential equations.'

'Really? What is the difference?'

'One of them,' he said, 'is incomplete.'

* * *

Pam had wandered off and Richard was trapped by two Trout Lake couples that Clarence had inflicted on him. One of the men kept trying to steer the conversation back to sports while the other, who evidently thought Richard was some kind of expert, hammered insistently on computer questions: Apple's survival, NT versus Windows, Zip drives, zzzzz. Richard had trouble following the thread. Why did Clarence always think he wanted to talk to computer addicts? The two men's wives stood quietly aside, wearing their boredom politely.

Mr. Computer Guy stopped talking abruptly when they heard a loud splash, as if something heavy had just been dumped into the irrigation ditch. Someone shouted, someone else screamed, and then they heard another splash.

Richard and the two couples ran toward the ditch. He felt a momentary clutch of fear. Was Miriam playing near the water? The children, ten or so, were crowded along the bank of the ditch just downstream of the water wheel that fed the pond. As he arrived a young girl jumped into the ditch and one of the women in Richard's group screamed. Her child, apparently. The water was about four feet deep, and the girl was swept rapidly away.

'What's going on?' Richard said. 'Where's Miriam?'

'I'm right here, Dad,' she said. He turned and saw her standing with the adults two feet away.

'Some kids were playing by the ditch,' Karen said, 'and one of the boys got knocked in. He was pretty young, so one of the older kids jumped in to go get him. They both got carried away.'

Richard felt an impulse to jump in after them. 'Why isn't anyone trying to save them?'

'Someone is. Look, he's fished them out already.'

87

Richard leaned in so he could see downstream. A few hundred feet away, a man stood in the center of the flow, handing out the girl who had just jumped in. He climbed out nimbly and started walking back towards them, herding the three soaking wet children before him. When they got closer, Richard saw that the man was Frank.

'Mom,' the third swimmer cried when they were still a way off, 'it was great. Can I go again?'

All the children began screaming that they wanted a water ride, too, and parents began yanking them away from the water's edge. The drenched children were taken away to find towels and fresh clothes. Frank walked up to the depleted crowd, dry above the waist but still dripping below.

'Richard,' he said.

'Frank. You're a hero.'

'Do you two know each other?' Pam said from behind him.

'Oh, we've known each other for years,' Frank said.

'But — Richard, I thought you said you didn't know Frank.'

'He just wishes he didn't know me.'

'What does that mean?'

'I'm just joking, Pam. Of course we know each other. I tried to hire him to work as a reporter a few years ago, but he said no, he was too busy.'

Frank had a mischievous look in his eye. Richard tried to look threatening.

'I'm not sure what he does with his time,' Frank said. 'Reading and playing with computers, I guess.'

'I know what you've been up to,' Richard said. 'I've seen your name on a lot of bylines lately.' On articles full of misspellings and grammar mistakes. 'Editing isn't enough for you any more?'

Frank shook his right foot. Drops flew, and the shoe squished when he set it back down. 'I can't afford to just sit around the office. I have to get out and work like everyone else. Besides, I like to snoop around. You know what that's like, don't you, Richard?'

'What do you mean?' Pam said.

'Richard has a curiosity streak wider than the Columbia. Haven't you noticed?'

'Not yet.'

'Oh, yeah, I heard you two were news. Watch out for this guy, Pam.'

'Why?'

'Oh, shut up, Frank,' Richard said.

'He's like Ralf over there. No one knows where his money came from.'

'I'm nothing like Ralf, you ink-stained paper pulp busybody.'

Frank smiled. It wasn't pleasant.

'Look,' Pam said. 'He's doing that shark smile I told you about.'

'Frank,' Clarence shouted from the porch. 'Get in here and dry off before you catch pneumonia.'

'I'd better go,' Frank said. 'See you later.'

Richard was trying to decide how to head off her questions when Clarence bellowed again.

'Food's ready.'

They followed everyone else toward the porch.

* * *

Clarence was a master of the mundane grill. He doled out hot dogs, hamburgers, and chicken breasts. Pam found enough vegetarian side dishes to make a meal, but Richard had two of Clarence's superb hamburgers, hot, thick, and juicy. Pam made a point of not watching him eat.

By the time they finished it was dusk and nearly everyone had pulled on coats or sweaters. In a sky midway between blue and black, the first stars glittered like lost fairies. The tip of Mt. Adams glowed faintly pink above the scarred, clear-cut ridge to the north. Miriam sat beside him on the picnic table with her head resting on his shoulder.

'What do you see?' he said.

Miriam raised her head and scanned the sky. 'There's the Dipper.' He nodded. 'And Virgo,' she said, pointing. 'And Leo, right next to her.'

'Where's Orion?'

Her head swiveled on her neck like a parrot's, looking up and back and left. Finally she pointed to the hills to the west.

'Behind that mountain.'

Richard put one arm around her shoulders and hugged her. 'Very good!'

'Dad, can I go back to the barn? Clarence has some new kittens.'

'Sure. I'll call you when the fireworks start.' Miriam squirmed off the fixed bench and ran off. Pam was staring at him. 'What?'

89

'Nothing. I was just thinking —'

But she wasn't looking at him any more. Richard turned in his seat and saw Ralf sauntering toward them.

'Gotta go,' Pam said sharply. 'Have fun.'

Ralf dropped onto the bench seat, spilling Miriam's unfinished can of Coke. 'Richard,' he grunted.

Richard didn't respond. There was no point in encouraging him by actually talking to him.

Ralf Doppman was a few years older than Richard, but he looked younger. He dressed like a young snowboarder, in droopy, baggy, unkempt clothes. The illusion was marred by his receding hairline. The hair he did have was long and shaggy. A narrow face, small eyes, and a prominent nose made him look like a rat that needed a haircut. May had been rather rainy, yet Ralf had a perfect tan.

'So,' he said, 'you're doing Pam, huh? I screwed her once. She was hot.'

That was either an outright lie or a drug-induced false memory. Richard looked for Pam and saw her sitting with A.M. near the door into the kitchen. He started to get up, but Ralf put his hand on his arm.

'You know the stars, huh?'

'What?' It was probably not a good idea to leave Pam and A.M. alone for very long. A.M. had an inexhaustible supply of embarrassing stories about him.

'I heard you talking with that little girl about the sky, man. There's something I want to ask you.'

Richard finally looked at him. The crash-head didn't even know that Miriam was his daughter. He resigned himself to trying to talk his way out of this.

'Okay, Ralf, what's your question?'

'Great. You know this theory that the stars are other suns, you know, like the sun, but really far away?'

'Yeah, I've heard that one.'

'And the planets, they're like worlds, like the Earth, man, but far away, too. And the Earth goes 'round the sun, and the other planets do, too.'

'Uh huh.'

'Okay. So here's my question. Is that just a theory, man, or is it true?'

Ralf had no discernible sense of humor, so he must be serious. 'Well, we know that the Earth and the other planets revolve around the sun. There's overwhelming evidence that the stars are suns, but no one has actually gone to check it out yet.'

'Huh? You mean it's not just a theory?'

'Have you ever heard of Copernicus? Kepler, Newton, Galileo?' Blank stare. 'We've sent probes to almost every planet in the Solar System, Ralf. The pictures were in the news. And maybe you've heard that a dozen men have walked on the moon.'

'No, man, that was faked.'

'What?'

'The man on the moon shit, that was fake. Hollywood. Special effects, like in the movies. NASA was just putting on a show so they could get more money to experiment on those aliens in Arizona.'

'You mean Roswell, New Mexico?'

'Uh... right.'

'Ralf, are you suggesting that the moon is green cheese and the planets are just lights in the sky?'

'That's it!' Ralf said. 'The planets, they're not real. Jupiter, and, and, uh... And there aren't any other suns up there. I mean, if the stars are suns, how come it's so dark at night, tell me that. And how could we send a spaceship to the moon, man? We can't even make a car that runs on batteries.'

'Right. So, Ralf, if there aren't any other suns, and the planets are just lights in the sky, where did the aliens come from?'

'Huh?'

'The aliens that NASA is studying. If there are no other worlds, where did the aliens come from?'

Ralf worked on that one for almost a minute before giving up. 'So, man, like I said, is it just a theory or what?'

Richard smiled viciously. 'Ralf, have you ever heard of the Greeks? Pythagoras, Aristotle, Socrates, those guys?'

'Ancient dudes?' he guessed.

'Right. You know what they believed? The Earth is surrounded by crystal spheres. The outermost sphere holds the stars, which are just torches—like patio torches. The planets are bigger torches, each one on its own sphere. The sun and the moon are bonfires in the back of magic chariots that are pulled across the sky by little boys driving a team of horses that can fly.' Ralf was nodding. 'People believed that for two thousand years, so it must be true, right?'

'Yeah,' Ralf said. 'Magic chariots. God damn, now that makes sense.' He clapped Richard on the arm. 'Thanks, man, I feel a lot better.'

'Glad to help.' He left Ralf smiling and nodding to himself and walked over to where Pam and A.M. had been talking, but they were gone. Clarence was just coming out of the house.

'Have you seen Pam?' Richard asked him.

'Not lately, but I've been inside. She can't have gone far—you've got the car keys, right?'

'That's not funny.' Clarence shrugged. 'Clarence—are you all right? You don't look so great.'

'I'm fine, Richard. I've been working pretty hard the last few weeks. And to tell you the truth, I still haven't got over Joe just up and running off like that. Why would a dog do that?'

Dog washes. 'I don't know.'

'Well, don't worry about me, I'll be okay. Hey, can you start rounding people up for the fireworks? I'll be ready to start in about ten minutes.'

'Sure.' Richard watched him walk behind the barn. Then he went to find the kids.

*   *   *

Except in winter when it was downright freezing, nights were always cool in this valley, less than twenty miles from the peak of Mt. Adams. People were huddled together under blankets or sitting in their coats on the picnic benches. It was very dark. The moon was below the horizon and Clarence had turned off all the lights. The only visible sources of light were the stars and the security lamps at the dairy farm half a mile away.

'This is how I remember my friends,' Clarence said quietly, but his voice was clear in the still night. He was barely visible as a darker smudge against the charcoal of the barn. 'I lost a lot of them in Viet Nam. On two separate occasions, a man saved my life only to lose his own within the next day.'

Clarence was silent for a moment, and a coyote somewhere on the hillside took the opportunity to yip and howl. The sound trailed off into a sad, thin wail that stopped abruptly.

'Well said,' Clarence said, and someone laughed. 'Okay, this is for Manny, Willie, Porkpie, Zipper, and Alphonse. I miss you guys.'

His dark shade vanished and there was no sound but the quiet murmuring of the crowd for several minutes. Richard realized that he hadn't seen any sheriffs here today. Normally someone came around to fine Clarence for illegal fireworks; they were only allowed on Independence Day. Clarence would accept the notice and offer the cop a beer, and the man would stay for the show. It was considered something of a perk to be sent out on this duty, but this year no one had come.

The fireworks were not the kind of thing you could buy at the Indian stalls just before the Fourth. Clarence ordered them direct from the manufacturers in New York, the same ones who supplied the major city displays. They cost him a substantial fraction of the yearly income from his mail order business.

A loud whump announced the launch of the first mortar shell. It whistled up into the sky, after which nothing happened. Some of the children started grumbling, but then the rocket burst, spreading brilliant red and white feathers all over the sky. Kids shouted and clapped, and one of the younger ones started to cry.

One after another, the fireworks burst over the neighbor's field. Every year Clarence asked permission, and every year they happily agreed to be the targets of the free show. That field had once been part of the same farm as Clarence's house, but now their only connection was the rocket fragments he dropped on their hay.

Mammoth white dandelions sprouted in the sky. Brief actinic flashes followed by deafening thunderclaps, whistling pinwheels that flung screaming sparks in all directions, wafting streamers of glitter. Everyone cooed and clapped, and blinked their eyes against the acrid smoke. Richard looked down from the sky for a moment and realized that the pole barn was on fire.

'Clarence!' he yelled, but another explosion drowned him out. He jumped up off the bench where he'd been sitting with Pam and Miriam and ran around to the back of the barn. Clarence was spraying water from a garden hose over the back wall. In a moment the fire was quenched.

'Damned sparks,' Clarence yelled. 'Go on back, it's out.'

A few of the adults were standing but no one else had followed him.

'Nothing serious,' Richard said. 'He put it out with a hose.' Everyone sat down and another mortar screamed up into the night.

A few minutes later the last one exploded. There was a long pause. Richard couldn't tell if it was over or if there was a grand finale coming. But then Clarence walked back to join them, so he started clapping, and everyone else joined in. Someone turned on the porch light, and Clarence stood off in the dimness with his hands in his pockets, not moving, looking at the ground.

Richard felt a shiver run down his back. Illuminated faintly by the weak lamp, Clarence's image seemed to shimmer, as if he were a ghost.

* * *

On the drive home, Richard wanted to tell Pam about his spectral vision, but it seemed too morbid, and he had a superstitious feeling that if he said it aloud it might come true. Instead he asked her what she had found to talk about with A.M.

'Lots of things,' she said. 'We discussed her shop. I think I have some ideas that might help her.'

'Really? Like what?'

'Sorry, that's a secret. Oh, and we're going to go windsurfing together on Wednesday.'

'Hmm. Can I come and watch?'

'Watch? There won't be much to see. We'll rig up and head out into the river.'

'I'd like to anyway.'

'Okay. I don't think A.M. will mind.'

'So what if she does?' he said.

'I'll tell her you said that.'

'Fine.' They fell silent for a while. The road was pitch black, and the high beams didn't seem to reach very far. Richard was a little paranoid about driving this highway at night. There were always a lot of deer crossing back and forth, and they didn't seem to be afraid of cars. 'Want to know what Ralf wanted?' he said after a minute.

'Sure.' So he retold the conversation. When he was done, she said, 'He's either got a really lazy mind or some very good weed.'

'Gak,' Miriam said from the back seat.

Richard had thought she was asleep. 'What, honey?'

'He's a gak. A hairball gakked up by the cosmic cat.'

Richard glanced at Pam and they laughed.

'The cosmic cat?' Pam said.

'Uh huh.'

'The cosmic cat,' Richard said. 'That explains everything.'

'Not everything,' Pam said.

He looked at her. 'What do you mean?'

'You've got some deep, dark secret, don't you?'

Here we go. 'What do you mean?'

'Frank and Val both said you're not what you seem to be. And A.M. implied that there were some bones in your closets.'

'A.M. lives in her own world. It's not the same one everyone else shares.'

'Sylvia seemed to agree with her.'

'Great, now I've got the Amazon twins ganging up on me. Sylvia is just jealous of my relationship with A.M. There are things we talk about that she can't share with Sylvia.'

'Yeah, there's that, too.'

They rounded a curve and the headlights of an oncoming car, the first they'd seen since leaving Clarence's, blinded him for a second before the other driver dimmed his lights. Then they were past it.

'So?' Pam said.

'So, what?'

'Do you have a secret? A sordid past, evil deeds in your youth, something black and tentacly inside?'

Richard drove quietly for a moment. Her voice sounded jokey, but her words didn't.

'I'm just a normal guy,' he said at last. 'Just like everyone else.'

* * *

95

Miriam was asleep when they got to Pam's house. He walked Pam to the front door.

'So I'll see you at the Hatch around noon on Wednesday,' he said. She nodded. 'Would you like to go out Friday night?'

'Absolutely.' She had not hesitated, which surprised him. After her probing in the car, he'd expected her to withdraw some, at least for a while. Perhaps she wanted to ferret out his secrets.

She kissed him, and took her time about it. Then she opened the door and went in.

When they arrived home a few minutes later, Richard unbuckled Miriam's seat belt and lifted her out of the car. She was asleep all the way into the house and up the stairs, but she woke up when he laid her on her bed.

'Dad?'

'Yes, munchkin?'

'How did you and Mom meet?'

Richard sat down on the edge of the bed and pulled the covers up to her chin.

'We were project specialists on the Space Shuttle. Your mom was studying the effects of zero gravity on the growth rate of mouse tails. I was trying to discover whether cats would land on their feet if you dropped them from orbit—in orbit, I mean. I had a little accident and one of my subjects met her objects and there was no more growing of mouse tails. But she forgave me, and since she had nothing else to do for the rest of the flight, she fell in love with me. We held hands all the way down through the ionosphere while the heat shield tiles blazed in fire.'

She was asleep. Richard stroked her forehead and went off to bed.

Chapter 9: Lucky Stars

The only happy woman's guilt

Dear Mrs. Bambi:

I've been feeling very guilty lately. All of my friends are having hard times, but my own life is so perfect that I feel like I'm living in the 'happily ever after' from a fairy tale. My kids are happy, healthy, and well-behaved. My husband and I both love our jobs. We have enough money and a comfortable home.

Everyone seems to be having problems with their car, their love life, or money. A lot of our friends are out of work. Three are going through painful divorces, one lost both of her parents and a brother within a single month, one had his house broken into, another had her house foreclosed. My dearest friend broke her leg bicycling and while they were X-raying her leg they found bone cancer.

I'm very grateful that my life is so tranquil, but it's uncomfortable to be an island of peace and joy surrounded by an ocean of pain and anguish. Is it weird to feel guilty about being happy?

—Giving Thanks

Dear Turkey:

When your life is perfect, shut up. The rest of us poor schmucks don't want to hear about it.

Don't waste your time feeling guilty, just thank your lucky stars. Help those of your friends that you can. Kiss your loved ones and tell them you love them. Enjoy the moment. Because, believe me, it won't last.

Dear Mrs. Bambi:

During the big snowfall last week, I remembered that every snowflake is supposed to be unique. Doesn't that imply some kind of communication between snowflakes, like, 'I've got design 23, everyone else back off.' So how would they communicate—by radio? Is it A.M. or F.M.? What about line-of-sight problems? Do they use satellites, and if they do, what did they use before we put the satellites up? Or is this uniqueness a new thing?

Communication implies intelligence—even insects have little tiny brains. Well, how does that work? Is a snowflake's mind encoded in its fractal lattice? What about before they choose a pattern, where is it then?

And finally, why bother? Who really cares if two snowflakes are identical? It's not like two women wearing the same dress to a party.

—Frosty the Snow Guy

Dear Flake:

This is like the identity problem in subatomic physics. Every electron is identical, but how? Is there a tiny electron waffle maker somewhere, or, like your snowflakes, are they communicating? Some people think that there is, in fact, only one electron in the universe, and it flashes back and forth in time over and over, uncountable zillions of times, appearing each time in a new location.

So maybe there's only one snowflake, and it travels in time too, and every time it shows up it chooses a new shape. This would explain why snowflakes appear to be unique: boredom. Obviously, the snowflake is a higher order intelligence than the electron, which is content to come back exactly the same every time.

Now that we have that problem solved, I can recommend a psychologist who can help you with your problem.

* * *

Once upon a time, before wind pagers, before weather service subscriptions, before Bart's Best Bet on the radio, and before Internet wind maps updated four times an hour, a frustrated windsurfer in search of a breeze discovered that the small road leading from Highway 14 to the fish hatchery passed by a perfect launch site. Some vagary of rock and river concentrated the wind on this small stretch of the north bank of the Columbia River, producing ideal windsurfing conditions.

He came back with friends, and, as is the custom with windsurfers, they bragged about their discovery to all of their friends. In no time the shoulders of the narrow gravel road were crowded with cars, the surrounding meadows were littered with trash and dog poop, and the native grasses and wildflowers were being trampled to dust.

The Fish and Wildlife staff waged a brief war against the intruders, but it was like trying to stop the advance of killer bees with a tennis racket. Very soon they succumbed to the inevitable and built a parking lot, installed trash bins, posted 'No dogs' signs and a bulletin board full of rules, and went back to their fish bunkers. The windsurfers, for their part, began treating the place with respect—now that it was theirs—and the 'Hatch' became one of the most popular launching sites on the Gorge.

The wind was even better just to the west, at Swell City, but that was privately owned land, and you had to pay for parking. No self-respecting windsurfer would hand over a penny for what he could get for free, so they crammed into the fish hatchery every time the wind was up.

* * *

The parking lot wasn't crowded, despite the perfect sailing weather. A good wind chased a few clouds across the otherwise perfect sky. The walls of the Gorge, like a two-hundred-foot-high levee built by giants, hemmed in the dirty brown, white-capped Columbia River.

Richard looked at his watch again. He'd been sitting for almost half an hour on a sunny rock in the hatchery parking lot. Pam had said she was meeting A.M. at noon, and it was a few minutes after. Punctuality was not just a dying virtue, it was fossilized. And he was starting to get hungry.

He glanced over his shoulder and saw Pam's Explorer pulling off the highway. A.M.'s beat-up, faded blue Subaru wagon followed her in. Richard was suspicious of the coincidence. Why were they arriving at exactly the same moment? Had they met somewhere else first? He worried that Pam and A.M. were becoming friends behind his back. A.M. was more like a sister to him than his own estranged sister: she knew him too well. It couldn't possibly help his romance with Pam to have them huddled together at pajama parties, swapping funny Richard stories.

They parked right next to him. Richard stood up and dusted off his rear. Pam flitted up and kissed him on the cheek, then walked a few steps away and frowned at the river. A.M. stomped over and kissed him on the same cheek.

'Turn the other cheek, baby,' she said, and joined Pam. 'What do you think?'

'Twenty, maybe twenty-five knots,' Pam said.

'Three-seven?'

'I'm thinking four-oh.'

'You're kidding,' A.M. said.

'Unh uh. Let's ask this guy.'

A tall, clean-cut windsurfer was just climbing out of the river, carrying his board and yellow and blue sail horizontally, still attached to each other, walking clumsily between them. He looked nearly dead from exhaustion.

'Hey,' Pam said. The man grunted in reply. 'What's it look like out there?'

'Twenty-three, gusting to maybe twenty-seven.'

'What are you using?' A.M. said.

'Four-five.'

'Really? Four-five?'

Richard tuned out and sat back down on his rock. Windsurfers could do this all day, swapping numbers like numerologists or crazed accountants. Like the rock climbers he had known in Seattle, windsurfers talked incessantly about what they were going to do, did it briefly, then talked all night long about what they'd done.

As far as he could tell, the larger numbers, eight or above, were the length of the board, measured in feet, and the smaller numbers, three to maybe six, were the area of the sail in square meters. It was idiotically charming how they mixed measurement systems, as if they didn't know the difference between length and area, or between the metric system and the English.

Pam and A.M. quizzed the sailor until he got tired, then they found someone else coming out and bothered her for quite a while, then they stood at the water's edge and debated sail sizes and wind speeds and lamenting that they had the wrong fin. Richard was getting a sunburn.

100

Finally they returned to their cars and opened up the backs. Like synchronized swimmers, each of them pulled out a two-part mast, selected a sail from the quiver, picked up a boom, and carried them across the dirt road to a grassy, shallow depression near the Fish and Wildlife bulletin board.

Richard had occasionally, over the years, watched windsurfers sailing, but he had never seen the rigging process before. Pam tossed out and unrolled her sail, a massive sheet of plastic that was half transparent, half brightly colored in bands of purple and blue. After locking the mast halves together, she slid a pocket on the sail over the mast and attached the universal joint. The boom, two bowed fiberglass tubes connected at their ends, slid over the sail to a cutout and clamped down to the mast. Then she attached the outside point of the sail to the boom and spent what seemed like a very long time adjusting the tension of the sail using long, flat ribs and velcro closures.

Richard followed Pam back to her car. Without any apparent shyness, she slipped out of her jeans and T-shirt. She was wearing a black one-piece suit underneath. The hips were cut high, making her already long legs look endless. Sitting on the bumper of her car, she struggled into a dry suit. The black fabric was thick and stiff. When she was done, she slipped her feet into booties and walked over to A.M.'s car.

'Can you zip me?' she said. Richard raised a hand to protest that he would have been happy to do the honors, but A.M. was already drawing the zipper of Pam's suit from one shoulder to the other. She turned around and Pam returned the favor. The suits were both black, with colored stripes like lightning running across them. Pam's had a pair of lime green and magenta stripes that climbed one leg and wrapped around her torso.

'Want me to braid your hair?' A.M. said. Her butt-length hair was already roughly knotted.

'No, thanks, I've got some bands.' In a few quick movements, Pam tied her hair back.

Each of them stepped into what looked like a jumble of nylon straps. With a tug and a few snaps, the cat's cradles became harnesses like a parachuter's or a rock climber's.

Richard stepped back as Pam loosened the straps holding her board to the Explorer's roof. The fin stuck up like a shark's dorsal. He wanted to volunteer to help get it down, but he knew she had done this a thousand

101

times without him. With one hand in a strap and one on the bottom of the board, she easily lifted the eight-foot-long board off the car and carried it toward her sail. A sudden gust of wind caught the board and threatened to jerk it out of her hands, but she shifted the angle and regained control.

Pam snapped the universal joint into its receptor on the board. When A.M. was ready, the two carried their boards, with the sail in front of them and the board horizontally beside them, toward the water.

Richard stood on a rock with the waves lapping at his feet. The women walked without hesitation right into the water and set their boards down. A.M. pointed her board up-river, set one foot on the board, and lifted the sail. She zipped off into the river. Pam turned back for a moment.

'See you later,' she said with a fairy grin. And then she topped A.M.'s launch with a graceful, utterly flawless beach start: she stepped up onto the board, stood the sail up, and took off.

Richard watched her set her feet in the straps and hook her harness to the boom. She leaned back and was suddenly lost in the school of gleaming, flashing sails gliding over the water like flying fish. He stood on his rock for a moment, watching the sailors dashing by, amazed at how easy they'd made it look after all the horror stories he'd heard about what a difficult sport this was. Then he saw one windsurfer crash and flounder in the waves, trying to get back on his board. Then another, and another. For all but the best windsurfers, the gorgeous, fluid grace and speed were transient, like everything else in the world—mere punctuation to the drudgery of rigging up and repeatedly trying to get back on your board after you'd fallen.

He looked at his watch. It had taken them almost an hour to rig up. He walked back to his car, thinking about where to eat lunch.

*   *   *

Standing on the small raised porch of Pam's house, Richard rang the bell and leaned back on the wrought-iron railing. She answered the door a moment later, wearing black jeans and a soft yellow blouse, barefoot and breathless.

'Come on in,' she said. 'I'm almost ready.'

Her toenails were painted bright red, cute as ladybugs.

She abandoned him in the living room, which did not look as he would have expected from the houses's Ozzie and Harriet exterior. Classy wallpaper—blue and white stripes with small yellow flowers—an expensive-looking Persian rug on the hardwood floor, a futon and frame serving as a couch, a single easy chair, a TV on a wooden cabinet.

The mantel of the bricked-in fireplace was decorated with a dozen or so framed photographs. Richard wandered over and started on the left side. Pam with an older woman, probably her mother, in front of a pink rose bush. Several recent-looking pictures of young children; nieces and nephews, maybe? He picked up an antique, crinkled, black and white picture of a rotund man with a thick handlebar mustache, wearing a three-piece suit and leaning on the railing of a wooden porch. Behind him a horse stood on a packed dirt street, its tail caught mid-twitch.

As he was reaching to set the picture back, his eye was drawn to another one. It was framed in ornate gold, given pride of place at the center of the mantel. The photograph showed part of someone's leg ending in a foot shod in a boot and a ski, standing in the snow. The shot must have been taken by the owner of the foot looking down her own leg. It was slightly out of focus, but Richard could tell that this was a child.

'That's my great-grandfather,' Pam said.

'What?' Then he realized he was still holding the picture of the fat man.

'He had a ranch in central Mexico somewhere. His sixth son was my grandfather. I guess there wasn't enough to go around, so my grampa came here to pick apples.'

'Is this your mom?' he said, pointing to the first picture.

'Yeah.' Pam walked over and touched the picture lightly.

He set the picture of her round great-grandfather back in its place. 'And what's this?' He picked up the boot and ski picture.

Pam laughed. 'That was my first skiing lesson, and the first picture I ever took. My dad took me to Meadows and brought his camera along, to record my first fall for posterity, or something. I asked him to show me how to use it. I was so proud of my new skis.'

'Do you still ski?'

'Not often. I prefer snowboarding now.'

That figured. Half the downhill skiers in the country were trading in their skis for boards. What was she doing going out with him?

'Are you ready to go?' she said.

Richard put the picture back on the shelf. She held the door open for him, and they walked into town for dinner.

* * *

'Did you read Mrs. Bambi today?' Pam unwrapped her silverware from the paper napkin and dropped the napkin in her lap. Richard nodded and scooped some salsa onto a tortilla chip. 'I liked her answer. Her father had no right to get her involved that way.'

'I guess you're right,' Richard said. He waited a discrete moment. 'Hey — maybe you can explain something that's always bothered me.'

'What's that?'

'Why are there no good Mexican restaurants in Hood River when so many Mexicans live here?'

'There's that taco stand over on Cascade.'

'Okay, that's not bad, but they only have three things on the menu. I mean sit-down restaurants.'

Pam munched a chip. 'I'd say that most of the migrants can't afford to eat out, so there's no demand for the real thing. The local people don't know the difference, and they wouldn't pay the premium for good food, anyway.'

'Windsurfers are cheap.'

'So are farmers,' she said.

'Don't forget the tourists.'

She laughed softly. 'Now that we've insulted everyone in the valley, what do you want to talk about?'

'Let's talk about us.'

'Uh oh.' She took a drink of water. The waitress came by and they ordered. 'Okay, then. What about us?'

'Doesn't it bother you that I don't windsurf? Or ski, or snowboard, or mountain bike, or any of that stuff?'

'Not at all,' she said. 'That's your third biggest charm.'

'Third? Uh... what are the other two?'

'Your daughter. And your hair.'

Richard ran a hand over the short bristles on his head. 'I'm serious,' he said.

'So am I. Look, Richard, I'm surrounded by windsurfers every day. Every time I go out sailing they circle me like sharks. Don't you think I would have one if that's what I wanted?'

'That's what A.M. said.'

'You should listen to her more often. I like windsurfing. I don't like windsurfers.'

'Why not?'

She looked at him for a moment. Maybe this conversation wasn't such a great idea.

'Do you know why the Gorge has such great wind?' she said. He shook his head. 'Starting just a few miles east of here, there's nothing but desert until you reach the Rocky Mountains. It's the rain shadow of the Cascades. The sun heats the desert, and the air rises. That sucks in air from the coast. The easiest way for air to flow into the vacuum is up the Gorge. So when you have hot air, you get wind. And windsurfers.'

'That's interesting.' What does that have to do with anything?

'What does that have to do with anything, right? They're like moths to a porch light, Richard. When I was in high school, some Canadians came down here and discovered the wind. They were doctors and teachers, a lot of them, but they were also windsurfers. They brought the sport to this place, and after a few years, you would have guessed that they were junkies, or vacuum cleaner salesmen, or bartenders—anything but doctors and teachers. Windsurfing makes people stupid.'

'It didn't make you stupid.'

'There are a few exceptions. Like A.M.' Their food came and they ate quietly for a while. 'Richard,' she said between bites of her vegetarian fajitas, 'you've just got to take this on faith. I don't like people because of what they do. I like them because of who they are.'

*   *   *

'Where's Miriam tonight?' They paused at a crosswalk as a van with a windsurfing board on the roof rack ran the stop sign and turned right directly in front of them, its tires squealing.

'She's with a friend who has an orchard in Parkdale.'

'Tiffannee busy?'

'I guess. Her parents said they couldn't do it tonight. This friend of mine, Nadine...'

'Uh huh.'

'She's having a birthday party for Miriam at her place, a week from tomorrow. I thought you might like to come.'

'She'll be ten, right?'

'Yes.'

A station wagon with a board on its roof stopped suddenly in traffic just ahead of them. The driver leaned out the window to talk to a group of people lounging on the lawn outside the library. The cars behind him waited politely for a moment, then started honking. The windsurfer ignored them. The first blocked car pulled out into the oncoming lane illegally and nearly clipped the windsurfer's body as he passed him. The windsurfer pulled his torso back into the cab of his car, screaming in rage. Four other cars passed him the same way. When the lane behind him was empty, he got out of his car and crossed the street to talk to his friends, leaving his car blocking the road and the door open.

'I'd love to come,' Pam said.

'Great. Miriam will be happy to see you.'

'She will, huh?'

Richard grinned. A few minutes later, he opened the door to let her into his house. The porch light was on but the living room was dark. He thought about turning on a light, but then Pam was standing in front of him and he forgot about anything but kissing her. He suddenly realized that they were almost exactly the same height, which made kissing her a little strange: awkward and perfect at the same time.

She took his hand and led him upstairs to his bedroom. He kicked the door closed as he stumbled after her and they fell on the bed together.

As he was falling asleep an hour later, he thought he heard her whisper, 'Sold,' but he couldn't be sure.

* * *

Richard awoke suddenly. Sunlight was spilling into the room like the water at Multnomah Falls. He could hear birds singing in the trees outside the open balcony doors.

Miriam was standing at the foot of the bed, grinning at him.

'Oh, shit,' he said, and snatched at the sheet. Fortunately neither he nor Pam had any embarrassing body parts showing.

'Morning, Dad,' Miriam said. 'Have a good night off?' She smiled again and walked out of the room, shutting the door softly behind her.

Oh, yeah, I had a good night. And a good morning. He rolled over and brushed curls off Pam's smooth, freckled shoulder.

'Wake up,' he said softly. 'We've been exposed.'

Chapter 10: Party Favors

From the Hood River Examiner
Friday, June 2, 1995

Mrs. Bambi Knows

Exposing scumbag no betrayal

Dear Mrs. Bambi:

I have to decide which of my parents to betray.

Yesterday my father called to tell me he would like to come visit me for a week—alone, without my mother. I was confused, but I said of course, he was welcome any time.

Then he told me he wants to bring his mistress with him! I didn't even know he was having an affair. He wants to stay in my guest room with some tart that he's cheating on my mother with!

It gets worse. He begged me to call my mother and tell her that I need to see him alone for a few days to discuss a problem I'm having. He wants me to lie to my own mother in order to set up an alibi so he can cheat on her.

And finally, he said he's dying to know what I think of his wonderful new woman, who is the love of his life. I thought my mother was the love of his life. Now he wants me to interview my new mommy, who's probably younger than I am.

He made me promise not to tell my mother what's going on. Now that I know what he's up to, I don't really want to see him, but how can I retract the invitation to stay? Whose feelings should I hurt? I don't know what to do. Please help!

—*Used and Confused*

Dear Bruised and Abused:

Are you kidding?

Put down this paper, call your mom this instant, and tell her everything. Who is the lying, cheating, worthless sleazeball, and who is the innocent victim? Your promise was made under duress. Your invitation was given before you knew that he would drip slime all over it.

You don't need a new mommy. Put an ad in the paper for a new father. The one you've got isn't worth the spit your mom is about to fling in his face.

Dear Mrs. Bambi:

I can't stand it any more. First, Bloom County gave up, then The Far Side, and now, after six months, I'm dying of Calvin and Hobbes withdrawals. Dilbert is funny but he's just not enough. Doonesbury used to be everything I needed, but now he's as satisfying as eating snowflakes.

What am I going to do without my favorite comics? I might as well cancel my paper right now.

—*Opus Mopus*

Dear Opie:

When did they let you out of Mayberry? How did you keep breathing before there was Calvin and Hobbes?

Buy the books. Read one strip a day, in order. By the time you get through them all, maybe a new genius like Watterson will have come along.

If not, there's always the final solution. It's painless and guaranteed lethal: brain death from an overdose of TV.

* * *

After obsessing all week, trying to decide if he should tell Pam that he was Mrs. Bambi, Richard was ready to either quit the column or spit out the truth. But he couldn't decide which. If he told her everything, she might just walk away; or if she didn't, and their relationship didn't work out, she could use the truth as a weapon against him. If he tried to keep his secret, sooner or

109

later she would discover it anyway—no secret was that secure, especially when he was still writing the column.

Maybe he should just give it up. Then there would be no chance it could hurt Pam, or his chances with her. Sometimes it was an imperial pain doing the column, but other weeks it seemed to be his only connection to the community; a lifeline. He wasn't sure he was ready to throw that away. He had thought that his life had some direction, but now he felt he had been drifting, like someone floating down a stream in an inner tube who wakes up from a nap to find himself adrift in the middle of the Pacific Ocean.

Pam rode beside him on the drive to Parkdale, holding his hand. Miriam sat in the back, unusually quiet; she had been subdued all week. Was it because she had seen him in bed with Pam? He had to keep fighting down the feeling that Miriam had caught him doing something perverted. The shame alternated with the conviction that he'd been touched by the divine that night.

He hadn't seen Pam all week. He'd spent last night, Friday, at Nadine's house helping her get ready for the party. He and Pam had talked on the phone only once: she called to laugh at him because he sent flowers to her office.

'No one has ever sent me flowers before,' she said. 'The office is buzzing like a jar full of hummingbirds. It's as if I went to sleep as Imelda Marcos and woke up as Princess Diana. Some of them seem to think I've made a deal with Lucifer. My broker came in to my room, shut the door, and asked me if I was pregnant.'

'Maybe the flowers weren't such a great idea.'

'Shut up. It was brilliant.'

In the clear afternoon light, the tidy farmhouses and parallel rows of trees parading up the hills looked like a watercolor painting. It was a perfect day for a birthday party.

* * *

There was no telling what Miriam had expected, but it couldn't have been what she got. As Richard pulled in to Nadine's driveway, Miriam looked up and then shot upright, pointing over his shoulder and yelling, 'Dad, look at that!'

A twenty-foot banner was draped from the tractor barn: 'Happy Birthday Miriam.' As usual, she was out of the car before it had quite stopped, but this time she hesitated on the gravel, gaping at the sign and unsure which way to run. Richard and Pam stepped out of the car just in time to see Miriam levitate off the ground when a crowd of people rushed out of the shop, screaming 'Happy birthday!'

A gaggle of kids surrounded her and they swarmed away into the orchard. Their parents were left behind, smiling and shaking their heads, and finally gravitating toward the food and drink tables set out near the house.

'Good one, Richard,' someone said at his shoulder. He turned and almost bumped into Tiffannee's dad, Sam, who put out a hand to keep him from falling. Richard shook it, but only briefly, because Sam seemed to want it back. There was something strange in his eyes.

'Nice to see you, Sam,' Richard said. That was just a small lie. He trusted Miriam with Tiff's parents, but he'd never really liked them. They had five TVs and they golfed.

'How did you orchestrate that? We'd been in the shop maybe three minutes when you drove up.'

'I called Nadine before we left.'

'Uh huh. Well, see you.' He wandered off.

'Friendly guy,' Pam said. 'Know him well?'

'That's Tiff's father.'

'You trust your daughter with a rude jerk like that?'

'He's not usually—'

'Hey,' Nadine said. 'Good timing.'

'Thanks,' Richard said.

'Want a beer?'

'Yes, I do.' She led them toward the drinks. Mt. Hood loomed on the horizon like a galactic ice cream cone that had been licked into asymmetry by a Titan child. The pear tree leaves were bright green pointillism beneath a cloudless blue sky.

Pam grabbed a Full Sail and went off to talk to a friend she'd spotted in the crowd. Nadine handed Richard a dripping bottle of Corona.

'I hear you're buying the shelter a house,' she said. Richard choked on his first swallow of beer.

'That's supposed to be confidential,' he said when he could catch his breath.

Nadine grabbed his chin and turned his face back to her. He'd been trying to spot Pam. 'Pam didn't say anything. Gail told me.'

'She wasn't supposed to tell anyone.'

'Yah, well, she told me. She knows we're friends, and she's upset that you won't let her acknowledge your support.' Richard shrugged and wiped beer off his chin. 'You can't take credit for anything, can you?'

'Let it go, Nadine. And tell Gail to let it go, too.'

'Fine. Have it your way. Go talk to Clarence.'

'Where is he?

'Around the corner there.'

Richard worked his way through the throng. He didn't recognize even half the people here, and it was his daughter's party. Nadine must have been pumping Miriam for months to build the guest list.

Clarence and Karen were sitting across from each other at a picnic table around the side of the house. Richard was relieved that Clarence didn't look any worse than he had two weeks ago at his Memorial Day picnic. But he didn't look any better, either. He was still dangerously thin, his face drawn and exhausted.

'Mind if I join you?' he said.

Karen smiled and shook her head and Clarence moved over to give him room. 'Surprised the hell out of her, didn't we?' he said.

'There was air under her shoes,' Richard agreed.

'So where's your girlfriend?'

Richard half-turned and waved back the way he'd come. 'Over there, somewhere.'

Clarence looked at him closely for a long moment. 'Ah ha,' he said. 'It's about time you got some.' Karen clucked disapprovingly and smacked him lightly on the arm. 'What?'

'Do you have to be such a boor?' she said.

'Congratulating him on getting laid is not boorish. Asking him what she's like in bed, that would be boorish.' He turned to look at Richard. 'So? What's she like in bed?'

'Get stuffed. Is this something you just figured out, or is everyone in town talking about my sex life?'

112

'Well,' Karen said, 'now that you have one...' She stood up. 'I'll see you guys later.'

They turned to watch her leave.

'Nice view, isn't it?' Clarence said. Richard made an agreeable face. 'I love her to pieces.'

'How do you even know her? I know you don't hang out at Pig's Wings.'

'Ah.' Clarence was silent for a long moment. 'She came up to my place a few years ago. Said she saw my catalogue and was about to call in an order when she noticed the address, and decided to drive instead.' He took a sip from a red plastic cup—it looked like water, which was unusual. He should have been holding a beer. 'I'll never forget that day. I was carrying a box and I dropped it. Stuff spilled all over the floor. Looked up from picking up the pieces and she was standing in the big barn door. A beam of light was coming through the window, it made her face glow like an angel's. Then a cloud passed by, and the light winked out, and I realized that I wasn't dead. She stayed the whole afternoon, bought some stuff, and we've been friends ever since.'

He drank some more water. 'I wanted to come to the bar, but she asked me not to. Some nights I'm sitting alone up there, watching my damned scratchy satellite TV, and I think, 'I can be there in thirty minutes.' It wouldn't bother me if the guys flirted with her. It wouldn't even bother me if she flirted with the girls. But she said it would bother her, to know I was watching. So I never go.'

Clarence fiddled with his cup, then pushed it away. 'I swear to God, if I was twenty years younger, and she was straight, and I wasn't—' He shook his head and closed his eyes.

Richard patted Clarence's arm hopelessly. He felt like an imbecile. All those evenings he'd spent with his friend, and he'd never even suspected.

* * *

Richard stood under a tree and watched Karen walk back toward Clarence. She sat down beside him, put an arm around him, and rested her head on his shoulder.

He turned back to the party and saw Val sauntering toward him, hand in hand with... Ralf. Ralf? She could have any guy in the Gorge—and she had; most of them, anyway—and she was with Ralf?

'Val?' he said. What is this, Shock Richard Day?

'Richard. You know Ralf, I think.'

'Yeah.' Sorry to say.

'Richard, man,' Ralf said, 'I got a question for you.'

'Well,' Val said, 'I'll just leave you two to your boy talk.' Richard watched her walk away. I'll get you for this.

'So you know computers, huh?'

'No,' Richard said, turning back.

Ralf's jaw went slack for a moment. He ducked his head and with one hand swept his long fringe of hair back away from his face.

'Val says you do some kind of computer shit for a living, man.'

'She's mistaken.' Richard took a swig of Corona. 'I'm retired.'

'Nuh uh, I know people, man, they said you set them up. Nadine, and... uh... um...'

'What's your question?'

'I was reading an article about computers—'

'In Highlights for Children, right?'

'Huh?' Ralf said.

'Go on.'

'Well, this dude said that in the twenty-first century, computers will be able to think.'

'I read an article, too. It said that in the twenty-first century, snow boarders will be able to think.'

Ralf frowned for a second, then broke into a belly laugh that snapped off abruptly. He slapped Richard hard on the arm, causing him to stumble. Beer sloshed out of his bottle.

'Good one, dude. No, really, here's my question. Can't they think already?'

'No.'

'Huh?'

'No.' Richard looked around for Pam, or A.M., or Nadine. Someone to rescue him.

'Oh, right. It's some kind of big secret, huh? All you computer guys are in on the conspiracy.'

'No.'

'Come on, man. What's the Internet all about? You hook up a billion computers, they're like brain cells, you know? Bam, you got an Einstein, Frankenstein, whatever. And HAL, man, what about HAL? He could think, he offed all those corpsicles.'

'Okay, Ralf, you're right. There is a secret. And since you're my pal, I'll tell you.'

'Cool, man. I'm all ears.'

And absolutely nothing in between. 'Ghosts,' Richard said.

'Ghosts?'

'Yep, it's all done with ghosts. They catch a ghost—'

'Like in Ghostbusters!'

'Just like in Ghostbusters. They catch them in a ghost trap and stick them in those little black chips inside the computer. Then the ghost has to work for food.'

'Oh, man. Ghost slaves.'

'Exactly. Like Roman galley slaves. But sometimes the chips leak, and the ghost gets out. That's what causes computer crashes.'

Ralf slapped his high forehead. 'Geez. That explains everything!'

'Right. Excuse me, I have to go find another reality.'

He found Val examining the brightly-wrapped presents on the gift table. 'This is quite a haul,' she said.

'Ralf? You're dating Ralf?'

'Oh, I wouldn't say I'm dating him, exactly.'

'How the hell did you get started with him?'

'Well, I knew who he was, but we'd never really met. We got to talking—'

'Talking?'

'Okay, we started necking at Clarence's party.' She took out a cigarette and lit up. When she turned her head to blow the smoke away from him, she looked like Lauren Bacall. 'One thing led to everything, like it does sometimes.' She took another drag and chuckled at his expression. 'Okay, I'll admit he's not the smartest guy I ever slept with.'

'Smart? Smart? If that guy eats a cantaloupe, it's cannibalism.'

She laughed. 'Yeah, conversation can be a little tough. But we don't spend much time talking.'

'What can you possibly find attractive about him?'

'Take a guess, Richard. He doesn't need any rhino horn, you know what I'm saying? He's got the rhino's other thing.' She took a deep drag and blew smoke into the wind. 'I figure I'll just screw him until one of us is dead. Then I'll stop.'

'You've got to be kidding,' Richard said.

'No. I'm not.'

'I give up, Val. Have fun with your new toy.'

'Thanks.' She smiled at him; it was scary. 'I will.'

* * *

The first domino was Jeremy falling out of a Bartlett tree.

A group of the kids, including, Richard later discovered, the birthday girl, had been daring each other to climb to the top of a tree. Pear trees are amazingly spindly considering the weight of fruit they can bear, and the wood is soft. Jeremy was the second one to reach the treetop. He was doing a Tarzan yell, beating his chest, when the branch snapped and he tumbled down, bouncing from one limb to the next.

The party went on hold for half an hour when a parade of screaming children interrupted the adults. They followed them back to the orchard at a run, where the chaos settled down as soon as it was clear that no one was dead—Jeremy had just fainted. Other than the compound fracture in his left arm, he was only bruised. His parents, faces stiff with anger and concern, loaded him into their station wagon and drove away.

The second domino fell a few minutes later, when Tiffannee, sickened by the blood and Jeremy's exposed bone, threw up all over the plate of cookies her mother had brought.

Number three was someone bumping into Sylvia as she was helping to clean up the mess. She stumbled into the food table and one of the folding legs collapsed, spilling all the pot-luck dishes into the grass, where small puddles of vomit still waited to be hosed away.

Some of the dishes were covered and could be salvaged, but by unspoken consent anything that had touched grass was garbage. Consuela, Nadine's partner, silently gathered Nadine's cousin Becky and her partner Jane, retired to the kitchen and went into hyperdrive.

They had a lovely Mexican dinner: three different salads, cactus soup, cheese and beef enchiladas, vegetable fajitas, and two moles. But it started two hours after the planned dinnertime, and several families had left by the time it was served.

'The hell with them,' A.M. said as she stood behind Miriam in the food line. 'More cake for us.'

'More happy birthday cake for me,' Miriam sang back.

It was dark by the time Richard called everyone inside for cake and presents. The remaining half dozen children ran inside immediately, followed at a more leisurely pace by their parents. Some of the adults paused at the gift table to grab an armful of presents and carry them inside.

If half the guests hadn't left already, there wouldn't have been space in the living room for everyone. As it was, they filled the sofas, the seats and arms of the chairs, and the floor in between the furniture. Several people stood against the walls.

Consuela carried in the tall white cake, candles flickering, and set it on the coffee table before the couch where Miriam, Tiff, and two of their friends sat, bouncing and kicking their feet. The tune to 'Happy Birthday' was not carried—it was fumbled, dropped, and intercepted by the other side. Miriam made her wish and blew out the candles, and pieces of cake were passed hand-to-hand around the room.

Richard was standing in the doorway between the living and dining rooms, snapping pictures now and then. When most people were done with their cake, he grabbed a present from the pile on the dining room table and passed it forward.

Miriam was not a gentle or patient opener of gifts. Shreds of paper and ribbon were flung all over the room. She did stop and dutifully read each card first, but the moment she had read the inscription aloud, the card dropped, forgotten, to the floor and the package it had been attached to was ferociously ripped apart.

She received toys, clothes, books, a soccer ball from Pam, and a short pair of pruning loppers from Becky. When the pile was gone, Miriam looked around politely, as if inviting anyone who had been too shy to offer gifts before to come forward now. Finally her stare came to rest on her father, who had so far given her nothing.

Richard smiled innocently at her for a moment, just to tease her, then he clumped down the stairs to the basement and came back up carrying a large, plain cardboard box with holes punched in its sides. He threaded his way carefully through the room and set the box down on the table in front of her. Something inside the box rustled.

Miriam hesitantly opened a flap of the box and looked in. A small black puppy launched itself at her face, licking her from chin to eyebrows. She yelped in delight and pulled the little dog out. It was utterly black, with silken, floppy ears and huge paws. As soon as it was clear of the box, it squirmed out of her hands and plopped into her lap, where it sat as if enthroned, surveying the room and yipping happily.

'Oh, Dad, he's great!'

'It's a girl,' Richard said.

From her place leaning against a desk, A.M. said, 'What are you going to call her?'

The puppy squirmed in Miriam's lap and looked around the room with cheerful curiosity. It yipped again, then tipped its head backwards and licked Miriam's chin, upside down.

'I'm going to call her Kobi.'

'Cobie?'

'Kobi, K-O-B-I. It means 'joy.''

Richard looked at Pam, who smiled at him. He smiled back weakly. It was just starting to sink in: his baby was ten years old.

* * *

Richard had been sitting for half an hour in the dark kitchen with Nadine, drinking coffee and companionably not talking, when he realized that the living room was silent as well. Miriam had been in there with her friends and her new puppy. If it was quiet, something must be wrong.

Nadine followed him out of the kitchen, still holding her big glass mug. Miriam was sleeping in a big chair, curled up around Kobi. On the couch, Pam and Sylvia had their heads together, whispering, while A.M. lay on her back with her head on Sylvia's lap, apparently asleep. Everyone else had gone home.

Pam looked up when they walked in. 'Time to go?' she said softly. Richard nodded.

He carried his daughter and Pam carried the pup. Nadine opened the back door of his car for him. He buckled Miriam into her seat belt and took the half-asleep puppy, laying her on the seat next to Miriam. The rest of the gifts had been loaded earlier, so they were ready to go.

'Thanks for doing this,' he said to Nadine. 'No way I could have surprised her like this at home.'

'Yah, no problem. You know she's welcome any time. And her dog, too.'

'Thanks. Don't stay up all night doing dishes.'

Nadine laughed. 'I don't do dishes. That's why I have farm hands.'

A.M. stumbled out of the house, rubbing and stretching her neck. 'Hey,' she said, 'you leaving?'

'Yep.'

'Didn't get a chance to talk to you much.'

'Yeah, you were too busy tormenting all the straight couples.'

'Um. So...' She watched Pam give Sylvia a hug and climb into Richard's car. 'You guys are an 'it' now, huh?' Richard just glared at her. 'That's good. But you owe me—I want details. Stop by the shop and tell me everything. And maybe you should take notes so you don't forget anything juicy.'

'A.M....'

'What?'

'Never mind. Go home.'

He hugged Nadine and got into his Subaru. It took half an hour to drive home, and he was getting pretty bleary by the time they pulled into the driveway. Pam carried the dog again, trailing him upstairs. Miriam lay in his arms like Raggedy Ann, sound asleep.

'Do you want the puppy in here?'

He thought about it for a few seconds. 'Yes. She might make a mess, but I want her here when Miriam wakes up.'

Kobi settled into a small pile of clothes at the foot of Miriam's bed and instantly fell asleep. Richard pulled the light blanket up to Miriam's chin and closed the door.

He hesitated for a moment, but then headed toward his room. Pam followed him and closed the door behind him.

'Does this door have a lock?' she said. He locked it. She started unbuttoning his shirt.

Chapter 11: Dirty Dog

From the Hood River Examiner
Friday, June 16, 1995

Mrs. Bambi Knows

Who's snooping whom?

Dear Mrs. Bambi:

I recently discovered to my horror that my oldest and dearest friend— I'll call her Beth—is living a double life. She's an accountant here in town with a great job. She has a doting husband, two wonderful children, a nice home. You would think her life was perfect.

Last week I was in the jewelry store, checking out the new watches, when I saw Beth come in. Before I had a chance to go over and say hi, I saw her drop a gold chain necklace down her bra. Then she walked out without paying, as cool as iced salmon.

I was too shocked to say anything to the store manager, but I started following her to see what else she might be up to. Here are some excerpts from my journal.

Wednesday, 2:47 p.m.: B makes phone call from pay phone near library. Drives to motel, rents room, enters room. Strange man drives up, knocks on B's door. B kisses him, lets him inside! One hour later stranger opens door, hands her a wad of cash, leaves.

Thursday, 9:19 p.m.: B walks down Cascade, stops, looks both ways. Doesn't see me hiding behind tree. Pulls long piece of metal out of purse, jimmies open car door. Not her car! Leans down in front seat, hot-wires car, drives off.

Friday, 4:32 p.m.: B leaves her office hanging on her boss. They get into his car, drive to same motel she was in Wednesday, get room! Two hours later, B comes out alone. Looks happy and flushed.

Saturday, 5:51 a.m.: B works down her street, picking through neighbors' trash cans. Keeps some items, stuffing them in blue canvas Gucci bag. Flings garbage into street, leaves can lids on ground.

As you can see, Beth is clearly a shoplifter, call girl, car thief, adulterer, and I don't know what you call it—a bum? What should I do? Should I tell her husband? Should I confront her? Maybe she's a psycho. Should I call the police? I thought I was her best friend, but it's clear I don't know her at all. I don't see how I can face her at our next weekly lunch. Help!

—*Ms. Sherlock*

Dear Snoop Hound of the Baskervilles:

I'd like to help you, but I don't have a psychiatrist's license. You need some professional assistance, girl. I suggest you drag yourself pronto into the office of someone who can prescribe some tasty drugs and maybe a long stay in a nice hospital with bars on the windows.

Or, plan B, this is a gag, right? In that case, I think you should still follow the advice above, because you are a very, very sick person.

Or, option 3, you're serious and the events you described really happened. In that case, please see the advice above. Don't you have anything better to do than follow your friends around night and day? Be like uranium: get a half-life.

Also, Beth honey, if your friend isn't fried or joking, please stay away from me. And you could use some chemicals, too.

Dear Mrs. Bambi:

I can't get my stupid dog to stay in the yard. He visits all of my neighbors every day, chasing their cats, digging up their gardens, and eating their geese. I have over twenty acres of woods, and there's just no way to build a fence. I've tried one of those radio fences, but he just ignores the pain and runs through it. I've tried tying him up, but he digs enormous holes, kills all the plants, and wraps himself around the trees.

122

He's five years old, and though I've tried hard I can't find him a new home. My neighbors have threatened to shoot him if he keeps terrorizing them, and I'm almost ready to off the mutt myself.

My vet is out of ideas. Do you have any suggestions? And yes, he's been neutered.

—*Dog Tired*

Dear Flea Bag:

Try this. Get one of those baby bouncers that people hang from the kitchen doorway. Cut two more leg holes where the baby's butt would go. Pick a tree with a branch that would be good for a tire swing, and tie a rope to it. Hook the rope to the back of the bouncer, then stick your dog in the bouncer. If you adjust the rope carefully, he shouldn't be able to reach the tree trunk or anything else. Be sure to put some food and water out there where he can get to it.

If that doesn't work, I've heard that a soy sauce, ginger, and lemon grass marinade will make even the toughest pooch palatable.

* * *

After an hour of signing papers, Richard's hand was numb but Gail had her new women's shelter. Her gaunt face, eyes dark with raccoon smudges, looked rather gruesome when she smiled, but he was happy to see her smiling anyway. Her life had not been easy. Gail's ex-husband, now in jail for armed robbery, had beaten her violently and often. The shelter she had started several years ago, Faith House, was named for her sister, who had been clubbed to death with a tire iron by her drunken husband.

When the papers were all signed, Richard gave the title agent a cashier's check for $287,845.93, and Faith House was back in business. Gail hugged him quietly, her tears soaking into his shirt. The title agent—a very cross-looking woman wearing a gray suit, her hair in a bun so tight it seemed to be pulling her face back—stopped on her way out of the room, set down her stack of papers, and also gave Richard a painfully strong hug. Then, without saying a word, she picked up her files and left Richard alone with Pam.

Pam raised an eyebrow at him. 'Want to go get a beer?'

'Uh huh.'

They walked the seven blocks to Pig's Wings. A storm was stalled at Cascade Locks twenty miles to the west, dark ominous clouds piled up high above the Gorge, but the sky overhead was clear. They climbed the shaky outside stairs and then the cramped inner stairway to the bar. Karen came by after they were settled at a small table. Richard asked for the Snout Stout, Pam ordered the Curly-Tail Ale.

'Have you read today's Mrs. Bambi yet?' Pam said.

Christ, here we go again. 'Yeah. Why?'

'That column's sort of a Freudian slip, don't you think?'

'What do you mean?'

'The double life. The hidden truth. Multiple personalities.'

'I don't see what—'

'Never mind. Let me ask you another question. Has Miriam stayed at Tiff's house lately?'

'It's been about a month, actually. Why?'

'Interesting. Where's she staying tonight?'

'A.M. and Sylvia went to Portland this morning for shopping and a movie. They took Miriam with them to celebrate. Yesterday was the last day of school.'

Pam nodded. Karen set down their drinks, looked from one to the other, and walked away without saying a word. Pam picked up her Ale.

'What's going on?' Richard said.

'You won't believe what I heard on the grapevine last night.'

Last night? They'd slept together at his house most of the nights this week, since Miriam's birthday party, but last night Pam had said she had some work to do.

'Really? Something juicy?'

'Very, very juicy. I heard that you, Richard Lantz, are really Mrs. Bambi.'

It took a moment to sink in. He wasn't sure he'd heard her right. Then the words toppled from his ears into his stomach like big lead weights. How? Who could have told her? Frank? Richard had planned to do something, he just hadn't had a chance yet to decide what. For a moment he considered lying, but it was too late.

'So it's true,' she said. He could only nod. 'You let me rant about her for weeks, without telling me? You must have found that very amusing.'

'No, not—'

'I never pegged you for a liar, Richard. Not just a liar. You were defending her. I don't believe this.' She sat back in her chair. 'The biggest bitch in town is my boyfriend.'

Richard took a deep breath. 'Pam...'

'What? You think what you did for the shelter excuses this?'

'What? No, I just—'

'Tell me something, Richard. How do you make a living doing your little bits of computer jazz?'

'What?'

'Where do you get your money?'

Richard had to close his eyes for a moment. He felt dizzy. 'What does that have to do with anything?'

'I want to know. I want to know how big a liar you really are.'

He touched a finger to the cold side of his beer glass. Little beads of condensation were gathering and running down the canted edge. He watched a drop slide all the way to the table top and merge with the small puddle there, and suddenly he felt calm. If this was the end, he would end it with honesty.

'When I lived in Seattle, I was an inventor, an engineer. I designed a little doohickey that ended up being used in a lot of brands of hard drives. The royalties weren't much, but it was enough to live on if I worked a little. Then, about four years ago, my father died. I hadn't spoken to the son of a bitch since he left us when I was in high school. We never knew what happened to him—the bastard went out and got rich selling used airplane parts. He left us all his money. Even split four ways, it was enough so that I never have to work again. Do you want to know how much?'

Pam inspected him closely for a few seconds. 'No,' she said. 'I want to hear about Mrs. Bambi.'

* * *

'Okay.' He took another deep breath and let it all come rushing out. 'I met Frank at one of A.M.'s weird parties. We were the only guys, and the only straights, too, so we got to talking. I was a little drunk. When he told me what he did for a living, I started ragging him about the rotten writing in the Examiner. He was just as drunk as I was. He says, okay Mr. Hot Shit, see if you

125

can do better. I didn't want to be a reporter, so we came up with the idea of doing an advice column.

'It was Frank's idea to use a pseudonym. Who's going to take advice from a thirty-year old unemployed guy? He wanted to call her Bambi. I think he knew a dancer in Vegas named Bambi. I said, who's going to take advice from a bimbo? She should be Mrs. Bambi. She used to be a bimbo, but now she's older and she's been around the marina a few times, she knows something about the world.

'We made up the first few letters, just to prime the pump. Then people started writing us, and everything was fine for a year or so, until the volume dropped off. I guess people didn't like my advice. We were down to a few letters a week, most of them unusable—unprintable, actually. Frank suggested maybe we should let it die quietly, but I had an idea. Why not write the letters that people should be writing me? However bad my advice was, it had to be better than the mess people were making of their own lives.

'So I started eavesdropping. After a while I got to like it. It's a thrill, like having secret powers, to listen to people's problems and know you could help if they'd only listen to you. It was fun. Frank didn't like it much, but I found plenty of material to keep doing the column. After a while, we started getting complaints and some buzz in the community, and it sold papers.

'Now he's torn between what it's done for circulation and the hassle of dealing with pissed-off, uh, subjects every week.'

'And what about you?'

He pushed his beer glass away. 'I've been debating lately over whether to stop.'

'Afraid you'd get caught?'

'Um...'

Pam took her wallet out of her purse and put some money down on the table. 'Richard, I really like you, but this might be too much for me.' She stood up.

'Pam, don't—'

'I need some time to think this through. I'll... I'll see you around.'

He watched her walk out. After a second's thought, he got up and went to one of the windows. He could see her going down the last of the steps and head uphill back to her office.

His imaginary tail was drooping. Maybe he should head up to Clarence's place. If he was going to be in the dog house, he could use a dog wash. But when he called, Clarence said that he'd had a hard day and was going to bed early. For the first time in quite a while, Richard had nothing to do on his night off.

* * *

On Monday, Richard stood outside A.M.'s shop, trying to make sense of the display window. Against a backdrop of draped fabric, a blue so dark it was almost black, a single mannequin was posed wearing one of A.M.'s designs. The insectile doll was formed of glittery gray plastic, its waist draped in a short, wrap-around skirt that could have been made from a throw rug—tassels included. Over its chest was a backless copper breastplate that Madonna would have rejected as too revealing, completely covered in Mayan symbols worked into the metal.

The mannequin hung suspended from the ceiling, upside down, on almost invisible threads.

Mayans in Space? Was she implying that the Chariots of the Gods had been made, or at least driven, by ancient Mayans? Richard shook his head and gave up.

It had been a few weeks since he'd visited her shop, but there were no changes that he could see. It was empty of people, as usual, but the floor space was filled with racks of bizarre clothing. Near the door hung blouses with only one sleeve. He fingered the shiny material, dyed in alternating teal and black stripes, peppered with white blotches as if a flock of very large birds had just taken flight overhead; it felt like normal cotton.

A.M. poked her head out from the back room. 'Come on back,' she said, 'I'm on the phone.'

As she finished her conversation, Richard looked for a place to sit. All of the chairs were covered with books, stacks of paper, bolts of fabric, and takeout food detritus. He lifted a pile of papers from one of the chairs and set it carefully against the wall.

A.M. hung up. 'Coffee?'

'Sure.'

She puttered at the coffee machine. Her very long black hair was braided and tied with an orange ribbon. He was a bit disappointed at her modest clothes today: a knee-length skirt of jaguar skin print and a spotless white sleeveless blouse with ruffles around the neck and down the front. No thighs, buttocks, or cleavage was visible. Tame.

She set two mugs of coffee down, swept a pile of cloth from the chair next to his, and sat. He blew on his coffee but didn't try it yet.

'So what are you and Pam fighting about?' she said.

Richard set his cup down, untasted. 'Do you have everyone in town spying on me?'

'Karen was working at the bar.'

True. And she'd noticed the tension between them.

She waited, but he said nothing. 'Aren't you going to tell me?'

'No.'

A.M. leaned back in her chair and sipped from her mug. 'Richard, you are a bitter disappointment to me. I don't even know why I like you. You've lived like a damned monk since before I ever knew you, unfairly depriving me of the titillation that is my Goddess-given right. The most exciting thing I've ever seen you do was to puke on a couchful of dykes. Finally, you've found yourself a lusty wench, and you won't tell me a thing. Not one detail about your sex life or even what you're fighting about. Is this fair? After all the stories I've told you?'

'I never asked you to tell me about your sex life with Sylvia. You don't tell me dirty stories for my benefit, A.M., you do it because you get off on it. You're a verbal exhibitionist.'

'I am, in fact, every kind of exhibitionist. What does that have to do with anything? We're friends, you bent-rod asshole. You're supposed to share things with me.'

Richard turned the mug around. There was a picture of Betty Boop on it. That figured. 'I can't tell you what happened, A.M.,' he said.

'Do you mean you don't know or you just won't tell me?'

'I won't. I'm sorry, it's private.' She snorted. He doubted that she understood what the word meant. Not that he, in his Mrs. Bambi persona, understood it any better than she did.

'Great,' she said. 'Let's talk about the weather. Hot enough for you?'

'Oh, fu—'

The shop door's bell rang. A.M. held up an index finger. 'Hold that thought,' she said, and went out front.

Richard followed her. He couldn't remember the last time he'd seen a customer in the shop, and he wanted to watch.

It was a young woman with short-cropped white hair. She turned to look at something on the wall, and Richard saw a wide purple streak running from the crown of her head to her right ear. It was surprisingly attractive. She wore snug black tights and a cropped white T-shirt that showed off her flat stomach. He expected A.M. to fawn all over the girl, but she simply said a few words and busied herself at the register.

Streaky took over ten minutes inspecting every display. When she passed the doorway where Richard stood, they nodded at each other and she smiled at him. Her tights were very tight. He tried not to stare, but the departing view was impressive.

'Very interesting shop,' the woman said to A.M. when she'd completed her circuit of the shop. She had a slight German accent.

'Thanks,' A.M. said. The woman headed toward the door. 'Come back.'

'Oh, I will.'

A.M. walked toward him. 'I saw you staring at her butt.'

'So were you.'

'Uh huh. If you don't tell Sylvia, I won't tell Pam.'

They went back to the table and sat down. Richard took his first sip of coffee. It was cooling.

'I'm sorry,' he said.

'It's okay. I understand, I guess. You know, if there's ever anything you need to talk about, you can call me. I'd really like to help.'

'I wish you could help me with this. But Pam and I need to get through it ourselves.'

'Okay, tough guy,' she said.

'What were you and Pam and Sylvia talking about at Miriam's party?'

'Pam's got some ideas for the shop. Some good ones, actually.'

'She mentioned something about that. What kind of ideas?'

'Oh, I'm not ready to talk about it yet,' she said.

'Well, just in general.'

'In general? Improving sales.'

'That wouldn't be hard.'

'Thanks, that's very kind. For your information, I sold something just yesterday.'

'Really?' he said.

'This six-foot tall Amazon came in and bought some boots.'

'Did you offer to lick them for her?'

'Oh, ha ha. As a matter of fact, I did, but she said she'd rather just give me all her money.'

'You're going to get in trouble with Sylvia if you keep coming on to the customers.'

'Oh, for Tlaloc's sake, Richard, you know better. You think I'm going to ruin the chance of a sale just for a quickie?'

'I was only joking.'

'Yeah, me too. Shut up.'

He took another drink of coffee, but now it was cold. 'How was Miriam on Friday?'

'She was fine. She's a hoot to go shopping with. She was all, 'Dad would never get that for me,' and 'Isn't that cool! I could never get Dad to buy that.' How come you're so stingy with her?'

'To make up for all the spoiling you and Sylvia do.'

'We don't spoil her.'

'Oh, really?' he said. 'What did you have for dinner?'

'Uh... Pizza, gum drops, and ice cream.'

'See?'

'Shut up. We're just trying to give her a good time.'

'I know. I think if I died tomorrow, my friends would roll my corpse into the gutter and then start fighting over who gets Miriam.'

'Not true,' she said. 'We'd bury your corpse in the back yard and time-share her.'

He sighed. 'I've got to go. She's going to be back from her swimming lesson soon.'

'Okay. If you want my advice—'

'Not really.'

'—you'll go buy Pam a big bouquet of flowers and a cute little sex toy and try to make up with her.'

'Thanks, A.M.,' he said sarcastically. 'That's a great idea.'

* * *

Early Thursday afternoon, Richard took a break from working on a glitch in the flower shop's point-of-sale computer. He walked across the street to the Pizza Plaza and ordered two slices of pepperoni pizza and a Full Sail. The large, floppy wedges came on a sheet of red-checked paper that he carried over to a tall stool at the bar looking out on Oak Street. There were a few tables open, and a loft upstairs that looked empty, but he liked watching the town go by while he ate.

Windsurfers and normal people strolled, jogged, and biked past the window. He was pretty sure he could tell the windsurfers, by the cultish hair (men: short and moussed, women: long, straight, and tied back), the clothes, the perfect, wiry bodies, and the too-early tans. Some of the pedestrians stared at Richard as if he were a fish in a bowl; others seemed unaware that they were the fish. A steady stream of traffic rolled by.

He was well into his second slice when Connie, his shrill nemesis, walked past, glanced up at him, and stopped dead. Richard groaned around his pizza.

Connie tottered back to the restaurant door and flung it open. 'Richard!' She pranced over to him. Why was she walking like that? He looked down and saw that she was wearing bright red sandals with six-inch heels.

'You're still alive!' Pity. He took another bite of pizza, not quite looking at her.

'I've been asking around and no one even knew you were sick, although I did hear that you broke up with your girlfriend, what's her name, anyway you look really good! Are you sure you should be eating that, and beer, I don't think you should be drinking beer if you're still on chemo...'

What was she yabbering about? It took him a moment to remember how he had ditched her last time, when he and Pam were having lunch at Vito's— by saying he had cancer.

Wait a minute. She'd heard that he and Pam had broken up?

'I'm in remission,' he said.

'Oh, that's good news. Now, before you go—I mean, leave here, not, you know, go, sorry—there's something I've been meaning to ask you, it's about my computer—now don't look at me like that, I deleted that program you told me to, even though it would have been better if you did it, it took me all afternoon and I'm still not sure I did it right—'

She broke off suddenly and ran her fingers through his stubbly hair. He shivered at the contact; it was like being petted by a leopard. She looked at her hand as if expecting to see loose hairs from the chemo. He went back to his pizza, even though there was a knot in his stomach.

'Anyway,' she continued, 'I'm having a horrible problem, I can't seem to find the on switch to my computer any more, I think it must have crashed somehow, and I need you to come over right away, but don't worry, if it takes too long I have some nice steaks we can barbecue and maybe you could help me fix the one leg on my bed—'

She stopped again and didn't continue. Richard looked up and saw Pam standing with her hand clamped firmly over Connie's mouth. The knot in his stomach evaporated.

'For your own safety, I think you should leave,' Pam said. 'If we happen to have an earthquake, you're going to topple off those fuck-me pumps and break your skinny neck.'

Connie's mouth was open but nothing came out. Pam sat down at the stool next to Richard and took a sip of his beer.

'Also, my dear, I don't think Richard will be able to help you with your silly computer any more. You might as well just throw the thing in the trash, or better yet, donate it to the high school. You see, he's very ill, and he may not have much time left, and I think he's going to be spending all his remaining days or hours, however few they may be, screwing his brains out. With me.'

Connie stumbled back a step, mouth still agape, utter surprise on her face. Richard smiled at her cheerfully, and she wobbled back outside and down the street.

'I am?' Richard said.

'Just until neither one of us can walk again.'

'I thought you needed some time to think about... um...'

'You think six days isn't enough? I can come back later—'

He grabbed her arm to keep her on her stool. 'Now is fine.' She settled back onto her seat.

'This is going to surprise you,' Pam said. 'But the more I thought about it, the funnier it got.'

'Funny?'

'Yes, funny. I went back and reread a lot of your columns. I was visualizing you hovering around in Safeway and Dairy Queen, taking notes. And sitting in front of your computer thinking up all those sharp retorts, while everyone in town tried to figure out who the Witch of the West really was. And Frank having to edit what he knew was fiction. It made me laugh.'

'I never thought I'd hear you say that.'

'Oh, I was mad at first. I felt like you'd lied to me, but I thought back to our first few dates, and almost from the very beginning I was raving about Mrs. Bambi. I tried to think, if I was Mrs. Bambi and you were raving, how would I have told you? I couldn't come up with a way to do it. So I decided to give you the benefit of the doubt.'

'It took you six days to figure that out?'

'No, it took me two days. Then I let you stew in it for another four, as revenge.'

'Consider yourself revenged.'

'I do. But I have a question for you. Does Miriam know?'

'No. I've thought about telling her, but it's too complicated to explain. And I'm not sure she could keep the secret.'

She looked at him appraisingly for a moment. 'So, are you busy now?'

'I was in the middle of helping Angela fix her computer. Uh... why?'

'I was thinking we could go back to my place.'

'Oh, well, I guess I could knock off, I mean, come back, um... tomorrow.'

'Good. Because we have some serious thinking to do.' She stood up and he did the same.

'Oh. Thinking?'

'You haven't got around to asking me how I found out your little secret. Or have you guessed by now?'

'No.'

'Tiff's father, Sam, told me. He said he was concerned after he saw us together at Miriam's party that I might not know who I was getting involved with.'

Sam? How the hell could Sam have known? But that would explain why they hadn't wanted to take Miriam on Friday nights lately. The last time had been over a month ago. Could he have known for that long? But if he knew...

'Ah,' Pam said. 'You've figured it out. Sam and Carrie aren't what you would call discreet. If they know who you are, pretty soon everybody in town's going to know.' She held the door open for him and he walked out onto the sunny street. The passing strangers—some ignoring him, some staring idly—suddenly seemed ominous. 'We have to go figure out what to do when people start throwing rocks at your house.'

Chapter 12: Last Harrumph

From the Hood River Examiner
Friday, June 23, 1995

Mrs. Bambi Knows

Kill TV, spare sporto husband

Dear Mrs. Bambi:

My husband is a sports addict, primarily TV sports because he doesn't even have the gumption to get off his butt and go watch a game live. He does occasionally wander down to the bar to watch games and drink beer with his buddies. That's an improvement, I guess, because then he's out of my sight.

He has no discrimination, either. Football, baseball, basketball, hockey, golf, championship aardvark wrestling, bowling for Jello, whatever. I don't think I can bear the Olympics next year—they're like one long orgasm for him, but I just get a headache.

I've decided to kill the worthless sack of pig crud, but I don't think I can do it myself. So I was wondering if you knew how to hire a hit man. I'm looking for someone discreet, reliable, and not too expensive. Any ideas?

—Killer

Dear Phyllis:

This is not a good idea. All you really want is for your husband to get off his butt and stop watching sports, right? So don't kill your husband.

Kill your TV.

Poetic justice demands that you do it with a baseball bat. I recommend a wooden Louisville Slugger; aluminum bats are for sissies, and they conduct electricity, too. If for some reason you can't find one around the house, Wal-Mart sells them.

Do it right in the middle of a big game. Be careful not to stand in front of the set when you hit it, because the tube is going to implode, and you'll get showered with glass. Strike one should be right in the middle of the tube.

When your husband shoots up off the couch, both of your objectives will be accomplished. Now wasn't that easy? The bat will come in handy then, too: if he comes after you, assume the batter's crouch. He will know exactly what that means. Explain to him calmly that you have had enough sports to last you until the Dodgers come back to Brooklyn, and it's time the two of you found some pastimes in common.

If he buys another TV, do it again. Sooner or later he'll get the idea. Then he'll either leave you or find a way to overcome his addiction. Either way you'll get what you want without any of those pesky inconveniences like a trial or jail time.

Dear Mrs. Bambi:

Was Tyrannosaurus rex a predator or a scavenger? There are good arguments for both sides, and I can't decide. It's hard to imagine something that big running down his dinner like a lion, but it's so demeaning to think of T. rex as nothing but a huge reptilian vulture.

—*Rex Fan*

Dear Dino Boy:

The latest biomechanical studies have shown that T. rex could probably run at thirty miles an hour or more. What's the point of speed if he was just going to walk up and snarf down someone else's leftovers?

Also, dinosaurs weren't reptiles any more than you are. Dinosaurs and mammals evolved at the same time from different reptilian ancestors. Bone structure shows they are more closely related to birds than reptiles, and they probably had endothermic metabolisms, so that makes them more like us than like a lizard.

My own theory is that T. rex was a carriage horse for intelligent velociraptors. Big legs, small arms. You figure it out.

* * *

Dogs and people traipsed around a dusty circle in the hot sun. The motley collection of mutts and one purebred German shepherd strained at their leashes, trying to coalesce into a pack. At the other end of the leashes, the humans, mostly children but also two adults already tight-faced with boredom and despair, struggled to walk the circle, constantly being tugged nearly off their feet toward the center. Heeling practice was not going very well, except for one happy black Labrador mix and her owner. Richard waved at Miriam as she passed by him again with Kobi trotting along obediently at her side.

'I told A.M. I was going to watch Miriam's obedience training,' Pam said. 'She said if her mother had known there was obedience training for kids, she would have had a leash on A.M. in a second and now she'd be stuck with a leather fetish.'

'She has enough fetishes as it is.'

'Really? Like what?'

He watched Miriam pass by again. 'I'd rather not say in front of all these tender ears.'

'I don't think the dogs are as innocent as you think. Look.'

A fuzzy mop of a Shih Tzu was trying to climb onto the shepherd with obvious carnal intent. It could have walked beneath her belly without ducking its head. The two owners and the 4H trainer were trying to disentangle the dogs. The shuffling circle dissolved into chaos.

'Anyway,' Pam said, 'I guess I'll get a chance to find out for myself tomorrow.'

'What?'

'A.M. and Sylvia invited us to a party.'

'Oh no!'

'Relax,' she said. 'It'll be fun.'

Fun? He'd been to dozens of A.M.'s parties. They were a little like public executions: revolting but impossible to turn away from.

The trainer called a halt for the day and pleaded with everyone to practice for next time. The adult students were so obviously fed up that they would never be back.

'That went well,' Pam said as Miriam walked up to them.

137

'Sit,' Miriam said. Kobi shrugged her rump and sat. Both of them beamed up at Richard.

'Treats,' he announced. At the Dairy Queen drive-through, a friendly young woman with buzzed red hair and a stud in her nose handed over a tray of Blizzards and a tiny, narrow ice cream cone for Kobi.

* * *

'Time to give it up, asshole.'

'Hello, Frank,' Richard said.

'You've really baked yourself into a pot pie now. I just got a complaint about your last column, naming you personally as the author. It's on the street, pal.'

Richard carried the cordless phone into the living room and looked outside. No mobs, no picketers, no snipers. 'So what do you suggest I do?'

'I think we should print an apology, shut down the column, and you should move to New Zealand—or Cleveland, whichever is farther away.'

'I'm not moving anywhere,' Richard said. 'And what's the point of stopping now? If everyone's going to know soon, it won't matter if I do a few more columns before they drag me to the guillotine.'

'It'll matter to the poor slobs you write about. And one of them might have a gun.'

'Everybody has a gun. The question is, do they know which end the bullet comes out of?'

Frank sighed. 'Why are you being so stubborn? I didn't think you even liked doing it any more.'

'I don't. But I do. Look, I know we're going to have to stop soon. Let me keep going as long as they'll let me. We have the rest of our lives to live without Mrs. Bambi.'

'You are a very sick man,' Frank said, and hung up.

Pam had also tried to talk him into abandoning the column. Maybe, she'd said, if Mrs. Bambi shuts up, the whole thing would die down in a few weeks and the scattered people who knew his identity wouldn't be able find anyone who cared any more.

He didn't see it that way. The end of Mrs. Bambi's column would be a much bigger sensation than its continuation. Everyone would wonder why she quit; then the hunt would be on for real, and the few who knew the truth would go tell it on the mountain, and in every bar and church in town.

Richard didn't know the right thing to do. But it was too late to just bow out and hope the curtain didn't crush him as it fell.

He went onto the porch and sat in a wicker chair. Miriam would be home from her swimming lesson soon.

Who had divulged his secret? It was impossible to believe that Tiff's parents had discovered it themselves. Sam was an electrician, Carrie was a substitute teacher. It was hard to imagine anyone in town less connected than they were. Except himself. So who had told them?

The cars and pedestrians streamed by. In two weeks, would he still be able to sit out here and enjoy the weather in peace?

*   *   *

The summer solstice fell on Wednesday that year—an inconvenient day for witches, lesbians, and goddess worshipers to party—so A.M. scheduled her annual pagan ritual for the following Saturday. Pam parked her Explorer in the first empty spot they could find and she and Richard walked the block and a half back. It was about 8:30. The sun was just setting below the hills to the west, but it would be another two hours before the sky was fully black.

A.M.'s neighborhood was a suburb of Hood River, itself a small town of five thousand people. This development was about a decade old, and the houses were typical Northwest suburban eighties homes: cedar siding, shingled roofs, big garages and windows, and too many small rooms inside.

Sylvia answered the doorbell. They could hear the music even before the door opened; once inside it was so loud that they experienced it more with their skin than their ears. Richard was well into the room before he realized that he recognized the song: it was the Indigo Girls. Trust A.M. to play acoustic rock so loud that it sounded like heavy metal.

There were over a dozen women in the great room, trying to talk over the singer's epic wailing, grazing at a table laden with finger food, and one couple was dancing what looked like a waltz, though the music was aggressively 4/4. Richard was the only man in the room.

Though not all of the females were women. In the doorway to the kitchen a woman in her late twenties was rather obviously seducing a girl in

139

her late teens, leaning in close to feed her sloppy tidbits of something with her fingers. The girl had the freshly-scrubbed, innocent look that Richard had always associated with cheerleaders until he actually got to know some. The cheerleaders he had met in college were as cunning as timber wolves and as cuddly as porcupines.

For a pagan solstice gathering, this was pretty tame. No outrageous outfits—just jeans and shorts with T-shirts or blouses, and a few dresses—no blood rituals, no brooms. Richard followed Pam into the kitchen, edging carefully past the seductress and her prey. Pam spotted a pitcher of margaritas and poured herself one. Richard found a beer in the fridge.

They wandered back out into the living room. A.M. was nowhere to be seen. Sylvia was leaning against the dining room wall, nodding as another woman yelled at her over the music. Richard didn't know these people, though he recognized some of them from other parties in the past. Then he spotted Karen sitting in a large tan leather chair, slowly and methodically pouring herself shots of Wild Turkey and slugging them back. He waved but she didn't see him.

Nothing about the house, other than the preponderance of women, suggested lesbian. No, he took that back. In a little art niche in the living room, a clear glass sculpture about two feet high showed two naked women. One had her head thrown back, her long hair brushing the ground. The other caressed the first's breast as she kissed her neck. But Richard had known dozens of men that would gladly have owned that piece if their wives had allowed it.

In the kitchen doorway, the seduction seemed complete: the older woman had a finger hooked in the waistband of the girl's jeans, and the girl's hand was on the woman's hip. The dancing couple swayed in place, locked so tightly together there was no air between them. Then the music cut off so abruptly that Richard thought for one panicky moment he had gone deaf. His ears rang with the echoes of near harmony.

He turned to see A.M. entering the room. She wore one of her lampshade blouses, closed tight at the throat but open below; it swung like a bell with every step. A cobalt blue breechcloth that barely covered her groin. Low boots with leather thongs that wrapped around her bare legs to the knee. A short jaguar-print cape that hung down to her ass, fringed with dozens of puffy white balls on short strings. Brightly-colored glass Christmas tree ornaments formed a thick necklace at her throat and a matching bracelet on her left wrist.

Richard felt a belly laugh trying to explode out of him, so he started clapping, and in a moment everyone in the room was applauding her audacious costume. A.M. glided through the room regally, pausing twice to kiss someone on the cheek, but heading straight toward Richard. The thick necklace made it hard for her to move her neck, giving her an aloof, queenly posture. Sylvia held a hand over her eyes in mortification.

When A.M. reached Richard and Pam, she slowly and deliberately leaned back. The blouse was open at the bottom and she wore nothing but a skimpy bra beneath it. As the lampshade tilted up, Richard was face to breast with her chest. Pam burst out laughing and Richard felt his face go hot.

'Better keep him, Pam,' A.M. pronounced majestically. 'Any guy who can blush like that is sure to be faithful.'

* * *

Pam had found someone she knew and was hunkered down in a corner with her, shouting over the resurgent music. Richard went to sit on the edge of the couch near Karen.

She looked ghastly. Dark rings circled her eyes like bad make-up. Her skin was pasty, her dirty brown hair pulled back into an indifferent ponytail. She might have been wearing the same stained 'Nuke Elvis' T-shirt and torn blue jeans for days. Richard sat watching her sip Wild Turkey for several minutes before she noticed him.

'Ah, Richard,' she said thickly. 'You and Pam get over your little fight?'

'You know, there are faster ways to kill yourself.'

'Not as much fun.'

'You look like a microwaved cow pie. Are you sick?'

She very carefully poured herself another drink. Richard put his hand on her knee. It rested over a large hole torn through the worn denim. White threads stretched tightly over her pink kneecap, weft without warp. Many of them had torn and hung listlessly like broken flower stems. Karen ran her fingertips lightly over the back of Richard's hand and took a drink.

'Can't talk about it,' she said. 'I'd like to, Richard, God knows I would, but I promised him.'

141

'Promised who? Clarence? Is something wrong with Clarence?'

The lights went out. Richard looked up. In the back yard, someone was lighting luminarias made from brown paper bags. Several women ran out the patio door from the dining room and immediately began shucking their clothes. It was the biannual solstice dance, traditionally done naked between the artificial stars below and the real ones in the sky, and secretly the only thing he actually liked about A.M.'s parties, but he turned back to Karen. She was gazing raptly outside.

'Yes,' she said. She stood up unsteadily and started walking toward the doorway, swaying a little on her feet. She tugged on her T-shirt but it refused to come out of her jeans. 'Baby dykes,' Karen called, 'I'm coming for you. Yoo hoo, sweet things!' She took another step and tripped on her own feet. Richard stood up, too late, but Sylvia came out of nowhere to catch her before she hit the floor.

'Help me get her into bed,' Sylvia said. Richard took Karen's left arm and helped Sylvia guide her into the guest room.

'Yes, bed,' Karen crooned. 'I need sex, Richard.'

'Uh huh.'

'You send me something, okay, Sylvia? Something sweet, something young? Please?'

'Sure, Karen,' Sylvia said. They covered her with the blanket; she was asleep before they closed the door. Sylvia leaned against the hallway wall. 'She's been drinking like that for hours.'

'What's wrong? Did she say?'

'She won't talk about it. A.M. said she hasn't been to work in a week. We thought the party might cheer her up, but the moment she got here she sat down with that bottle and wouldn't talk to anyone.'

'She said she promised 'him' that she wouldn't talk about 'it.''

'Him who?'

'Clarence, maybe?'

'Could be.' She thought for a moment. 'He hasn't looked so great lately.'

'He's looked like shit for a month.'

They stood without speaking. Sylvia flicked off the hall light and they stood some more in the near darkness, blaring music ricocheting off the walls.

'He won't talk to me about it,' Richard said. 'But he looks sick. AIDS, maybe? Cancer? He was in 'Nam for two hitches. Who knows what he was exposed to over there?'

Sylvia shrugged. 'You know about them, right?'

'Not until Miriam's party a couple weeks ago. I never saw them together before Memorial Day.'

'Sad, huh?'

'Tragic is more like it.'

'Yeah.'

'I don't know,' Richard said after a minute. He rubbed his eyes. 'Is it good or bad to find your soul mate, if you can't actually be together? Is it worth it to know them, to know they exist, but not be able to do anything about it?'

Sylvia pushed herself off the wall. 'I can't think about this now. Let's go get a beer and watch the naked girls dance.'

'How about a Scotch?'

'You're on.'

* * *

When the clothes were on again and most of the women were back inside, the music turned down so that conversation in the living room was possible without yelling, Pam sat next to Richard on the couch and teased him about watching the dancers.

'I wasn't ogling,' he said. 'I was observing a religious ritual.'

'I'm sure. You looked like you were concentrating on spiritual things.'

'I was.'

'Like what?'

He was searching for an answer when a woman walked up to them and stood looking down at Richard, one hand holding a glass of beer and the other cocked on her hip. He looked up at her. She was dressed in a thin blue skirt, white T-shirt, and sandals. He didn't know her.

'Is your name Richard Lantz?' she said.

'Yes.'

'I heard that you're the asshole who writes that Mrs. Bambi column.'

Richard's ears rang. It seemed that all conversation in the room had stopped. He saw several other women staring at him.

143

'Do you deny it?' the woman demanded.

'Wait a—' Pam began, but the woman tossed her beer into Richard's face and stalked away. Richard wiped his face on the sleeve of his shirt. 'Time to go,' Pam said, and yanked him up off the couch and out the door before he knew what was happening.

When the baby sitter had been sent home, they lay face to face in bed. They were naked but Richard felt no erotic impulse whatsoever. He was still numb.

'Now A.M. knows,' Richard said.

'It's only going to get worse,' Pam said.

'Thanks. That's a cheerful thought.'

'You might as well face it and start coming up with a plan.'

'What kind of plan? A running away plan? A chicken shit plan? I don't even know where to start.'

'So you're just going to wing it? Crash by the seat of your pants?'

'That's it,' Richard said. 'That's my plan.'

'Okay,' she said. 'I'll do what I can to help. But you and Miriam are going to have to take most of the heat yourselves.'

She rolled over and he snuggled up against her back. He couldn't remember falling asleep.

* * *

The next morning was Sunday. Richard called Clarence.

'I saw Karen last night,' he said.

'Really? How is she?'

'She looked terrible. She was upset about something and her idea of dealing with it was to drink herself unconscious.' Clarence said nothing. 'So how are you?'

'I'm fine,' Clarence said. That might be the clumsiest lie Richard had ever heard.

'Maybe we should get together for dinner and some chess soon. You haven't had a chance to kick my ass since the day Joe left.'

'Old Joe. What a traitor he turned out to be.'

Richard waited for Clarence to say something else, but there was complete silence. 'So what about dinner?'

'Sure. Let me call you in a week or so.'

'Well, what about Friday?'

'Yeah, maybe. I'll call you. I gotta go now.'

Richard hung up the phone and stared at it for a moment. He thought about driving up to see him, but he couldn't justify the intrusion. Clarence obviously wanted to be left alone for a while. Whatever was wrong, he'd just have to wait to learn the truth.

Chapter 13: Bears and Wolves

Camping casualty craves cash

Dear Mrs. Bambi:

My husband and I spent several months planning a week-long backpacking trip. At the last minute, he announced that a good friend of his was coming along. I complained, because one reason for this trip was to try to put some passion back into our marriage, which lately has been showing as much life as a rattler run over by a logging truck. But he demanded that I be charitable; this person was going through a rough time right now and needed our help.

His friend met us at the trailhead, and it was a woman! A very young woman, with long black hair and—oh, never mind about her perfect figure. I don't need to tell you that the hike was a nightmare. They couldn't stop touching each other: a helping hand on the elbow here, a friendly pat on the rump there, a swift caress whenever they thought I wasn't looking.

He did everything but suggest that the two of them share a tent. Every evening they went off together for an hour to 'gather firewood.' Sometimes they forgot to actually pick up any wood. I was so humiliated I cried myself to sleep every night. Several times he got up in the dark and I could hear them going off into the woods. Twice in one day? I prayed for a bear to find them, or maybe a pack of wolves, but every morning the creep was back in his sleeping bag, snoring and grinning in his sleep.

My question is this: should I kill him or just cut off his nuts ? Or should I kill them both?

—Crying Camper

Dear Goatwife:

What's the point of killing him? Then his suffering would be over. And taking away his equipment isn't enough; you want to get him out of the game.

If you really want to hurt both of them, don't kill him, don't maim him, and don't divorce him. Impoverish him. If you took him to court, you could never get it all, so my advice is this: spend it. All of it.

Max out the credit cards. Take out a second mortgage. Empty the bank account. Cash in the savings bonds. Sell the stocks and bonds. And spend all of it on things that he wouldn't want, like new kitchen appliances, long getaways to a New Mexico spa, stuffed animals, makeup, clothes, and a retainer for a good divorce lawyer.

In my experience, younger women are almost exclusively attracted to older men who have money. When you've spent it all, she'll desert him. He'll want a divorce. Fight it all the way; he won't have any money left to hire a lawyer. Wait until he's reached utter despair, then kick him over the divorce cliff.

Your half of the debts will leave you poor for a while. You'll have to work hard to get back on your feet. But it will be worth it.

Dear Mrs. Bambi:

My cat gets hairballs, and she insists on hawking them up on the carpet. I have perfectly good linoleum, which would be a lot easier to clean, but as soon as the urge hits her, she runs for the wall-to-wall. It's bad enough when I'm around—the noise is disgusting, not to mention the smell. But coming home to these dried up messes on the rug is making me consider Meow Shu Cat for dinner. How can I get her to puke on the linoleum, or better yet in her litter box?

—Retching Ralph

Dear Felis Vomitus:

I sympathize, but there's no easy solution. Cats are not just a law unto themselves; they own the universe. Here are some ideas, for what they're worth.

Get rid of the little vermin.

Shave her: no hair, no hairballs.

Yank out the carpet and cover the whole place in linoleum.

Lock her in the bathroom when you go out.

Pour mineral oil down her throat.

Explore the Zen aspects of acceptance.

* * *

Richard spent most of Sunday afternoon bemused. Pam and Miriam sat together on the floor in his living room, surrounded by backpacks, boots, socks, rain gear, sweaters, capilene underwear, maps and compasses, water bottles, a cook stove and folding cookware, ropes, sleeping bags, a tent, and a small mountain of other gear. In a few days, Miriam was going on the first backpacking trip of her life, and he wasn't sure how he felt about it.

They would leave Friday morning. It was about an hour's drive to Bonneville, then a five hour hike to their first campsite. If all went well, they'd be home in time for dinner Sunday.

If all went well. There were reports of bears, and even worse, a cougar in the hills above the Bonneville Dam. Miriam had brand new gear, and Pam had a lot of hiking experience, but how would they deal with a hungry wild animal?

'What if you run into a cougar?' he said.

'Cool!' Miriam said.

'We'll shout and ring our bear bells,' Pam said.

'Oh, that'll scare the pants off him.'

'Well, if it doesn't, I'll persuade him with this.' She reached into her pack and pulled out a pistol.

'Oh my God!'

'Wow!' Miriam said. 'You've got a gun!'

'Do you know how to use that thing?'

She frowned at him. 'Of course, dummy. I'm a crack shot.' Was there any sport she wasn't an expert in? 'I use nine-millimeter Hydra-Shok ammo. It'll kill a cougar. It might not kill a bear, but it'll sure make him think twice.'

'Okay, but what about accidents? There could be a rock slide, or she could fall off a ledge—'

'Daddy!'

'Richard! Lighten up. We're going backpacking in the Gorge, not in Tibet.'

She was right, but every year people died hiking and climbing in the Cascade Range. He didn't say it. Richard's idea of exciting outdoor activities was a stroll up Post Canyon Road. He'd taken Miriam camping several times, more out of a sense of a father's duty than because he enjoyed it, but that had been years ago. And it had been car camping, in a state park, with rangers and toilets nearby.

Pam leaned toward him. 'Richard, she can't learn to take care of herself by reading books. She has to live it. The point of this trip is for Miriam to start learning how to safely plan and execute a trip into the woods. How to use a map and compass, to provision and protect herself, to anticipate the unexpected—to survive. Okay? You want that for her, don't you?'

Of course. He just wanted her back, too. Miriam was staring at him expectantly. 'Sure,' he said.

'Okay.' They huddled again. Pam checked out Miriam's pack one more time to be sure she had the Ten (or Twelve, or Fifteen, depending on how you counted) Essentials. They put their heads together over a printout from a computer program Pam used to find hikes, and then a Green Trails map to check their route.

'What's the name of this trail again?' Richard said.

'Tanner Butte,' Pam said. 'I'll leave a copy of this with you when we go.'

'Dad, here's how to remember the name. If you forget again, I'll Tanner your Butte.'

Pam laughed and Richard dutifully chuckled. He wasn't very happy about this. But he had to admit that if Miriam had to go into the back country with anyone, he was glad it was Pam.

There was some irony here somewhere. His daughter and his girlfriend were going off to brave the wilderness, while he stayed home with the dog and had dinner ready for their return.

* * *

The opening ceremony for the new Faith House took place Monday afternoon. Richard had to ask Pam to help knot his tie. He hadn't worn one since his father's funeral, and he'd forgotten how. She smiled during the entire enterprise, whether at his fumble fingers or his paisley blue silk tie he didn't know, and he wasn't keen to ask.

They walked the half mile from Richard's place. The house looked much better than the last time Richard had seen it, a month ago. The grass had been mowed, the shrubs pruned, and bright flowers were planted around the maple tree in the center of the yard. Although the house had not been repainted, the white clapboards looked cleaner; perhaps they'd been pressure-washed.

Pam and Richard joined a crowd of a few dozen people milling around patiently on the sidewalk. The front door was closed and Gail was not to be seen.

'How's she doing on her grants?' Pam said.

'She sent in the paperwork, but it's going to take a while. The good news is that the insurance company paid off and the old lot's up for sale. And she's had so many donations she had to borrow one of Nadine's barns to store them in.'

'I hope the grants don't take too long.'

'You know how slow—' He stopped as he saw Frank walking toward them. 'Heads up, it's our favorite grouch.'

Frank was smiling as he approached. 'Pam, good to see you.' He dropped the smile like a rock to say, 'Richard.'

'Nice to see you too, Frank.'

'Nice tie. Did Pam tie it?'

Pam laughed lightly but Richard was not amused. 'What do you want, Frank?'

Frank jerked his head at Pam. 'Does she...'

'Yeah, she knows about the column.'

'And you're still together? Huh.' He scratched his buzz-cut scalp. 'I'm going to have to pull the plug on you soon, my friend. I've been getting half a dozen calls a day, wanting to know if the rumors are true that Mrs. Bambi is really a nobody named Richard. Maybe after they string you up we can start a new column, "Poor Dead Richard's Almanac."'

'Very amusing. You're the editor, Frank. Do what you have to do.'

'I don't understand you, Richard. This town is about ready to boil over, and when it does there's going to be a lynch mob after you. And you want to keep writing your stupid column. Why?'

'I told you. If I quit, that'll be the catalyst that makes them boil over.'

'Bullshit.'

'Richard,' Pam said, 'maybe Frank's right. It's time to let it go.'

He looked from one to the other without a word.

'You and I used to be friends, Richard,' Frank said, 'and if you'd stop being such a dickhead maybe we could be friends again. So, as a once and future friend, stop bullshitting me and give it to me straight. Why?'

Richard looked away from them. There was still no sign of Gail. They'd been on the edge of the crowd when Frank first joined them, but now the mass of people had drifted closer to the house. They were alone on the sidewalk beside the street.

'Mrs. Bambi is everything I'm not,' Richard said.

'You mean, female and a bitch.'

'I mean, she's original, she's quick, she's witty, she's sarcastic, she's helpful. When I'm her, I'm all those things, and there's no other outlet for that in my life. You want me to give that up forever, and maybe I should, but it's not so easy.'

Frank stared at him for a moment. He seemed about to say something when Gail opened the front door of the house and stepped out. He turned back to Richard.

'One more week,' he said. 'That's all.' He rushed toward the porch where Gail stood, pulling a small recorder out of his pocket and holding it up.

'Thank you for joining us on this beautiful afternoon,' Gail said. 'I see so many faces of people who have helped us in the past. I'd like to thank the people who have made this rebirth possible. First, this house, our new home...'

She gestured behind her. Richard stopped breathing.

'I can't tell you the name of our generous benefactor, because he or she has asked to be anonymous. But I want you all to know that this person will be in my prayers every day.' She smiled over the crowd right at Richard. He started breathing again until he saw Frank follow her gaze, and they locked eyes. Oh shit.

'Because of this angel's help, our new house is completely paid for.' The crowd muttered and a few people applauded. 'That's right, no mortgage! That means that our operating expenses will be so low that we can continue to run the house for at least five years even if we never get another dime of government money. As soon as we do get the grants, we'll be able to hire a part-time counsellor.'

This time the entire audience applauded. Richard clapped too. He hadn't realized that Gail had received so much in donations. If she got her grants again, which was very likely, she might never have to worry about funding again: Faith House would be self-supporting.

'Next I'd like to thank Pam Castle, who found this house for us. She also helped enormously in getting the conditional use permit approved so quickly. Thanks, Pam!'

Pam waved and the audience applauded again.

Gail thanked the men and women who had helped clean and repair the house, the people who had donated money and furniture, Nadine Szabo for letting her store furniture and household goods in her tractor barn, everyone who had helped her move in, and the insurance agent who had swiftly processed the claim against the old house that had burned down. It seemed that nearly everyone in town received some benediction. When she was done, someone handed her a broom and Gail symbolically but vigorously swept the threshold clean.

'Come on in,' she cried. People crowded around the steps leading up to the front door. Richard and Pam were nearly the last to enter. Gail met them at the door and hugged them both.

'You bastard,' she whispered in Richard's ear. 'You should have let me tell them it was you. And I think it's great that you're Mrs. Bambi.'

Shocked, Richard stumbled after Pam into the living room. The house was completely furnished, in old but serviceable Salvation Army furniture. Every room looked freshly painted, except the dining room, where the old-fashioned floral wallpaper was still in good condition.

There was wine, but Richard didn't really care for wine. After tasting it, Pam said the Merlot was not a good one. They walked through the kitchen and into the fenced and treed back yard, where Pam poured out her glass into the shrubs as a libation to the goddess.

'Deities aren't as picky about vintages as I am,' she said.

'I'm ready to go whenever you are.'

'Fine with me. Let's go.'

On their way back through the house, Richard grabbed a handful of coin-sized cheesy things. They were still warm and very tasty. They had almost made it out the front door when Frank stepped in front of them.

'Richard,' he said. 'Leaving so soon?' They glared at him, but he refused to move. 'Maybe you can help me clear up a mystery. Boy, this town has a lot of mysteries, doesn't it?'

'Would you mind letting us past?' Pam said. 'We're late for something.'

'Sorry. I'll just keep you for a second. Richard, what do you know about this secret benefactor Gail talked about?'

'Why should I know anything?'

'I thought you'd say that. No clue as to who she's talking about?'

'It could be anybody.'

'Anybody with a couple hundred thousand dollars to spare. What about you, Pam? Any ideas?'

'Goodbye, Frank,' Pam said. She pushed him out of her way.

They left him standing in the doorway. Richard could feel the reporter's eye drilling into his back all the way to the car.

* * *

At lunchtime the next day, Richard walked to the Heave Ho. That wasn't the restaurant's real name. Some people called it the no-name restaurant, because the big sign above the door just said, 'Restaurant.' Richard had his own names for it: Lotus Vomit, Lai Lo, General Choke's Chicken, War Sue Regurge. It was, without reservation, the worst Chinese food he had ever had in his life. Worse than the restaurant in a little town near Mt. Rainier that featured Chinese and Texas BBQ, in which the patrons poured ketchup over their fried rice; worse than the one in the Canadian Rockies where every dish came smothered in Nuclear Meltdown Red sweet-and-sour sauce; far worse than the one in Kentucky where the cook, who was also the town's auto mechanic, served you with grease-stained hands.

He had objected to eating at a restaurant where the food could also serve as an industrial lubricant, but A.M. had insisted.

The exterior of the place was so badly done it was almost Smithsonian material, as if the owner had demanded a replica of the Forbidden City but refused to spend more than $200. A red-painted plywood bas-relief of cupolas and towers was outlined in neon. The inside was all worn linoleum, faded travel posters for Beijing and Shanghai, and rickety booths. To the left as he entered, the 'banquet room' was equipped with folding tables and chairs. The tables in the main room were covered in frayed and stained white cotton tablecloths and bent flatware. Somewhere in the back was a bar that offered karaoke five nights a week, but Richard had never bothered to check it out.

Three tables were occupied, by a solitary man with unruly white hair, an old deaf couple shouting amiably at each other, and a pair of young women near the window with their heads nearly touching in whispered conversation. The waitress breezed by, leaving 'Sitwheveryawan' echoing behind her as if it were the answer to a question everyone asked. Richard took a seat at a booth that faced the doorway. A.M. walked in a few minutes later and flounced down into the seat across from him.

She was dressed almost normally today, in a sleeveless red knit vest over a very short, tight black leather skirt. The waitress whisked up to the table. She was a portly Caucasian with thin red hair teased out like a dandelion, dressed in a soiled orange uniform with white trim. She wore a huge Mickey Mouse watch on her left wrist.

'Beer!' A.M. said.

'I'll just have water,' Richard said. The waitress slouched away. 'Are you okay?'

'I don't know. I'll be better when the beer gets here.'

He searched her face. Something was bothering her. He had a very bad idea what it might be, but he didn't see the point in opening doors that he couldn't shut.

'Your earrings don't match,' he said instead. They were golden images of the squat Mayan gods that represented numbers, sitting above one another like totems on a pole, but her right ear had five of them and the other had four.

'They're supposed to be that way, dummy.'

'It looks like one of your gods fell off.'

'The Mayans counted base twenty.'

'So?' he said.

'So five times four is twenty.' The waitress set down their drinks and stood waiting. 'Egg roll. Lemon chicken. Steamed rice.'

'I'll have the hot and sour soup, Kung Po chicken, and steamed rice.'

The waitress looked as if she'd been raised on an Iowa pig farm, but she wrote the order in Chinese ideograms.

'Okay,' he said, 'five and four makes twenty. That means your head is a multiplication sign. That's good to know. If it had been a subtraction sign, you'd get one, or a plus sign you'd have nine.'

'Shut up.'

'Okay.' He waited for her to bring up a new subject, but she didn't. In a moment their first course arrived. A.M.'s egg roll was wizened and small; it had probably been sitting on a counter in the back since yesterday. His soup was lukewarm, with nothing recognizable swimming in the thick broth: no wood ears, green onions, meat, tofu, bean sprouts, nothing but small colorless lumps. There were two cellophane packets of saltine crackers on the plate beneath his cup.

'Do you think they expect you to actually use these...' At a noise, he looked over at the white-haired man, who was crushing crackers into his cup of soup.

A.M. dipped her withered egg roll in mustard sauce and began eating it methodically. Richard couldn't get more than halfway through his tasteless soup before he had to stop. It was neither hot nor sour, nor anything that he could identify.

Their main course came quickly. A.M.'s chicken was slathered in a thick yellow goo. His dish had been made with peanuts instead of cashews, and the tiny chunks of chicken and vegetables swam in a greasy brown sauce. He tasted it. How was it possible that it wasn't even hot? They'd only ordered five minutes ago. Did they have platters already made up and sitting under a heat lamp: Chinese fast food?

A.M. didn't speak again until she was halfway done with her food. 'I've got a question for you.'

'Okay.' He put down his fork. He was afraid he knew what was coming.

'If you and Pam got married...'

'Whoa!' That wasn't what he'd expected. 'Wait a minute. We've only been dating for five weeks.'

A.M. looked at him expressionlessly and he raised his hands in submission. She started again. 'If you got married, would she be Mr. Bambi?'

That was what he'd been expecting. But it didn't help that he had: he couldn't think of anything to say.

'You've been Mrs. Bambi from the beginning,' she said. It wasn't a question.

'Yes.'

'You made up all the letters.'

'No, not at first,' he said. 'But lately, well, for the last couple of years, yeah.'

'No one ever knew it was you.'

'No one except Frank and Clarence.'

'And you never told me, your goddamned best friend!'

'A.M., I—'

She threw her beer in his face. What was it with people throwing beer in his face? First at her party, now this. Maybe it's a lesbian thing; maybe it's just a female thing. He let it drip for a moment until he was sure she wasn't going to attack him, then he used his sopping napkin to try to dry off his face.

The waitress was standing beside their booth with her mouth open.

'I need another beer,' A.M. said. Her voice was so calm, yet so intimidating, that the woman scurried off without saying a thing. She returned in a moment and cautiously set the glass down on the table before running away again.

'I'm sorry,' Richard said.

'That's not going to do it, Richard.' She took a sip of her beer. He braced himself for another faceful, but she set the glass back down.

'I don't know what else to say. What do you want me to do? Grovel?'

'Groveling would be good. Look, you shithead, Miriam is like my own daughter. I see her more than you do. I share everything with you. You hear about every yeast infection, every fight with Sylvia, every problem with the shop. And what have you given me back? Nothing, not one damned thing about you and Pam, and now I find out that you're balls-deep in the middle of the biggest piece of gossip this town has ever known, and I had to hear it from the partner of an ex-lover at my solstice party.'

'I never—'

'Shut up! I'm through with you, Richard. Go fuck yourself!'

She swept out of the booth and stalked out of the restaurant. The other diners were staring at him, whether in disapproval or amusement he couldn't tell, and didn't care. The waitress came by with a towel and a smirk.

'I guess you're paying,' she said.

* * *

The dreaded day came at last. Richard waved at Pam and Miriam as they backed out of the driveway for their camping trip. He wondered if he would ever see them again.

'Don't be stupid,' he said to himself. 'It's just a weekend camping trip.'

That night he went out alone to the Big River Saloon for very loud, very bad music and a lot of Scotch.

Saturday afternoon, just to be perverse, he took Kobi for a walk up Post Canyon Road. The woods in the canyon were beautiful, but they were scarred by the frequent mounds of trash. Hundreds of people had mistaken this beautiful, winding road through the forest for the county dump. He saw an old stove, piles of tires, a hot tub, several sofas, and a whale weather vane littering the slope just off the road. If the forest lasted long enough it would bury the trash, and future archaeologists would thrill at finding a twentieth century midden. In the meantime, it made Richard sick.

Kobi loved the long walk. Every tree, every chunk of garbage, every human, the foursome clopping by on their quarter horses, and especially every dog was greeted with joyous barking and exuberant sniffing. She didn't miss a single opportunity for puppy networking.

After lunch on Sunday, Richard started a complex Indian dinner, consisting of two main courses, a side dish of fried onions, flavored rice, and homemade bread. By five o'clock he was ready to start cooking, but they hadn't arrived yet. By six he was starting to worry that the bread had risen too long and that his daughter had been eaten by a mountain lion, but then he heard a car in the driveway.

Miriam burst through the door; it was impossible to say whether Kobi tackled her or vice versa. They rolled on the living room carpet for a moment before Miriam sprang up and ran outside again. Richard followed her out. After kissing Pam briefly but intensely, he helped them unload the car.

'You're still alive,' he said.

157

'Yes, but stinky. Is there time for a shower before dinner?'

'Sure.'

He started cooking his meal, listening to them take turns in the shower. They came downstairs together, arguing happily, but he couldn't make out the words until the disagreement spilled into the kitchen.

'Wolf,' Miriam said.

'Coyote.'

'Wolf.'

'It was a coyote.'

'Wolf.'

'You saw a coyote?' Richard said.

'Wolf. And a bear,' Miriam replied.

'You saw a bear?'

'Yes,' Pam said, 'a black bear.'

'What did you do?'

'We stood still,' Miriam said, 'and it walked away. Then we saw a wolf.'

'Coyote.'

'Wolf. And Pam burned her dinner. My dinner came out perfect.'

'I didn't burn dinner,' Pam said.

'Did too. It was all black on the bottom.'

'It was supposed to be like that. Anyway, how could you tell? It was night.'

'You saw a bear?' Richard said.

They stopped arguing long enough to tell him what happened. On their long hike Saturday they came into a clearing and a small (according to Pam) huge (according to Miriam) black bear was standing at the far side, watching them. They stood perfectly still for several moments until the bear snuffed once and walked away. An hour or so later they were walking along a talus slope and saw a coyote (Wolf!) up the ridge. It loped off almost immediately.

'We went up to the top. You could see five big mountains from up there, Dad! And we had a snowball fight!'

On July first?

'We found a snow field at the base of a cliff,' Pam said. 'She put snow down my neck and I got her in the face with a snowball. It was grand.'

Richard watched them tease each other as they told the story, and felt a twinge of something that was almost pain. Miriam's mother had died the day after Miriam was born, so he had never seen them together. Perhaps this playful arguing would have been their life together, if Rosalind had lived to see her daughter grow up.

They were all exhausted. Right after dinner, Richard carried Miriam, who was already half asleep, up to her bed. He pulled the sheet up to her chin and sat down beside her.

'Dad?'

'Yes, kitten kaboodle?'

'How did you and Mom meet?'

'Well.' He thought for a second. 'I was out hunting for mastodon. I bagged a big one, enough meat for the whole tribe for a month, but I got lost coming home. Compasses hadn't been invented yet, you know. I rode into a strange village on the back of my tame saber-toothed tiger, with my giant camel train all loaded up with mastodon meat behind me, and asked if I could spend the night. We roasted mastodon steaks on sticks over the fire and they gave me rough mead to drink. We sang songs and told stories all night long. There was one girl, the prettiest girl in the tribe, the prettiest girl I had ever seen, and I couldn't take my eyes off her. When I left in the morning, she came with me as my bride.'

She was asleep. He stood up and turned to the door. Pam was standing there, watching him. He smiled sheepishly. She gestured to him; he took another step. She took his hand gently and led him down the hall into the bedroom.

Chapter 14: Red Rockets

From the Hood River Examiner
Friday, June 30, 1995

Mrs. Bambi Knows

Saboteur or spook? Listen up

Dear Mrs. Bambi:

My wife is sabotaging my life. It has to be her.

One day last week I was running late for work. I gulped some coffee, kissed her on the cheek, and ran into the garage, but the car wouldn't start. The spark plug wires had all been pulled—but not viciously. They were laid out neatly on the carburetor, as if Martha Stewart had turned to vandalism.

On Saturday, I was all set for a nice afternoon of watching baseball, but I couldn't get anything but static on the TV. The coaxial cable had been cut clean through. She said it must have been mice, but mice chew through stuff, they don't use wire cutters.

I was getting dressed for work yesterday and picked out my favorite tie. There was a hole burned right through it. It looked like a cigarette, or maybe a soldering iron.

This morning there was motor oil in my coffee cup. You know, it won't mix with cream.

She denies doing any of this, but who else could it be? Why is she ruining my life? Should I have her committed? Is this grounds for divorce?

—Shook up

Dear Milqueshake:

You're pretty quick to mention divorce and doctors. It sounds to me like you're looking for an excuse to get rid of her. Are you having an affair?

My guess is, it's all your fault. Shape up, shut up, and try listening to her for a change. Then she won't have to go to such lengths to get your attention.

Then again, it could be a poltergeist.

Dear Mrs. Bambi:

My garage is an utter mess. I try to keep it organized, but there's so much stuff in there that I really can't make a dent in it. How can I get it cleaned up?
—*Buried*

Dear Deddan:

Rent a Bobcat, one of those small front-end loaders. Or leave the door open and hope that thieves come along. Or tell your in-laws you heard a rumor that the house's previous owner left a sack of gold coins in there but you just can't find it. Or buy one single stick of dynamite.

Or you could have a yard sale. Come on, do I have to think of everything?

* * *

Monday's mail had a thick envelope from the Examiner. Richard hefted it; usually there was just a sheet or two, with a snide note from Frank.

This week he didn't even bother being snide. Under the Examiner letterhead was a single word: Adios.

The rest of the packet was all hate mail. Some were addressed to the paper, some were addressed to him care of the Examiner. Some were typed, some were neatly hand-written, many were scrawled and almost illegible, and one was written in crayon. That one said, 'My mommy hates you. Me too.'

'Someone ought to do to you what they did to Bambi's mother.'

'What kind of gutless coward hides behind a woman's name?'

'I'd like to cut off your head and hang it over my fireplace. Too bad you don't have any antlers.'

'They ought to chop off your balls, you fairy. Then you WOULD be Mrs. Bambi.'

The invective grew numbing after a while. But near the bottom of the stack, one short note in flawless, elegant script said, 'You're the funniest transsexual in town. Keep up the good work.'

Despite Frank's warning that he would publish no more of Mrs. Bambi, Richard went upstairs and wrote his column for the week. He was damned if he was going to stop now.

* * *

The next day was Independence Day. Pam and Richard lay in bed in the morning discussing whether to go to the annual Fourth Party.

At a particular small house on the hill above Hood River, the view to the marina was completely unobstructed. This made it the perfect place from which to watch the fireworks, and for almost ten years, no matter who owned the house, all of the windsurfers, snow boarders, and mountain bikers in town converged on the house and its expansive deck, six-packs in hand, for a day-long party. Several of the past owners had objected to the trespassers, who simply ignored them and partied without hosts.

'I went last year,' Richard said.

'I've been there five years in a row.'

'Really? Why didn't I see you last year?'

'You were probably just watching bikinis.' That was fashion de rigueur for stylish women at the Party, no matter what the weather was like. 'I was wearing normal clothes.'

'Bikinis don't talk to people like me,' he said. 'I must have been in a corner somewhere drinking with A.M.'

'So, do you want to go?'

Richard had actually been to several installments of the Party. He remembered wandering around the stunted lawn, where a displaced bathtub and a children's pool served as the water sports arena; trying to start conversations with people who asked him if he'd been up on the mountain today and turned away when he said no; listening for half an hour to a round robin discussion of summer snow conditions on Mt. Hood.

'No. I'm tired of wearing beer.'

162

'I'm not really interested either. It's exactly the same party every year.'

'Let's just spend the day with Miriam, then.'

'That's fine with—'

The door popped open.

'Everybody decent?' Miriam said. She stood in the hallway with her head averted.

'Go away!' Richard shouted.

'Okay, but breakfast's almost ready.'

'Breakfast?' Pam said. 'We'll be down in a few minutes.' They heard her clumping down the stairs. 'I thought you said that door had a lock?'

* * *

Breakfast was cinnamon muffins and fresh fruit.

'Where's the coffee?' Pam said, and Miriam handed her a mug. 'Ahh. You're my goddess. Where did you learn to bake like this?'

'Dad and Betty Crocker.'

They packed a picnic lunch, books, and blankets and walked to the city park. It was a few blocks west on Oak and a long trudge up the hill almost to the hospital. Kobi walked beside them without a leash, jaunting off every now and then to sniff a telephone pole or a bush, then trotting back happily. It was unnatural how well-behaved she was. Perhaps there was something wrong with her.

As soon as they picked out a shady spot, Miriam dropped her shopping bag full of books, sun hats, and other stuff and ran off toward the swing sets. A swarm of children, most of them younger than she, was already climbing and defying gravity there. Pam spread a blanket and Richard helped her smooth it out before dropping down onto it. He was still a little winded from the steep climb uphill.

'What's wrong with the weather?' he said.

It was warm. Pam looked up at the blue sky; clouds ran across it in packs. 'Nothing. Why?'

'It always rains on July Fourth. This is the only day of the year you can count on rain.'

'Nothing's dependable any more.' He grunted. 'You know, I don't think the parade is going to go by here.'

'I know. I asked Miriam if she wanted to see the parade and she just shrugged. She used to love parades.'

'Kids go through phases,' she said.

Please, God, don't let this be the start of her sullen teens. She's only ten! Richard closed his eyes and let the sun soak into his body. After a minute he reached into Miriam's bag and pulled out the new biography of Edison he was just starting. Pam had her paperback. For a while they sat side by side reading in the sunshine.

Miriam flopped down beside him and announced that she was tired. Kobi curled up next to her on the blanket, scorning the grass, and instantly fell asleep. But a few minutes later Miriam jumped up and ran out into the sunny, grassy middle of the park, where a large group of children thronged like a school of fish. Kobi waited a moment, then with an air of resignation went charging off after her. There didn't seem to be any reason for the ebb and flow of the kids: no identifiable game was in progress. Flocking was its own reward.

At lunch time, Miriam came back. They ate spicy sesame noodles, carrot sticks, fresh crusty bread, peaches, and Snapples.

'You forgot the pickles,' Miriam accused him.

'Sweet or dill?' Pam said.

'With spicy noodles? Sweet pickles.'

'I'll remind him next time.'

When Richard opened a bag of cookies, Miriam grabbed a handful and ran off again, Kobi trailing behind her like the tail of a kite. They were soon lost in the crowd.

'Look at that,' Richard said. He pointed down the hill a ways.

'Is that Val? And... Ralf? Are they still together?'

'I guess so. I gave them three nights, tops. It's been almost a month.'

Pam stood up and grabbed his arm, pulling him to his feet. 'Come on. We have to go say hello.'

Val was lying on her back, exposing almost everything in an extremely skimpy blue string bikini. She had obviously spent a lot of money on wax treatments. As they approached, she shaded her eyes and looked up.

'Val,' Richard said, 'don't you think that outfit's a little extreme for a family park?'

'Hi, Pam.' She turned to him slowly. 'Richard, what do you mean? Where do you think families come from? Weren't you born out of a woman's body?'

'Not one like that.'

'I believe that,' Ralf said. Richard turned his attention away from Val and was startled to see that Ralf had had a makeover. The shaggy balding look was replaced with a trim, rakish haircut. He wore nothing but long baggy shorts, but he wore them on his hips, not halfway down his buttocks, where you would expect to find them on a snow boarder.

'Haven't you guys heard about ozone depletion, UV, melanoma?'

'That's a scam by the cosmetics industry, man,' Ralf said.

'Val,' Pam said, before Ralf could start off on one of his rants, 'this is some kind of record for you, isn't it?'

Val sat up a bit, resting on her elbows. Her taut stomach creased, her breasts threatened to pop out of the minimal top. Richard consciously yanked his eyes away and looked at her face.

'I don't keep records,' Val said, 'but I guess you're right.' She looked at Ralf with an expression of placid ownership. He grunted and closed his eyes, leaning his head back to expose his neck. 'As long as he keeps me satisfied, I guess we're still an item. Who knew itemhood could last so long? But what about you two? You're past itemhood and into couplehood, aren't you?'

Pam grinned. Richard felt himself blushing.

'It suits you, Richard,' Val said. 'I've never seen you look this good.'

'But you need some new threads, dude,' Ralf said without opening his eyes. 'Those drapes are way too Cartesian.' Richard looked down at himself. He was wearing a polo shirt and cotton slacks. Cartesian? That was Val's influence. 'Talk to Val, man, you wouldn't believe how she's helped me.'

No doubt. Val was smiling as if she'd just found a diamond ring in a Cracker Jack box.

'Well, we'd better get back,' Pam said. 'Nice to see you again.'

'Bye,' Val said. Richard turned away, but she called out, 'Oh, Richard.' He turned back. 'Good column on Friday.' She lay back down on her beach towel and closed her eyes.

He must be getting used to it. He didn't even feel upset, let alone startled.

'You were staring,' Pam said as they reached their blanket.

'No, I wasn't.'

'Yes, you were. But it's okay. Look if you must, but keep your hands to yourself. Or better yet...' She took his hand and pulled his arm around her waist. He kissed her, standing up in the sunshine.

'Can you believe they're still together?' he said when they'd settled back down.

'Ralf's never looked so good.'

'Yeah, but he's still Ralf.'

'Well,' she said, picking up her book, 'I guess it takes all kinds.'

'No, it doesn't. It doesn't take all kinds. It's just that we've got all kinds, so we might as well make the best of it.'

*   *   *

They left the park in late afternoon and Pam cooked dinner at her place. As dusk fell, she bundled them into her Explorer. After they dropped Kobi off at Richard's house, Pam drove them across the toll bridge to Washington. They headed up the road to Trout Lake, but turned off it onto a street that Richard had never traveled before. On their right, small suburban homes were surrounded by scraggly lawns. Across the street, small, dirty horse farms hunkered down against the hillside.

'I thought we were going to see the fireworks,' Miriam said.

'We are,' Pam said mysteriously.

'Usually we just walk to the marina. You can lie down right underneath the fireworks. It's cool.'

Pam laughed for no apparent reason. Richard decided to be patient.

The road wound up a hill, threading through woods and farms. It was getting dark, and there were no streetlights on this country road, nothing but the twinkling of house lights seen through the trees. Some of the homes, set well back from the road, had signs at their mailboxes announcing small businesses: auto repair, saw sharpening, machine shops. After a few right-angle turns, they veered off onto another road that climbed even more steeply up the hill. Richard was utterly lost. He was fairly certain they were still in Washington, but only because they hadn't crossed the Columbia again.

Pam pulled into a long gravel driveway with a For Sale sign at the street. They stopped at a large, darkened A-frame house. By the light of the crescent moon hanging over the trees, she led them to the front door and punched

166

some numbers into a key box hanging from the doorknob. The front popped off and she used the key inside to let them in.

'Be careful,' Pam said. 'I don't want to turn the lights on.'

'Why not?' Miriam said. 'Are we breaking in?' Pam shushed her, took her hand, and led her into the kitchen and up some steps to the living room.

That room occupied most of the volume of the house. Above them loomed a vaulted ceiling with exposed beams. There was enough light to see a wood stove in the corner, and there was no furniture. That was fortunate, or else they would have been stumbling over it. Pam took them to the far end of the living room, and Richard finally understood what she was doing.

The entire south wall of the house was glass, broken only by the dividers that held the huge panes in place. The Columbia River wound away beneath them. Straight ahead were the lights of Hood River, climbing the hill up away from the river. The moon hung just above the crest of the Gorge.

'I thought you might like to do something a bit different this year,' Pam said. 'Instead of looking straight up at the fireworks, you can look down on them.'

The scene before them was quiet and still for what seemed like a long time. Then they were startled by a brilliant flash below them in the Gorge. Another burst of light blossomed into a luminous dandelion. The fireballs were clearly beneath them. Miriam laughed and Richard grunted in surprise as a red and blue explosion lit up the walls of the Gorge.

He had never before seen fireworks from above. They looked different somehow: flatter. Gravity pulled the embers down, and the trajectories apparently looked different depending on your vantage point. The bursts were probably specifically designed to be seen from below...

'Stop analyzing it,' Pam whispered in his ear. 'Just enjoy it.'

He took her hand. The three of them stood before the magic window, watching gigantic sparks flare and die in the sky below them.

* * *

The drive back to Hood River was quiet. Miriam seemed to be asleep in the back seat, slumped against the door. Richard held hands with Pam as she drove, tired but feeling as if he'd been wrapped in a fuzzy happy blanket. The mood lasted right up to the moment when, from three blocks away, he saw the flashing lights of a fire truck parked in front of his house.

Pam pulled over a few houses away and a young cop ran toward them. 'You can't park here,' he said.

Richard got out of the car. 'That's my house.'

'Oh. Well, okay. Park your car here and I'll take you to the chief.'

'Can you keep an eye on Miriam for a few minutes?' he asked Pam.

'Sure.'

The cop led him onto his front lawn, which was soggy and strewn with hoses and debris. He was relieved to see that the house itself was intact, but the garage was a smoking ruin. Several firemen were rolling up hoses and gathering equipment. There were no flames, but wisps of smoke rose from the collapsed roof of the garage.

'This is the owner,' his escort said to one of the firemen standing in his driveway. Without waiting for an answer, the cop walked back the way they'd come.

'Mr. Lantz, is it?' Richard nodded and they shook hands. 'I'm Claude Jackson, assistant chief. I'm in charge of this circus.'

'How bad is it?'

'Not very bad. The garage is a total loss, I'm afraid, but it didn't spread to the house. You've got a good fire door. There's also a broken window in the house. I'm not sure if we did that or not.'

'Do you have any idea how this happened?'

'Not yet. I've got a few men poking around, and a couple more on standby in case it flares up again.'

The garage doors were simply gone, but he could see nothing but pitch black inside. Then he saw flashlight beams zapping around in the darkness, illuminating charred two-by-fours and men with shovels. Much of the roof had caved in, and the timbers poking up from the hole looked like scorched bones. Everything was dripping wet.

'Mr. Lantz,' a voice said behind him. Richard turned around to see another cop, this one older and heavier, wearing thick glasses in dark plastic frames. 'I'm Detective Olvera. I have a few questions, if you've got a minute.'

'All right,' Jackson said, 'I'll be back shortly.'

Olvera waved him off and turned back to Richard. 'Were you gone all day?'

'Yes, we were at the park, and then we watched the fireworks.'

'Was your house locked?'

'No, I never lock it.'

'I see. What about the garage?'

'Yes—no. The doors are on, uh, I have a garage door opener. But there's a door around back that's always unlocked.'

'Uh huh. Mr. Lantz, have you been getting any threatening phone calls lately? Hang-ups, hate mail, anything like that?'

'What? Why?'

'We're pretty sure the fire was set on purpose.'

'What, you mean arson?'

'Yes, arson.' He waited patiently for a moment. 'So, can you think of anyone that would want to hurt you?' Richard thought of the thick batch of letters he'd received yesterday. 'What?' Olvera said. 'Did you think of something?'

'Well, just yesterday...' How was he going to explain this?

'Was it because you write the Mrs. Bambi column?' Olvera said. Richard stared at him in astonishment. 'So you have received some kind of threat?'

'Uh, yes. I used to get one or two irate letters a week, but yesterday I got about thirty of them. Some of them obviously knew I'm— I mean, that I write Mrs. Bambi. They mentioned my name.'

'I'll need to see those letters first thing in the morning, sir.'

'Okay.'

Jackson came strolling back.

'Well?' Olvera said.

'Definitely arson. Very amateur: wadded rags and gasoline. You're lucky they didn't wedge the breezeway door open, Mr. Lantz, or you might have lost your house, too.'

Olvera handed Richard a business card. 'I'll expect to see you in the morning, Mr. Lantz. Call me tonight if you think of anything that might help us.' He clapped Jackson on the arm and the two men walked toward the street. Frank Morris from the Examiner ran up to them with a tape recorder.

Richard went back to Pam's car.

'What's going on?' she said. Miriam was sitting up in the back seat, staring at the commotion surrounding their house.

'The garage is gone. They said it's arson.'

169

'Arson!'

'Dad!' Miriam said frantically. 'What happened to Kobi? Is she okay?'

'I'm sure she's okay, honey. I'll go and get her.' He looked back at Pam. 'Can we stay with you tonight?'

'Absolutely. Do you need some help?'

'Dad!' Miriam said. 'My bike was in the garage!'

'I'll get you a new bike, Miriam.' Richard rubbed his face. He felt as if he hadn't slept in days. 'Okay, I'll just grab some things and be back in a few minutes.'

'Go on,' Pam said. 'We'll wait here.'

Richard went up the walkway to the front door. One of the living room windows was shattered, as if someone had hit a baseball through it. He turned on the lights and saw a rock lying on the floor. It was a smooth, light gray river rock, and on it was written in black magic marker, 'Mrs. Bambi knows dick.'

He grabbed the rock and turned the light off. Cleanup would have to wait, but he didn't want Miriam to see this. He ran upstairs and tossed the rock into the trash can in his office, then grabbed a change of clothes from his dresser and stuffed them into a small duffel. He was in Miriam's room, doing the same for her, when the doorbell rang. He ran back down the stairs.

It was Frank. 'I'm kind of busy, right now, Frank.'

Frank muscled past him and glanced at the glass-strewn Persian in the living room. 'I warned you, Richard.'

'Skip the lectures for later, okay? I've got to go. Pam and Miriam are waiting for me.'

'Uh huh. Any idea who did it?'

'The cops think it might have been one of the wackos who wrote the letters,' Richard said.

'What do you think?'

'Is this on the record?'

'Absolutely.'

'I think you should get the hell out of my house.'

'Can I quote you on that?' Frank said.

'Please do.'

'Richard—'

'What?'

'Calm down, pal. I just wanted to say that if there's anything I can do to help—'

'Right now, I just need to get out of here. Please?'

'Okay, I'm going. By the way, I got your column for this week. I'm not running it.'

'I don't care,' Richard said.

'I know. But you will be on page one in Friday's paper. I got some great pix. See you.'

As Frank turned to leave, the phone rang. Richard walked over, intending to answer it, but thought better of it. He let the machine pick it up. It was A.M., calling to see if everyone was okay. He didn't want to talk to her, so he let her babble on—but then he turned back. The message light was blinking. It might be from the arsonist. He waited until A.M. hung up, then pushed Play.

The first message was from Connie, his stalker, whining about why didn't he ever tell her he wrote the Mrs. Bambi column. He erased it. The second one was a hang-up. The third message started out with a sound like weeping. He pushed the volume button.

'Richard, it's Karen. I'm really sorry you had to find out like this. Clarence has been admitted to the hospital, here in Hood River. He's—' There was a muffled sound and a long pause. 'I'm sorry. He made me promise not to tell anyone. It's brain cancer, Richard. Terminal. He's known for months. They don't think he'll last more than a few days. You can see him tomorrow if you want, after one o'clock. I'm... I'm sorry.'

The machine beeped.

Richard turned away from the phone. He felt as if there were weights inside his forehead. He trudged back to the door and picked up his duffel. The phone rang again, but he ignored it. He had his hand on the doorknob when he remembered Kobi. He hadn't seen the pup yet; she should have been bouncing around him from the moment he stepped through the door. They'd left her in the house—could she have got into the garage somehow? The thought of having to tell Miriam that her puppy had burned up in the fire made him want to throw up.

'Kobi!' he called. No response. He walked upstairs and looked in Miriam's room. 'Kobi?' He heard a whimper from the closet. The door stood ajar; when he pulled it open, he saw her hunkered as far back into the corner as she could get. 'Come on, girl, let's go.'

He had to pull her out by the collar, but then she followed him downstairs with her tail drooping. They walked across the yard to where Pam was parked.

'Kobi!' Miriam shouted. Richard opened the back door and the dog leaped up onto the seat. He tossed the bag back there too and got in.

Pam was half-turned in her seat, looking at him. He faced the front, watching the firemen clean up their stuff, leaving his yard trashed. He hadn't noticed before that all of the neighbors were out: some standing around, some sitting in lawn chairs, drinking beer and watching the show.

'What?' Pam said.

'It's... I can't... There was a phone call. From Karen. Clarence... is in the hospital.'

'Is he okay?'

'No, he's not. He's dying.' Pam sucked in her breath. 'Brain tumor. She said he's got a couple days left.'

'Oh, Richard, I'm so sorry.' She leaned over to hug him. It took him a moment to remember to hug her back.

Chapter 15: End Game

Mrs. Bambi Knows (Archive)

Off the baby-sitter

Dear Mrs. Bambi:

We had the best baby-sitter in the world. She was an angel, a gift straight from God. She loved our baby boy, she was reliable and careful, and she was an excellent student—so she had a limited social life and was always available when we needed her.

Last week she ran off with my husband.

We've been married for five years. I thought we were happy, but apparently what he really wants is not me—not the devoted, loving 30-year old mother of his child—but a shiftless, conniving, contemptible teenage vixen. If she was two years younger I could have him arrested for statutory rape.

He confessed everything. They've been doing it for over a year—on his Wednesday 'boy's night out,' every time he drove her home after sitting, and sometimes in our house before he drove her home, while I was upstairs getting ready for bed!

And now, as if the humiliation weren't enough, I need to find a new baby-sitter.

I know he'll be back eventually, and I'll be able to hold this over him for the rest of his life. I'm just not sure whether I want him back after this.

—Betrayed

Dear Helen Keller:

Are you crazy? Are you actually considering taking this slime bag back? Open your eyes and get your head examined.

He'll be back, all right, when he finds out that teenage girls are only half-baked, but even if he gets down on his knees and begs, kick him out. No man with his priorities and gonads so far out of whack can be trusted again.

As for the new baby-sitter, find a 70-year-old grandmother. The odds are better that she'll be able to keep her panties on.

Dear Mrs. Bambi:

My wife refuses to take the Christmas tree down. The few needles that haven't fallen out on the carpet are completely brown.

The kids think she's nuts. I think the thing's a fire trap. But she says she can't live without the spirit of Christmas any more. What should I do?
—Up a Tree

Dear Mr. Squirrel Monkey:

What's your problem? Is she asking so much? Is your last name Scrooge?

Go get a fresh tree. The Forest Service will gladly sell you a permit.

After she's gone to bed one night, take down the dead tree and put up the new one. Decorate it just like the old one. Think of the expression on her face when she comes downstairs in the morning. And stop being such a crotchety wretch.

* * *

The next morning, Richard walked to the police station and dropped off his collection of hate mail and the stone that had been thrown through his window. The desk clerk gave him a receipt. The detective wasn't available. He walked slowly back home and puttered around, cleaning up the living room and trying to find something to keep him occupied until visiting hours began.

A Hispanic woman at the hospital's front desk gave Richard the room number. He took the elevator up to the third floor and followed the signs. The hallway was eerily lit by fluorescent fixtures behind waffle grills in the ceiling. Shadows seemed to lurk everywhere, but when he turned to look, everything was sterile and bright.

An old Japanese woman shuffled by him, clutching her thin silk robe tightly to her chest. A doctor in pale blue scrubs strode by, frowning at an open file folder and avoiding obstacles by some trick of peripheral vision. Empty wheelchairs were lined up against one wall like the luggage carts at an airport: pay a dollar, get a ride.

The door to Clarence's room was open but no one was visible inside. It was a semi-private room, with an unmade bed near the door and a shabby curtain blocking his view of the back. Richard knocked.

'Clarence?' He heard a faint sound and walked past the empty bed and the privacy curtain.

His friend lay propped up on pillows. The head of the bed was inclined, to raise him into a half-sitting position. He looked dead already: the skin of his face and arms was gray, with a strange translucent quality, and it hung loosely on him. He was spectrally thin, like a late-stage AIDS victim. Richard had never seen him without glasses before. He could almost make out the skull beneath his face.

He realized that Clarence was staring at him, too. A thin arm raised off the covers and a finger like a chicken's pointed to the chair beside the bed.

How could he have deteriorated so quickly? A month ago, at Miriam's birthday party, he had looked like a middle-aged man who was just recovering from the flu. Now he tottered on the brink of the grave.

An IV dripped clear fluid into a tube that snaked under a bandage on Clarence's right hand. The heart monitor hummed and beeped quietly. Clarence breathed in and out, slowly.

'You should have told me,' Richard said.

'Why?' Clarence wheezed. He coughed weakly.

'Because we're friends.'

'Could you have done anything about it?' Richard winced. 'Sorry.' His voice was growing stronger. 'No time left for being gentle and polite.'

'You should have told me.' They stared at each other stubbornly, like old times, for over a minute. 'Does it hurt?'

'Not any more.' Clarence raised the hand with the IV. 'I feel light-headed most of the day, and sometimes a little confused. But it's worth it. It hurt like hell all the time.' He coughed again, more forcefully this time. 'I always swore I'd never die in a hospital, but look at me now. I feel like somebody's science fair exhibit.'

'When... How long...'

'February. I started getting these unbearable headaches. It felt like my eyes were going to boil out of my skull. I went to the doctor, and he gave me blood tests, then X-rays, then a CAT scan. He showed me the inside of my head, pointed to a blob and said, 'See here, you've got a brain tumor, it's very advanced, and there's nothing we can do about it.' He's a very subtle guy.'

'What about surgery?'

'Too advanced.'

'Chemo?'

'It's too late, Richard.'

'What about those new tumor-shrinking drugs?'

'Richard.'

'What?'

'Shut up.' Clarence fumbled for a moment before finding the control box for his bed. He raised the back so he was sitting upright. 'You think I haven't been over all this already? I talked to the guy they have here, who's pretty good, and somebody even better in Portland. There's nothing they can do. End of story.'

'I can't believe—'

'Shut up, okay? I have a couple of favors I want to ask you.'

Richard pulled his chair closer to the bed. There was a faint smell coming from Clarence, as if he'd already started to decompose.

'Sure,' he said. 'Anything.'

'Don't be too hasty.' Clarence coughed again. 'You're not going to like either of them.' He reached for a large water bottle on the table, but it was just out of his reach. Richard handed it to him and he drank through the straw. 'First thing. You know I don't have any family, so I made you the executor of my estate.'

Richard jerked in surprise. Clarence smiled at him, showing his skull even more clearly; the effect was horrible.

'It's not going to be simple. I have the farm in Trout Lake and a rental property in White Salmon. Pam can handle those.' Richard nodded. 'The house is full of junk that needs to be sorted out. Then there's my business. Believe it or not, somebody offered to buy me out a year or so ago. My lawyer has all the information. They'll probably still be interested.'

'I'll take care of it.'

'Are you sure? If not, I'll have the lawyer do it.'

Richard imagined the days it would take him to sift through all of Clarence's effects, the weeks or months it would take to sell the business and the properties, all the while surrounded by his friend's aura and feeling the pain of his loss. Dealing with lawyers and who knew what else. Then he thought of how he would feel if he knew someone else was doing it.

'I'll do it,' Richard said finally. 'I don't want a stranger rummaging around in your life.'

Clarence relaxed back into his pillows. 'Thank you. I'd really rather it was you.'

'Do you have a will?'

'The lawyer has it. He'll call you after—'

They stared at each other silently for a while.

'What's the second thing?' Richard said.

'Leave.'

'What?'

'I want you to leave right now, and don't come back.'

Richard stared at him. He had planned to spend several hours here every day until his friend... died. 'But—'

'I mean it. Go now. It's bad enough you had to see me this way once. I don't want you, or anyone else, remembering me this way.'

Richard couldn't make himself move.

'Please,' Clarence said. Richard stood slowly. 'I know, you had more to say. Me too. That's the breaks, my friend. But think of this. Either one of us could have been killed in a car crash any day of our lives. I almost bought it three times in 'Nam. Instead we lived long enough to say goodbye today.'

Clarence held out his hand. Richard took it and squeezed. Clarence gripped his hand hard, then let go.

'Say goodbye to Miriam for me,' he said as Richard turned away. 'I'll miss her.'

Karen was leaning against the wall outside the room, crying. Richard opened his arms and they hugged fiercely for a moment. When she let him go, she walked around him into Clarence's room. Richard shambled down the interminable hallway to the elevator and pushed the button. It seemed like a week before the doors opened to let him out of hell.

177

* * *

Richard stood in his driveway, contemplating the ruin of his garage. The spine of the roof had been broken, as if a tyrannosaur had stepped on it. Parts of the siding were still intact, in fact the entire right side of the structure looked undamaged, but the middle was a charred, soggy disaster.

So what? He never put his car in there; last night it had been safely parked on the street in front of Pam's house. What had he lost? Some gardening tools, their bikes, boxes of junk he hadn't opened in years—and a certain sense of security. He considered whether he should start locking his doors and decided that whatever sick cretin had done this, he wasn't going to win the war by turning Richard paranoid.

He went inside and called the contractor that had remodeled his house ten years ago, when he'd first moved to Hood River. The office manager answered. Richard described the problem and she promised him that her boss would stop by that day to look at the damage.

There were two more messages from A.M., asking him to call her, and three hangups. He erased them all and phoned Nadine.

'Can you take Miriam this Friday?' he said.

'Sorry, I can't. We're going... out.'

'Really? You never go out. Where are you going?'

'Ah... Oh, sorry, Richard, Becky's calling. Got to go.'

Going out? Bullshit. He punched in the number for Tiff's parents. It was a long shot; he hadn't spoken to them since Memorial Day, but maybe they'd got over being upset by now. Tiff's mother, Carrie, answered.

'Oh, I'm sorry, Richard, but we have family visiting. We really can't.'

Sure. Well, that left A.M., and he wasn't up to talking to her yet. He sat in the back yard for a while, listening to the breeze ruffle the leaves of the oak trees and watching the sunlight filter through them. Then he heard the squeal of tires, close. He went back through the house and opened the front door. The outside of the door was dripping raw eggs, and the big tree in the middle of the yard had been draped with toilet paper.

'Well, now I have something to do,' he said to himself. He was impressed that the vandals had been able to do this in the middle of the day. But perhaps the passersby and even the police had stopped to help.

178

The egg wasn't hard to clean up, but he had to get a ladder to reach all of the TP. It took over an hour, and when he was done he'd come to a decision about A.M. He went back inside and called her shop.

'Are you and Miriam okay?' she said.

'We're fine. The garage is wiped out, and someone just egged and TP'ed the place.'

'Kind of early for Halloween.'

'Yep.'

'Come on over?' she suggested.

'I'll be right there.'

She was sitting on a stool at the cash register when he entered the shop, looking over a ledger. She set the small book down and put her hands in her lap. Her tight cobalt blue blouse was cropped, low-cut, and only covered one shoulder. As he came closer he caught sight of her skirt: trim at the hips and flared at the knees, where a feather boa seemed to have been stitched to the hem.

'Where's Miriam?' she said.

'She's with Pam at work today, learning how to be a realtor.'

'She wants to be a realtor?'

'No,' he said. 'But we thought it would keep her mind off the garage.'

'What happened, Richard?'

'Somebody burned the damned thing down. I must have pissed off someone who needs psychiatric help.'

'You pissed off just about everyone in the valley.'

'Yeah, I know.' There was a clear spot on the wall near the counter; he leaned against it.

'Sorry about the beer in your face.'

'Well, I'm getting used to it, after your party.'

'Yeah, that's where I got the idea.'

'I'm thinking about drinking all my beer like that from now on,' he said. 'It cuts down on the calories.'

'Higher laundry bills.'

'True.' They looked at each other for a moment. 'I thought you were through with me.'

'Nah, I was just pissed off.'

'You didn't burn down my garage, did you?'

179

'Not my style. If I were really mad at you, I'd pour hot wax into your computer. Or just kick your ass.'

'Then I'm glad you're not really mad at me.'

'I got over it,' she said. 'Want some coffee?'

'Sure.'

They went into the back room and she fixed him a cup. He had to move a stack of fabric bolts off a chair before he could sit down.

'Is Nadine angry, too?' he said when they were both settled.

'Yeah, but she'll calm down in a day or so. You know, lying your little dick off like that is not considered acceptable behavior between friends.'

'I'm sorry,' he said. 'It won't happen again.'

'Don't give me that sorry crap. Why'd you do it, Richard?'

'What? Mrs. Bambi?'

'No, needle brain, why didn't you tell me that you were Mrs. Bambi?'

He spread his hands in a helpless shrug.

'You know,' A.M. said, 'I think it's kind of cool that you wrote the column. I went back and reread some after I found out it was you. Did you know that I saved a bunch of them—ones that flicked on people I knew?'

Richard shook his head.

'Yeah,' she said. 'You were pretty funny. And sharp. You'd make a great lesbian if you weren't a guy.'

'Thanks, I guess.'

'But I don't get it. I could have helped you, stumblebutt! You know I'm completely tuned in to this town. All the times I begged you to open up to me, not only were you holding out on your own pathetic little life, but on this great alter ego of yours, too.'

Richard set down his cup and leaned forward in his spindly chair. 'A.M., I don't know if I can explain this clearly.'

'Try.'

'I kept Mrs. Bambi a secret... because she was mine.'

'What do you mean?'

'When I was her,' he said, 'I was connected. It was a link between me and this community that I don't fit into very well. And it had nothing to do with Miriam, and nothing to do with computers—and nothing to do with you. It was just pure me.'

'Bullshit. It was a pure lie.'

180

'No, it wasn't,' he said. 'Mrs. Bambi is me, and I'm her. But we were also separate people, and she was all mine. I didn't have to share her. I didn't owe her to anyone else.'

'You were playing with yourself.'

He started to protest.

'No,' A.M. said, 'I know masturbation when I see it. And now I get it. She was one of those guilty pleasures that priests warn kids about.'

Richard sat back. She had it all wrong, but he didn't think he could explain it any better, and if that explanation satisfied her, he'd let it ride.

'It's okay, Richard,' she said. 'Everybody either does it or lies about not doing it. You just have a more elaborate method of getting off than most people.'

'Thanks for being so understanding.' He had a feeling that she was going to tease him with this for the rest of their lives.

'I'll take Miriam on Friday,' A.M. said. 'I think you need to go get drunk.'

* * *

The Big River Saloon was a dump. It was located on the first floor of what had once been a nice hotel, but was now a vacant fire trap that, for over seven years, had been scheduled to be remodeled 'starting next spring.' Just around the corner from the saloon, in the same building, was a small, dingy restaurant that closed and reopened under a new name every few months. The man who owned the building had big plans for the place, but no organization skills worth mentioning and not enough money. No one in town expected anything to improve: the building would just keep getting more and more run down until it collapsed or was condemned.

The saloon was a large, dark, jumbled space, with a long bar along one wall, beat-up tables and chairs scattered everywhere, and a bandstand tucked into a corner where it couldn't be seen from half the floor. Richard paid the cover and went in alone. The band was tuning up, if that was the right word; the drummer took random whacks on his set, and someone was trying in vain to find the right tension on his electric guitar strings: twang, adjust, repeat.

Richard sat in a booth as far away from the band as he could get. A waitress came by, looking exhausted already at the start of her shift, and he ordered a beer.

When the band started playing some kind of Texas bluegrass very loud and still not in tune, he switched to Scotch, working his way through the bar's roster of single malts. After an hour of that he was feeling nearly deaf, a little dizzy, and his bladder was full.

The bathrooms were in the back, which meant that he had to walk directly in front of the band's speakers. He stuck his fingers in his ears and tried not to watch the couples dancing; swing dancing always gave him vertigo when he was drunk.

The men's room was run down, but reasonably clean. As he was washing his hands, someone came in behind him. He didn't look up.

'Hey,' a slurred voice said, 'you're him.'

Richard hurried out of the restroom, but he'd only taken a few steps beyond the door when a hand landed on his shoulder. He turned to see a short, muscular kid in black jeans, cowboy boots, and a white T-shirt. The man said something, but Richard couldn't hear him over the band.

'What?'

He spoke again, what sounded like 'sucking bike,' but that couldn't be right. Richard smiled, shrugged his shoulders, and turned away. The man grabbed his arm and yelled something that might have been 'twisted Camry.' Richard grimaced, pointed to his ears, and was about to turn away again, but the band abruptly stopped. His ears rang like church bells on Sunday.

'I said,' the kid screamed, 'you're the asshole who writes that advice column, aren't you?' Richard let his face go blank. 'You dissed my girl, you damned queer.'

'Did I? I'm very sorry.'

'You're going to be sorry, you mean.' Without warning, his fist drove into Richard's stomach, knocking the air out of him. Richard sat down hard, clutching his belly. All he could see were the kid's shiny black cowboy boots on the scuffed and ancient wooden floor, with their polished silver tips, and stitching that was really quite handsome. He wondered if the guy was going to kick him with those boots. Then he threw up on them.

There was some kind of scuffle that he really couldn't follow, but when someone finally helped him up he couldn't see the little muscle-bound rodent anywhere.

'You'd better get on home,' the bartender said. 'Do you need a cab or can you walk?'

'I'll walk,' Richard said.

The bartender was an old-timer at the saloon, a middle-aged windsurfer with no hair and huge arms who over the years had served Richard too many beers to count. He helped Richard to the door. When Richard looked back half a block later, the man was still watching him. They waved at each other and Richard stumbled home and fell into bed.

* * *

The phone woke him just after eight. It rang three times before he managed to pick up the handset.

'A.M., I'm going to kill you.'

'Mr. Lantz?' It was a man's voice. 'This is Leo Karstetter, Mr. Hoskins' attorney? I'm sorry, did I wake you?'

Hoskins? He meant Clarence.

'Ugh,' Richard said. 'Who is this again?'

'Leo Karstetter. I'm an attorney in White Salmon.'

'Uh huh.'

'I'm very sorry I woke you, Mr. Lantz, but I thought you would want to know as soon as possible.'

'Right. Know what?' Richard looked down at himself. He was lying, fully clothed, on top of the blankets.

'I'm sorry to tell you that Mr. Hoskins passed away last night.'

Richard sat up. His head swam, but he ignored it. 'What did you say? Clarence is dead?'

'Yes, I'm sorry. He died last night in his sleep at 2:15.' Richard leaned forward and rested his head on the heel of his palm. 'Mr. Lantz? I think we need to talk.'

'Not now,' Richard said, and hung up.

Chapter 16: Legal Rites

From the Hood River Examiner
Friday, July 7, 1995

Mrs. Bambi Knows

Mrs. Bambi's column will no longer appear in this paper. The Examiner regrets the sarcastic tone often displayed in this feature and offers its sincere apologies to anyone who may have been offended.
—The Editor

Fire destroys Oak St. garage

Two pumpers and an emergency medical truck responded to a fire at 915 Oak St. at 9:53 p.m. on July 4. The flames were extinguished quickly, and the blaze was restricted to the garage, where the fire began. Damages are estimated to be around $9,000.

Initial conjectures that the fire was caused by bottle rockets were later disproven when evidence of arson was discovered. An investigation is underway.

Additional damage included a broken window caused by a thrown rock.

The house's owner, Richard Lantz, and his ten-year old daughter were not home at the time of the fire. No injuries were reported.

Additional photos on page A-8.

* * *

Clarence's memorial service was held in the small United Methodist church in White Salmon, a town about half the size of Hood River and almost directly across the Columbia River from it. Richard rarely visited White Salmon; there was no reason to. The downtown was a strip a block wide on either side of

184

the main street, populated by struggling clothing stores, a small grocery, a tiny library, a few dreary restaurants, a pharmacy, a lot of churches, and the requisite video rental. The Inn of the White Salmon was the only interesting thing in town.

Miriam looked around with interest as they walked up the aisle together. They almost never went to church except on Christmas Eve, to hear the singing. She craned her neck to squint up at the choir loft, and stumbled. Pam steadied her with a hand on her shoulder.

A few dozen people huddled together in the front pews. Richard scanned them quickly, recognizing about half of them. The rest were probably friends of Clarence's from Trout Lake. Richard led Pam and Miriam to an empty pew at the back of the herd.

More people straggled in behind them, mostly in pairs but occasional loners, too. Soon the minister entered from a door behind the altar and stood at the podium. He was a young man of perhaps thirty, with a face prematurely lined and hair that was starting to gray.

'Friends,' the minister said in a surprisingly rich baritone, 'we're here to give thanks for the life of Clarence Hoskins. He was a quiet man, a veteran who rarely spoke of the war; a private man, who lived by himself all his life, but had many friends...'

Richard had trouble paying attention. Had this guy even known Clarence? It would be better if someone who really knew him was speaking, but that probably meant Richard, and he had declined when Karen asked him if he wanted to say something.

'Dad?' Miriam whispered.

'What, honey?'

'Where's the coffin?'

'It's not a funeral, baby. Clarence has already been cremated. We're just here to remember how much we loved him, and how much we're going to miss him.'

'Oh. Okay.'

He drifted while waves of sound washed over him meaninglessly. Finally the service was over. He and Pam each took one of Miriam's hands, and they walked out into the blinding sunlight.

As they went down the steps to the sidewalk, a plump man in an expensive suit came toward them. 'Mr. Lantz?' he said.

185

'Yes.'

'I'm Leo Karstetter, Mr. Hoskin's attorney? We spoke on the phone.'

'Oh, right. I was going to call you back.'

'No need. I know this is a trying time for you, and you'll probably be unsure what to do next. I just want to let you know that I'm going to be taking care of things, the safe deposit box, entering the will in probate, and so on. All you need to do is handle the disposition of Mr. Hoskin's belongings, and that can wait until you're ready. I'll...' He paused to fish a business card out of his coat pocket, eventually stuffing his whole chubby hand in and coming out with a small wad of papers and cards. He handed one to Richard. 'I'll contact you in a few days. We'll read the will some time next week. In the meantime, don't worry about anything.'

'Fine. Good. Thanks.' And as the lawyer turned away: 'Bye.' He felt like a pre-verbal caveman. 'Let's go have some cake,' he said to Miriam.

He had offered to host a small gathering at his house after the service. Perhaps Karen should have done it instead, but her apartment was very small and she didn't really seem up to it.

It was not a success. Richard, Pam, and Miriam had made the food—vegetable plates, homemade soup, sandwich stuff, chips and dips, and a chocolate cake—and everything turned out fine. But the mood was somber and no one seemed willing to talk or to linger. Nadine, Consuela, Becky, and Jane left after only half an hour, having spoken no more than a handful of words to anyone. Val and Ralf, looking like a high society couple from the twenties in their matching dark suits, left soon after. A.M. and Sylvia kissed Richard on the cheek as they walked out the door.

That left only the four of them: Richard, Pam, Miriam—and Karen, who sat in Richard's rocking chair without rocking, looking at her shoes. She seemed to want to leave but couldn't find the strength to actually get up. Finally she looked at Richard. Tears were leaking from her eyes.

'Tomorrow?' she said.

'I'll pick you up at ten.' He stood and offered her his hand. She let him pull her out of the chair.

* * *

As he slowed down to go through a small town, Richard started laughing.

'What?' Karen said.

'The sign!'

In front of a log cabin restaurant, a hand-painted sign board said:

Baker's Doz.
Worms
$1.50

'What do you suppose a baker would do with them?' Richard said. 'Pie? Focaccia?'

Karen sighed and didn't laugh. Richard felt stupid, but he didn't regret trying to make her smile.

When they neared Trout Lake, they could see the bare crag that was called Sleeping Beauty. From a certain angle, especially if the observer was a farmer who'd been alone too long and had a bit too much to drink, the outcropping looked like the head and hair of a giant sleeping maiden; a nearby peak stood in for a breast, and a ridge made her hips.

Despite Richard's distaste for hiking, they were headed for the crown of Beauty's head.

They drove through the hamlet of Trout Lake, past the Forest Service ranger station, and up into the woods. After several miles of gravel roads, he parked the car. They shouldered their packs and started up the trail.

Richard had hiked this trail before, once with Clarence and once with Miriam. It was only a mile and a half long, but unrelenting from the first step: not as steep as some of the knee-crackers that Clarence had dragged him on, but steep enough to require frequent rest stops.

The trees here were mature enough to look like old growth, although they weren't. Half an hour into their ascent, Richard and Karen stopped for a water break in a place that looked like a forest cathedral. Enormous Douglas firs stood like ancient columns on the steep hillside. There were enough breaks in the canopy to allow sunlight to filter through, dappled and always changing. The trail curved in a long right-hand turn, hugging the side of the slope, through a gigantic open space bounded on all sides by the tall, straight trees.

'This is scheduled to be clear-cut,' Richard said when he'd recovered his breath.

'Oh, no. When?'

'I don't know. It's been on the list for a while, but since they haven't been logging in the National Forest here for the last few years, I'm not sure when they'll get to it.'

'Maybe never,' Karen said.

'We can hope.'

Ponderosa pines had given way to red cedar, Douglas and grand fir, and hemlock. The undergrowth was huckleberry, trillium, ferns, and dozens of things that Richard couldn't identify. He tried to concentrate on the beauty around him instead of the pain in his legs.

This trail, like most in the forest, was blocked by deadfall every winter, and they passed many two- and three-foot thick fallen timbers that someone had cut through, this spring, to reopen the path. Sawdust from the chain saws still lay in neat piles beneath the raw, fragrant ends of the severed trunks.

Finally they left the woods behind and came out onto open switchbacks. Mt. Rainier, still completely snow-covered, was visible peeking through gaps in the ridge line to their left. The trail was loose rock here, the trees stunted, grotesque, wind-shorn. Farther up, someone had dry-stacked thousands of slate-like rocks into short walls on the downhill side of the trail. Richard couldn't imagine the effort required to haul and place all those rocks by hand, but he was grateful: on his second slip on the leftover scree he might have sailed right over the edge if not for those walls.

After the last switchback, the trail seemed to dead-end in a wall of rock, with another talus slope on their left. Karen had never been here before, so Richard led the way up the obscure path across the loose rocks, scrambling on hands and feet.

They emerged on top of the world. A stiff, cold breeze blew from the southwest, welcome after the dusty heat they'd endured since leaving the forest. The sky was a cloudless, washed-out blue from horizon to horizon. To the west the stump of Mt. St. Helens brooded over its desolation; to the north Mt. Rainier was partially visible over the edge of the ridge; to the south Mt. Hood hunkered over the wheat-colored desert like a giant white meringue.

But to their east, Mt. Adams dominated the sky. It was broad and misshapen, the lobed peak still covered in white snow, dirty glaciers showing bare gray ice lower down, with crevasses like stretch marks. The mountain was wider than Richard's outstretched arms.

Below, verdant forest, feathery-looking from this distance, was interspersed in a checkerboard pattern with brownish blocks of clear-cut. The bare spots must have been replanted, but at this distance there was no sign of new growth, just the raw, dusty tan of bare earth and slash. The giant's checkerboard slunk away towards the horizon in all directions.

Directly south of them lay the Trout Lake valley, walled on both sides by high ridges, chopped up into small farms. The tiny village was hidden from view. An enigmatic mound rose out of the middle of the valley: Little Mountain, the locals called it, a cinder cone, a baby volcano that had never grown to maturity. Just off the left shoulder of Little Mountain, Richard thought he could pick out Clarence's house, but the valley air shimmered in the heat and he couldn't be sure.

'Ready?' Karen said.

Richard opened his pack and took out Clarence's urn. He handed it to Karen and they walked to the edge of the bluff, standing with their toes only inches from a seven-hundred-foot vertical drop. Richard looked down: the cliff face fell away invisibly, slightly overhung, until the slope broadened out far below and regained its cover of trees.

Karen peeled off the duct tape they'd used to keep the urn closed. She handed the curled tape and the lid to Richard and without a word dumped the ashes into the wind. They sailed off in a cloud toward the mountain, thinning out in just a moment until they were invisible. She gave the urn a final shake, dislodging a little more grit, and gave the dull gold urn back to him.

They sat on the edge of the cliff and ate a silent lunch. Richard stared out over the valley, trying to convince himself he could see Clarence's house, although it was probably a dozen miles away and surely invisible without binoculars.

The hike out was easier, but still tough on his legs. They had to stop occasionally, not to catch their breath but to ease the pain of trying to walk slowly down a steep trail. The muscles just above his knees felt inflamed.

It took over an hour to drive back to Hood River. Richard parked his car in front of Karen's apartment and they got out together.

'Richard,' she said, 'I...' She hung her head for a moment, then looked up. 'Thanks. Just... thanks.'

She leaned over stiffly and kissed him lightly on the cheek. He got back in his car and drove home. The feeling of that feather touch refused to fade.

* * *

In the days before the reading of Clarence's will, the low-grade lynching of Mrs. Bambi continued. Frank called to say that Richard had been named in three lawsuits against the paper. Richard's lawyer informed him that two suits had been filed against him alone. Returning from grocery shopping, Richard found a three-point set of deer antlers nailed to his front door. Miriam came running into the house one afternoon, crying because the kids at her swimming lesson were teasing her about her father being a woman. Piles of what he hoped were dog droppings kept appearing in his front yard, a problem he had never had before. He received several hate letters in the mail every day. And the day before the reading, the power at his house went off and stayed off for seven hours. All of his neighbors still had power. It took half a dozen calls to the electric co-op until they told him there had been a computer error; an hour later he had light again.

Leo Karstetter's office was in a decrepit two-story building in White Salmon. Mortar was missing from between the dirty bricks, and a faded, weathered sign announced the offices of Karstetter and Bloom on the second floor. Richard and Miriam stumped up the worn linoleum steps by the light of a single dim bulb.

It was a shock to step into the office's well-lit, clean, elegantly decorated reception area. As the receptionist went back to announce them, Richard sank onto a comfortable couch flanked by two large and vigorous plants.

They had to get right back up again. Leo came bounding down the hallway, dressed in deep blue slacks with a white pinstripe shirt, red suspenders straining over his huge gut, and a solid blue tie.

'Mr. Lantz—Richard,' he said. 'Miss Miriam. Come on back. Everyone else has arrived.'

The conference room was nearly filled by a massive, dark wood table. The indirect lighting was focused on several original oil paintings of Columbia River Gorge scenes: windsurfers and Mt. Hood.

Leo took a seat at the end of the table. Richard sat down next to him, with Miriam at his right and two couples he didn't recognize on their side of the table. On the other side were almost all his surviving friends: A.M. wearing a crisp white blouse, Nadine with one booted foot up on the table's edge and her chair tilted back so her shoulders rested on the wall, Val sitting primly at attention, Karen in an olive T-shirt and black jeans, a distant look in her eyes.

Leo handed Richard a tall stack of stapled documents and gestured for him to pass them around.

'Everyone please take one,' he said. 'Miss Miriam, you may take one, too.' Miriam looked surprised and pleased.

Richard glanced through the sheaf. On top was a single-page summary, followed by a fairly lengthy, official-looking last will and testament, and then a one-page letter signed by Clarence.

'Thanks for coming today,' Leo said. 'Except for the tax people, who were not invited, the people in this room constitute all the beneficiaries of Clarence Hoskin's estate. Let me explain what we're going to do here today. Well, what we're not going to do is read through Clarence's will line by line. You all have a copy of it there, and you can read it later if you like. All we need to be concerned with is the first page, which describes in plain English what Clarence wanted. Any questions before we begin? No? All right then, let's start with Miriam Lantz.'

Miriam jerked her head up and stared at the lawyer, eyes wide.

'Miss Miriam, Clarence has left you his library—in other words, all of his books.' Miriam nodded, frowning. 'Furthermore, he also wanted you to have his TV and VCR and all his videotapes.'

Miriam squeaked in delight and her face erupted in a huge grin. Richard closed his eyes and shook his head.

'I have a few messages concerning this bequest. Miriam, Clarence said, and I quote: "Spend more time with the books than the TV or your dad has my permission to smash it with a baseball bat."' Richard started; that had to be a reference to the Mrs. Bambi column about killing the TV. 'And Richard. I quote: "Get over it. It won't kill her."'

'Is it okay, Dad?' Miriam said.

Richard had to admit he'd been outfoxed: there was no way he could refuse. Clarence had always been a better chess player. 'Okay.'

Miriam clapped her hands and several of their friends smiled.

'And now, Richard. This is for you.' He handed Richard a sealed white envelope. Richard held it for a moment, trying to decide whether to open it then and there, then slid it under his stack of papers, unopened. He could tell that A.M. and Nadine were disappointed, their curiosity unslaked, but Leo nodded in approval.

Then the others. To A.M. Clarence left his old grandfather clock. Richard remembered that baroque old thing, all burnished cherry, beveled glass, and brass; it had been in Clarence's family for three generations. One of the men Richard didn't know, Bill Pond, seemed delighted to get Clarence's car. The other stranger, Al Steffen, got the plans and working model of Clarence's dog wash. He looked surprised and perplexed at what might or might not be his good fortune. Val was to get Clarence's abacus collection. Richard hadn't known that he had an abacus collection, but apparently Val did, because she was obviously stunned.

'Ms. Szabo,' Leo said. 'Clarence always admired the way you ran your farm, and especially your work as an out-placement home for the women's shelter. Therefore, he wants you to have anything from his farm that could be of use on yours, specifically the farm equipment and implements, household appliances, computer equipment, furnishings, and so on.'

Nadine nodded impassively, but Richard could see her eyes gleaming with arrested tears.

'And finally, Ms. Blanchard.' Karen sat up straighter, nervously smoothing out her shirt. Leo handed her an envelope like Richard's, which she held tightly in one hand that she dropped into her lap.

'Our instructions—myself as Clarence's lawyer and Richard as his executor—are to carry out the bequests we've already discussed, then to allow you to select from Clarence's home any personal effects you might care to own. The remainder of the estate, which constitutes the farm in Trout Lake, a rental property here in White Salmon, his mail-order business, and some securities, are to be liquidated and the entire net amount is yours.'

Karen inclined her head as if listening, but the room was silent. The hand not holding her letter fluttered up off the table, then fell back.

'How much?' she said quietly.

'That will depend on the sale price of the properties,' the lawyer said. 'But I've built a spreadsheet using quite conservative estimates. I believe the net will be somewhat over three hundred thousand dollars.'

Karen stared at him without speaking for a long time.

* * *

Richard drove back across the bridge to Hood River, and past their house.

'Where are we going, Dad?' Miriam said.

'I need to stop at the hospital for a few minutes.'

'Are you sick?'

'No, I just need to talk to someone.' When he parked in the hospital lot, he said, 'Do you want to wait here or come in?'

'I'll come in.'

Clarence could have gone to the hospital in White Salmon, but he chose to come over here because the Hood River hospital had a very well-respected oncologist. Richard asked the receptionist if he could speak to him. The heavy-set woman told him that since he didn't have an appointment, he would have to wait.

They sat on molded plastic chairs. Miriam picked up a woman's fashion magazine and began studying an article on how to apply eye makeup. Please, God, not yet, I'm not ready for that! Richard tore open the envelope Clarence had left for him. The note inside was written in a scratchy, feeble hand that Richard could barely recognize as Clarence's.

> Richard,
>
> You're a wimp hiker and a pathetic excuse for a chess player, but no one could have asked for a better friend. I'm not sorry I kept my illness from you, but I am sorry I won't be around to give you shit any more.
>
> The Mrs. Bambi fallout may get a bit rough. Just be Mrs. Bambi and you'll get by: keep your chin up, your tits out, your ears open, and your tongue sharp.
>
> You hang on to Pam. You've been alone too long, and she's good for you, and for Miriam, too.
>
> Take good care of your daughter. She's the best thing you'll ever have, or ever know.
>
> Clarence

'Mr. Lantz?' someone said. Richard looked up. A doctor was standing over him, white coat over dark pants, blue shirt, red tie. He was of medium height, very trim, with wavy hair and eyebrows that looked like black caterpillars. 'I'm Dr. Monrad. You wanted to see me?'

'I was a good friend of Clarence Hoskins.' He folded the note and put it back in its envelope.

'Ah.'

'I wonder if we could talk somewhere private for a moment?'

'Um, I suppose.' The doctor glanced around, irritated. 'We can go to my office.'

'Miriam,' Richard said, 'could you hang on to this for me?' He handed her the envelope.

'Sure.'

'I'll be back in a few minutes.'

'Okay.' She stuck her nose back in the magazine.

'Your daughter?' the doctor said. He was walking briskly down the hallway away from reception. Richard almost had to trot to keep up. They sped down one hall after another, until the doctor shoved open a glass door. 'Well, here we are.' He whisked around the desk, plopped into the chair, and steepled his fingers with his elbows on the chair arms.

'I know you're busy, so I'll get right to the point,' Richard said. He took a folded check out of his shirt pocket and handed it across the desk.

Dr. Monrad took it without unfolding it. 'What is this?'

'I know there was nothing you could do to save Clarence's life.'

'Yes, an unfortunate case. By the time he exhibited symptoms serious enough to bring him to us, there was no hope.'

'But you did what could be done. You made him comfortable. A mutual friend told me how much he appreciated how well you treated him.'

The doctor waved the check, still folded. 'And this is... what?'

'That is a donation to the hospital foundation.'

'Mr. Lantz, the foundation has an office right down the hall.' He reached out to give the check back.

'I know that, Dr. Monrad. I've been there. I want you to give them the check.'

The caterpillars over the doctor's eyes levitated. 'And why is that?'

'So that they'll understand it was your work that prompted the donation.'

Monrad looked down at the check in his hand and slowly opened it. 'Holy shit!' he said. 'A hundred thousand dollars!'

'There are two conditions,' Richard said. The doctor glanced up, as if seeing him for the first time. 'This money is to be used for the cancer ward somehow.' The doctor nodded. 'And this is very important. I want this contribution to be anonymous. My name is not to be mentioned or used in any way. Understood?'

'I understand,' the doctor said warmly.

Richard stood up. 'Then I'll let you get back to work.' They shook hands.

'I'll take care of this for you,' Dr. Monrad said. 'I can take you back—'

'I'll find it,' Richard said, and walked out of the office. He had to wander for a few minutes before he saw a sign that led him out of the maze.

Miriam looked up as he returned. 'Dad, can I get my ears pierced?'

Chapter 17: Moving Daze

Mrs. Bambi Knows (Archive)

Primitivism cures holiday pests

Dear Mrs. Bambi:

My brother, his wife, and their six children came unannounced for Thanksgiving, and they won't leave. They live in Idaho, and we thought perhaps they would stay for a few days, but they're still here two weeks later. They eat everything in sight; their youngest even chews on the wallpaper.

They've repeatedly refused our offers to put them up in a hotel. They say that would be impolite of them, and they couldn't think of putting us out, by which they mean taking our money, as if the locusts they call their children weren't costing us a fortune in groceries.

And the kids are vicious. They tore the door off the refrigerator, duct-taped the cat to the ceiling, and tied our son to a branch high in a tree. Now he can't sleep except on the floor beneath our bed.

My brother has an inexhaustible supply of racist jokes and he beats his kids in public, not that I can blame him much for that. His wife is actually very nice, but I can't get past the fact that she spawned this herd of malevolent wolverines.

How can I get rid of these vermin?

—Plagued

Dear Blacky:

You have to make them want to leave. Convince them that whatever they were fleeing in Idaho was paradise.

Turn off the hot water heater and pretend that it's broken. You might get it fixed in a month or so, but cold showers are so invigorating, aren't they?

Empty your cupboard and refrigerator of food; your church will be glad to accept the donation. You're starting your annual holiday fast, when you just take water and vitamins for two weeks.

Turn off the heat. We're having such a mild winter this year, it's almost like spring, isn't it?

Take your TV over to a friend's house and leave it there. Tell them the basement trolls must be acting up again.

Trust me, they'll be gone in three days.

Dear Mrs. Bambi:

I love Italian food but I can't eat it without getting it on my clothes. Any kind of pasta, the sauce ends up in little spots on my shirt. I hate to tuck my napkin into my collar like some dork, but what else can I do?
—*Bibbed*

Dear Babyface:

Take another shirt along. One for eating, one for after dinner.

Or go to the used book store downtown. They have a great selection of small buttons with slogans on them. ('Jesus is coming, look busy.') Buy half a dozen and pin one over every food spot. Your friends will be laughing too hard to wonder what's under the buttons.

* * *

It was becoming dangerous to go out in public. When Richard stopped at the Safeway to get ingredients for banana splits, a wild-looking woman with gray hair and slumping white cotton socks whacked him across the head with a family pack of chicken breasts, breaking it open, knocking him on his butt, and spilling raw meat all over him. He went to the coffee shop for a latté the next morning and three people, one after another, perhaps inspired by stories from the no-name Chinese restaurant, threw lukewarm cups of coffee in his face. At least they weren't scalding. The barista, a young woman with whom he had many times chatted amiably, laughed out loud.

Often now when he walked out his front door, a stranger, different each time, would be standing at the street, watching him.

Richard and Miriam left the house early in the morning two days after Clarence's will was read, each carrying a small sleep-over bag. Kobi trailed after, sniffing at every pebble and plant. A few days spent in Trout Lake, sorting through Clarence's stuff and avoiding flying coffee and chicken parts, would be fun for Miriam and restful for him.

It had taken the construction crew only two days to tear down his garage. The scorched, dirty foundation had lain bare and forlorn until now. This morning two men in torn jeans and scruffy T-shirts were fussing around the place, one taking measurements with a long tape that he rolled up with a silver crank, the other unloading two-by-fours from a flatbed truck. The workmen waved at them without speaking. Richard drove away, hoping the house would still be there when they got back.

*   *   *

The car had not fully stopped in front of the pole barn when Miriam leaped out and ran toward the main barn to check on the kittens, forgetting all about Kobi. Richard let the puppy out and she raced after her mistress, barking wildly and, no doubt, scaring off the cats.

At first, the task seemed Herculean; the irrigation ditch was far too small to flush out these stables. Richard wandered through the big barn, the pole barn, and the house, wondering how he was ever going to make sense of the clutter. Yet within an hour everything seemed straightforward. There were half a dozen items he needed to set aside for specific bequests: the car, the clock, the damned TV, the dog wash, the abacus collection if he could find it. Nadine and Karen would pick out the things they wanted. The business stuff would be set aside for its new owner. The ancient, rusting equipment in the barn could sit where it lay, as it had for decades. The rest he would sell, recycle, give away, or trash, and then he would be done.

Simple. It looked like only three days of superhuman effort.

He started by calling everyone who had been at the reading to ask them to come pick up their gifts. When he reached Karen, she hesitated for a moment and told him there was nothing in the house worth the pain of coming back up there. But everyone else committed to a time.

As his first chore, he tackled Clarence's office, copying the business data onto a series of floppy disks and then deleting it, as well as the few personal files, from the hard drive. Now the computer was ready for Nadine, if she wanted it. He sorted through the mounds of paper on the desk, the bookshelves, and in the filing cabinets, making three piles: business, personal, and recycle. He was nearly done when Miriam leapt through the door and said she was hungry.

After lunch he set out to find the abacuses. He had never seen or heard of them before the reading, which meant they must be either in the root cellar or upstairs, places he had rarely gone when visiting Clarence. Guessing they wouldn't be in the damp cellar, he climbed the steep stairs and got a surprise: he'd forgotten that this house had a third floor. The second story had three bedrooms and a bath, and a narrow, twisting stairway that led to a finished attic from which four small bedrooms had been carved.

In the tiny closet of the smallest of these, Richard found a small sea chest. The old-fashioned bronze skeleton key hung on a leather lanyard. Richard opened the chest and saw a cracked and weathered leather pouch. Within it rested an antique Chinese abacus, the size of a coffee table book: lacquered wooden frame with gold leaf highlights, intricately carved ivory beads, shining brass wires. There were five others below it, all carefully wrapped, none as magnificent as the first but all beautiful in their simple or baroque utility.

Richard carried the heavy chest downstairs and went out to the barn. Clarence had a huge supply of cardboard shipping boxes in many sizes, folded flat and strapped down to pallets. He was going to need dozens of them for Nadine and for all the leftover stuff. He found a tape gun and began making boxes, tossing the completed ones behind him until he had a pile of them twenty feet wide and taller than he was.

The Trout Lake beneficiaries came that afternoon. Al Steffen, dressed in jeans, a dirty shirt, and scruffy sneakers, helped Richard pick up the dog wash and carry it to his pickup. It was a lot heavier than it looked; Richard was breathing hard as he walked to the office to get the plans. He handed over the rolled blueprints and Steffen weighed them in his hand as if wondering whether to burn them.

'You know what happened with Joe?' Richard said as Steffen slammed the tailgate closed.

'Yeah. Poor old guy ran off after his first trip through this thing. Makes me wonder whether it's worth trying to develop this commercially.'

You can't be serious. But Richard smiled and waved as the doomed inventor-designate drove away.

The new owner of Clarence's car, Bill Pond, dropped by some time later, while Richard was sorting through Clarence's mail at the desk in the living room. Pond barely said a word, but smiled like a kid at Christmas when Richard gave him the keys to the beat-up old Taurus. *If he thinks this is great, what's he driving now?*

Richard hadn't seen Miriam since lunch and it was almost dinnertime. He wandered into the kitchen to see what raw materials were available when he heard a car in the gravel driveway. Miriam and Kobi popped up out of the small, weedy field and ran toward the house. Richard looked out the tiny kitchen window. It was Pam.

'Hey,' she said and gave him a big kiss, ignoring Miriam, who was standing with her hands on her hips, grinning at them. 'I brought the For Sale sign. And dinner.'

'Dinner?'

Dinner was vegetarian lasagna, salad from a bag with homemade dressing, a fresh baguette from the wine shop, and ice cream. Miriam helped Pam clean up while Richard finished sorting through Clarence's papers. They watched Miriam's video of Who Framed Roger Rabbit? on Miriam's TV using Miriam's VCR, then Richard carried her, half-asleep, up to the small bedroom on the second floor and set her down on the pale yellow quilt. Kobi took up station at the foot of the small bed.

As he was pulling off her shoes, she said, 'Dad, how did you and Mom meet?'

Richard tucked her under the quilt and sat down beside her.

'I was minding my own business, sitting in a tree in the jungle, eating a banana. Suddenly a beautiful girl came swinging by on a vine. She dropped down onto my branch like a gymnast and squatted right there in front of me. I almost choked on my banana, because she was wearing a skimpy little fur outfit that barely covered her up. 'Hello,' I said. She said, 'Me Rosalind, you Richard.' Well, I almost fell out of the tree, but she grabbed my arm and saved my life. And that was that. We got married and for a while I was King of the Apes. But then she wanted to move to Seattle and have a baby, so...'

She was asleep. Richard turned out the light.

Pam was standing outside in the hall. 'Which was Clarence's room?' Richard pointed next door, then took her hand and led the way to the third bedroom.

The larger of the guest rooms had a nautical theme: everything was blue and white, the books on the built-in shelves were all about sailboats, knot-tying, and the lore of the sea. The wall was decorated with a life preserver and photographs of tall ships and racing schooners. They got undressed and held each other in the dark under the anchor-and-dolphin blanket.

'How did it go today?' she said.

'I made a start. It's easy if you don't think about what you're doing and why.'

'Want to stop thinking for a while?'

'Oh, yes, please.'

She showed him a way to switch off his brain.

*   *   *

Pam left early the next morning, after making a date to meet at the Bistro for dinner tomorrow, which was Friday, Richard's night off. By the time Richard wandered out to the barn, Miriam had already disappeared with Kobi. There were several orders from customers on the business answering machine and in the mail. Richard recorded a new message saying that the company was no longer accepting orders, then went to fulfill these last few. He had watched Clarence do this so many times that he had no trouble locating the items, packing them, and setting the boxes out for UPS. Miriam showed up as he was finishing.

'Would you like to help?' he said.

'Sure. What do you want me to do?'

'How about packing your new books?' They carried several boxes into the house. Miriam stood in front of the living room bookcase, a half-height rough-hewn affair that looked as old as the house.

'Do I have to take all of them?' she said.

'Of course not. They're yours.... Do you want some advice?'

'Okay.'

'Take all the fiction and all the biographies, even if they look boring. Pick and choose among the rest. If you think you might ever be interested, pack it, otherwise leave it.'

She looked dubious, but she began sorting through the hundreds of dusty volumes.

With business out of the way and Miriam occupied, Richard started working through Clarence's personal things, putting clothes into bags for the Salvation Army. He stripped the bed in Clarence's room and was starting the laundry when Kobi started barking. Val was walking toward the house when he went outside. She was wearing cut-off shorts and a cropped white tank top.

'I guess you're here for your calculators,' Richard said, trying not to stare.

'Did you find them?'

He nodded and showed her the sea chest. 'Want me to carry them out for you?'

'Yes, thanks.'

She was probably stronger than he was, but he manfully carried the heavy chest out to her car and set it down carefully in her trunk. 'Have you got someone to help you unload it at home?'

'Ralf can do it, thanks.'

'So Ralf is still... helping you out, huh?'

She laughed and said, 'Goodbye, Richard.'

Nadine showed up right after lunch, driving a huge flatbed tractor-trailer combination, followed by her pickup and a twenty-four-foot rental van. Becky and Jane hopped out of the van and started attaching a ramp to the rear of the flatbed. Nadine sauntered over to Richard, slowly pulling her work gloves off her large hands. They stood toe to toe for a minute before she slapped him lightly on the shoulder with her gloves.

'That was a shitty thing to do,' she said.

'Which? Writing the column or not telling you I was writing it?'

'Not telling. What do I care if you flip off a bunch of whiners who don't know any better than to discuss private business in public? But you don't hold things like that back from your friends.'

'I'm sorry. You want to knock me down?'

202

She considered the offer. Consuela walked up to them and stood off to one side.

'Nah. I'll have Consuela take revenge on you with one of her spicy casseroles. Long-term paybacks are better.' She turned to Becky and yelled, 'Load them tractors, okay?'

Becky and Jane both waved and headed off to the pole barn, where the vintage red International and the merely old green Ford hunkered down in the dim light and dust. Richard led Nadine and her partner into the house and they walked briskly from room to room.

'Okay,' Nadine said when they'd seen it all. 'We'll take all the furniture, the linens, the appliances that can be moved, and all the kitchen stuff, including the food. We'll leave you the knickknacks and the artsy stuff.'

'What can you possibly do with all that junk? Your house is already stuffed.'

'It's not for me, bingo brain. It's for the shelter, and I know two women who just moved into town with nothing but the clothes I lent them. Let's see the barn.'

She took the computer and, astonishingly, several of the rusty ancient implements that Clarence had used for paperweights.

'Good God, I haven't seen one of these in years,' she said, holding up an angled open-hexagonal wrench.

'What is it?' Richard said, but she just smiled and patted him on the cheek.

Richard asked Miriam to gather up all the kittens. Before long she had all five collected, mewling piteously, in a cardboard box with a blanket and a small bowl of water.

In just a few hours, Nadine and her crew gutted the house. They left Richard and Miriam enough blankets so they could make a nest, but they took almost everything else except A.M.'s clock and Miriam's TV. One corner of each room was filled with neat rows of dust catchers and artistic whatevers. When they were done, the rental van was packed solid like a three-dimensional jigsaw puzzle, and the pickup was crammed full.

'I'd like you to take the kittens,' Richard said to Nadine as they walked out to the flatbed.

'Yah, okay. Maybe I can train them to eat gophers.' Nadine pulled herself up into the cab and Miriam sadly handed her the box, but she cheered up when Nadine said, 'You come and play with these little guys any time.' She waved and drove off at the head of her convoy.

It didn't take long to pack up the leavings. Since the food had all gone with Nadine, Richard took Miriam out to the Trout Lake pizza place, one of the two more-or-less normal restaurants in the village. The other was a greasy spoon that didn't tempt him in the slightest. There were also, unaccountably for such a tiny town, two fancy places. The first had such irregular hours that you could never guess whether they were open, and proprietors who would, given the chance, either try to convert you to some obscure Christian sect or sell you pagan magic magnets that would cure whatever ailed you. The other was a local B&B that served a prix fixe Northern Italian dinner that required reservations. Miriam was perfectly happy with pizza.

They watched another video, The Mask—which Richard despised— sitting on the floor in the dark living room. Before it was over, Miriam was asleep. He carried her upstairs and put her to bed in a cocoon of ratty blankets.

* * *

Richard awoke to a pounding at the door. It took a moment to unbind himself from the mummy rags his blanket bed had become in the night, and he almost fell on his face trying to get his pants on. All through this Laurel and Hardy routine, the pounding continued without a pause. He stumbled down the stairs and opened the kitchen door to see A.M., smiling, with a big brown sack in one hand. The coffee and muffins inside it were all that saved her life.

Miriam and Kobi wandered downstairs after A.M. shouted at them to get up, and the four of them sat on the floor in the empty dining room and ate breakfast. A.M. insisted on feeding Kobi parts of her muffins even though Richard objected each time she did it. Dust bunnies rolled around the edges of the room like mouse ghosts, occasionally exploding into view when they crossed a morning sunbeam.

'I hate this house,' A.M. said.

'Why?'

'It's too cramped, it's drafty, this damned floor is hard, and Clarence doesn't live here any more.'

After breakfast, Richard helped her carry the grandfather clock out to a long-bed pickup she'd borrowed from someone. They wrapped it in the blankets he and Miriam had slept in.

'Hey, Miriam, you want to come with me?' A.M. said.

'Dad?'

'Sure, go ahead, you're all done packing. I'll bring your books when I come.'

'And the TV!'

'Of course, the TV.'

'And the VCR. And all my tapes.'

'Yes, I'll bring everything. Go on.'

'See you tomorrow, Dad!' She climbed up into the tall cab and they drove away.

Richard carried eight boxes of books out to his station wagon, then a box of videotapes and the accursed TV and VCR. He stuffed his and Miriam's bags in the back and slammed the hatch closed.

The house was empty except for two shelves of books that Miriam hadn't wanted. Richard glanced over the titles and saw nothing she should have taken, just titles on Viet Nam, tractors, and remodeling.

He walked upstairs and looked in all the closets and cabinets, then up to the attic. There was nothing left. The sun was high now, shining full force into the void that had once been his friend's life. He went outside and looked over the flower gardens. They hadn't been watered in a while and the stems were starting to droop. It wouldn't rain for two more months, so Richard found a hose and soaked all the beds. The lawn, though, was on its own.

He glanced around once more. The pale yellow house stuck up out of the ground abruptly, unsoftened by landscaping, as if it had been extruded by some tectonic process. The weathered pole barn was probably going to collapse in a few years. The majestic old cattle barn loomed over the smaller buildings like Hades brooding over his dark lands.

Richard called Kobi and let her into the back with the boxes. He promised himself he would never come up here again.

* * *

Where his garage had once been a wooden outline now stood, looking from a distance like one of the popsicle stick houses he had built as a child. The framing appeared to be almost done. Only some of the rafters were missing—and so was the work crew. It was one o'clock on Friday, past quitting time, apparently.

Someone had stuck a plastic deer lawn ornament in his front yard. Its head lay a few feet away, severed with a chain saw. There was no other evidence of vandalism. He tossed the pathetic, broken thing out back with the trash cans.

Richard let Kobi into the back yard and lugged Miriam's loot into the house. He couldn't prevent Clarence from leaving Miriam his TV, but he was damned if he was going to have it in his living room. He carried the thing upstairs to her bedroom and hooked it all up, then tested it with a tape he chose at random—Ghostbusters.

He spent the afternoon on his front porch, reading. If this were the old frontier, he'd have his rifle across his lap, defending his house against poachers and bad guys. Instead, his presence and the latest book of essays by Stephen Jay Gould were going to have to be enough.

At 5:45 he arrived at the Wind Bistro for his six o'clock dinner date with Pam. The Bistro had been in business for over a decade, under four different names but always the same owner, a moderately famous windsurfer. The upstairs, the 'loft,' had a small L-shaped bar, half a dozen tables, and a pool table at the far end. Downstairs offered more formal seating, but Richard liked it up here. In the summer you could sit on the deck under the overhanging branches of a huge oak tree.

The place had undergone an extensive remodel during its annual two-week closing at the last new year, but fortunately they had preserved the wall and ceiling paintings when they repainted. Brushed directly onto the plaster by some unknown artist were reproductions of the horse and bison cave paintings from Lascaux, van Gogh's Starry Night, Botticelli's Venus, God and Adam from the Sistine chapel, a Chinese dragon, and several others. Richard had no idea who had done them, but he found them charming, perfectly suited to the quirky nature of the bar. A triptych ad on one wall showed smiling Hollywood stars from the fifties extolling the virtues of Chesterfields cigarettes, with a hand-lettered sign below that read, 'This is as close to smoking as you will get in this bar.'

Richard sat on a stool at the bar and ordered a Hefeweizen. The only drawback to the loft was the TV in the corner by the door. Richard turned away and looked over the half-dozen diners as he sipped his beer. He didn't recognize anyone. It was still a bit early for the dinner rush; on a beautiful summer afternoon like this, with a good breeze, everyone would be out on the water until dusk, when it became too dangerous for all but the most experienced windsurfers.

Pam showed up at his elbow without warning, right on time. 'What are you drinking, big boy?'

'Hefeweizen.'

'Half a bison? You can drink a buffalo?'

'What'll you have?'

'The same.'

Richard raised a finger at the girl behind the bar, a thin little thing with spiky black hair who looked too young to drink beer, let alone serve it. She nodded and fetched a pilsner glass from the wood-framed cooler on the wall behind her.

'Are you hungry?' he said.

'Very. I have a potential buyer for Clarence's rental already.'

'You're kidding.'

'Nope,' she said. 'It's a nice little place. Ever seen it?'

'I try not to go across the bridge if I can help it.'

The bartender brought Pam's beer. They carried their glasses outside onto the deck and sat down at a dusty white resin table on matching dusty white resin chairs. It took a few minutes to order their food, but then Pam leaned back in her chair and gave him a look.

'What?' he said.

'I think you should let me tell people how much you've helped this town.'

'What are you talking about?'

'You know what I'm talking about. The shelter. The donations to the hospital, the schools, the theater group.'

'That's my private business. How the hell do you know it?'

'I have my sources. You might get away with anonymous philanthropy in a big city, but this is a very small town. Everything comes out sooner or later. Just like Mrs. Bambi did.'

Richard sulked for a moment. 'I don't want people to think I'm some Rockefeller or Carnegie, and I don't want people calling me up all the time to ask for money.'

'No, instead you have people nailing antlers to your door. You're a public figure now, whether you like it or not. Wouldn't you rather be revered than reviled?'

'No.'

'Why not?'

'I just want them to leave me alone.'

'They're not going to do that, Richard. You think the people suing you and the paper are just going to go away?'

He didn't answer. They sat silently until their waitress brought their food, a blackened salmon sandwich for Richard and vegetarian Phad Thai for Pam. She reached over and stole some of his seasoned french fries, and they ate without talking.

'So you won't let me tell the truth about you?' she said when they were nearly done.

'What truth?'

'That you're not just a retired rich guy who enjoys yanking people's tails while hiding behind a pseudonym. You've done more to help people in this town than maybe anyone in its history. You're a good, if somewhat weird, father. You're a nice guy and you don't deserve the crap that people have been dumping on your lawn.'

'Thanks. But let it alone.'

Pam tossed her napkin on the table and stood up. 'God damn it, Richard, you can be such a blockhead.'

'Are you leaving?'

'I'm going home to cool off. I'll call you tomorrow.'

Richard watched her walk back into the loft and out the door. The couples sitting at two other tables on the deck were staring at him. He ignored them and took his time finishing his beer.

Chapter 18: Shelter Skelter

Mrs. Bambi Knows (Archive)

Coping with groping boss

Dear Mrs. Bambi:

My boss at the T-shirt shop is a letch. When he asks me to model new shirts for him, he gives me samples a size too small and tells me to be sure to take my bra off so he can get the full effect. He's always stroking my arms and my hair, and he 'accidentally' brushes up against my chest and my rear a couple times a day. How can I get this groping gomer to leave me alone?
—*Pawed and Peeved*

Dear Prancer:

It's very simple, but you're going to have to screw up your courage. The next time he asks you to model for him, come out of the dressing room without the shirt. Without ANY shirt. When you have his attention, say:

'Is this what you want? Take a good look, because this is as close as you're ever going to get. And if you ever lay a finger on me again, I'll have you in court on sexual harassment charges so fast it'll take your stiffie a month to find you.'

Be brave. Take charge. Stop being a victim.

Dear Mrs. Bambi:

My dog goes after the mailman every single day. He's almost bitten the guy five times. He doesn't bother anyone else, usually he's very friendly with strangers.

The mailman is threatening to sue and he's started carrying pepper spray. Now the Post Office is telling me that if I don't take care of the problem, they'll refuse to deliver my mail. What should I do?
—*Mailless*

Dear Brainless:

What's wrong with you? Tie the dog up. Leave him in the house when you're expecting the mail. Put him down (the dog, not the mailman). Find him a new home. Move to the country. Get a post office box.

No, I have a better idea. Let the stupid mutt kill the mailman and see what happens next.

* * *

The phone rang early the next morning. Was there some fathomless, cosmically crucial reason he could never sleep in on Saturday?

'What?'

'Richard, it's Gail.'

'Uh. Can I call you back? I'm not—'

'Richard, I need you to come over here right now.'

He sat up in bed. 'What's going on?'

'There's a man outside the shelter waving a gun.'

'Jesus Christ! Call the cops!'

'I did, but they said it would be at least ten minutes.'

'Do you know the guy?' he said.

'I think he's the husband of one of our women.'

'I'll be right there.'

Richard threw on the clothes he found on the floor and ran outside to his car. There was a single stop sign between his house and the shelter: he ran it. He pulled up across the street and got out of his car.

A young Hispanic man was pounding on the front door of Gail's house with his left fist. In his right hand he held a revolver. Richard had no idea what to do. He didn't want to get shot, and he knew nothing about fighting. The man pounded again and shouted something unintelligible, then he raised the gun and shot at the door. Splinters flew and the man screamed and grabbed his right leg. He couldn't have been hurt badly because he reared back and kicked the door with the injured leg, without any visible effect.

Richard had to do something, even if it was only to distract the maniac until the police arrived. He walked slowly up to the house. When he was about thirty feet away, the man turned and saw him. He pointed the gun in Richard's general direction, but he was swaying on his feet, probably drunk, and very likely couldn't hit him if he tried. Richard raised his hands anyway.

The man waved his gun. 'Who the fuck are you?'

'I came to see my friend Gail.'

'Bullshit. You're here for Maria—fucking slut. Go away.' He turned back to the door and pointed the gun at the lock. 'Maria! Come out!'

He was going to shoot again. Maybe this time the lock would give. Richard said quickly, 'She won't come out?'

The man lowered the revolver and half-turned to look at Richard. 'I told you, go away.'

'Maybe I can help you.'

'You can't help me. Nobody can fucking help me. Can't find work, she won't stop spending money, come home Friday and she's gone, man, just gone.' He raised the gun again. 'Maria.'

Richard sat down on the concrete walk. It was all he could think of to do.

The drunk man turned around at the plopping sound. 'Hey, what the fuck you doing?'

'I don't want to get shot,' Richard said.

'Not going to shoot you, man, not going to shoot anybody. Just going to get that fat-ass bitch home and teach her who's boss. Thinks she can run off on me. Bobby saw her here, told me, I come over right now to get that whore back home.' He leaned against the door for a moment and closed his eyes, then jerked upright and raised the gun again.

'Don't shoot,' Richard said.

'Why the fuck not?'

Richard could hear sirens in the distance, getting closer. 'You might hit somebody inside.'

'Nobody in there but my fat slut wife.'

'No, my friend Gail's in there, too.'

'Gail? Who the fuck is Gail?'

A police cruiser sped up the street, its sirens and lights off, and stopped abruptly at the curb behind Richard. Two policemen got out. One took a position behind the hood of the car, with his gun aimed steadily at the drunk. The other walked up the lawn to Richard's left, his pistol held in both hands but pointing at the ground.

'Drop the weapon,' the cop said. Maria's husband stared at him as if he'd never seen anything so astonishing. 'Drop the weapon!'

The man took half a step away from the door, then let go of his gun. It fell in the shrubs to the side of the porch. The cop advanced, frowning at Richard as he passed him. By the time Richard had clambered to his feet, the man was handcuffed and being led, stumbling, toward the cruiser.

'Who are you?' the other cop said.

Richard got out his driver's license. 'My friend Gail runs this shelter. She called me and told me she had an emergency.'

'She should have waited for us. What were you doing on the ground?'

'I thought he wouldn't shoot me if I didn't look threatening.'

'That was stupid. Wait here. I have some more questions, and you'll need to file a statement.'

He went to retrieve the dropped revolver while his partner knocked on the door and told the people inside that it was safe to come out. Gail led a dark young woman, thin and tall, with shoulder-length black hair, out onto the porch. A wail went up from inside the cruiser. One of the cops went to tell the husband to shut up while the other began asking Gail and Maria what had happened.

'What's up, Richard?'

Richard turned and his heart plummeted. 'Hi, Frank.'

'A little excitement, huh? What are you doing up so early?'

'Gail called me. That guy was trying to get his wife out of the shelter.'

Frank peered at Maria. 'Yeah, I can see why. So why did she call you?'

'I guess the cops were held up and he was starting to shoot the door down.'

'Uh huh. Does she always call you when she needs help?'

'Frank—'

'Yeah, I know. Fuck off. See you later.' He walked off toward the cruiser to talk to the cop standing there.

It took another half hour before they let him go, making him promise to stop by the station later to make a statement. Frank was still prowling around; Richard wanted to leave before Frank could try to interview him.

'I've got to go,' he said to Gail. 'Miriam's going to be home soon.'

'You look like you slept in those clothes.'

'Close.'

'Go home. Clean up. God is going to shower you with blessings for what you've done for us.'

'The only shower I need right now is a long, hot one.'

She kissed his cheek and turned away. On the way home, he stopped at the stop sign. He was just finishing getting dressed when Miriam ran into his room and jumped on his bed.

'Hi, Dad. You're up early. You won't believe what A.M. let me do last night. She said not to tell you. What did you and Pam do? Is she still here? What's going on?'

* * *

On his way out the door to go to the police station, Richard glanced at the big oak tree in the front yard and stopped with his hand still on the doorknob. Someone had made a scarecrow out of an old pair of denim overalls and a flannel shirt, with a crudely painted face on a burlap sack head—and crucified it on his tree.

The remodelers were busy hammering plywood onto the framing. He ducked his head into the half-enclosed garage and said, 'Can I borrow a hammer for a minute?'

One of the men handed him a claw hammer and Richard pulled the nails out of the scarecrow's hands and feet. It still hung limply; there was another nail at the crown of its ugly head. He had to stretch up high to pull it out. He picked up the five nails and the dummy and tossed them in the contractor's dumpster.

'Was that up there when you got here?' Richard asked as he handed the carpenter back his hammer.

'Yup. Thought it was kind of early for Halloween.'

'Thanks for the hammer.'

'No problem.'

It took only fifteen minutes to give his deposition. When they were done and the paralegal had put away the tape recorder, he asked if they had any leads on his garage fire. The woman, a young, serious-looking blonde, vanished for a moment and returned to say that he would have to wait for the detective, Olvera, to get off the phone. Soon the stocky cop walked out to where Richard was waiting, pushing his glasses up his thick nose.

'Ah, Mr. Lantz. I was going to call you on Monday. I'm afraid we've dropped the investigation.'

'I'm sorry?'

'It's been two and a half weeks, and nothing new has turned up. No one's volunteered any information since the fire, and I doubt the arsonist is going to come in and confess. There's simply no way we're ever going to find out who did it.'

'What about the rock they threw through my window?' Richard said.

'We got some smudged prints, but most of them are yours.'

'So that's it?'

'I'm sorry. We talked to everyone we could identify as authors of your hate mail, and we're stuck. There's nothing else we can do.'

Richard sighed. 'Okay, thanks.' He turned to go.

'Oh, Mr. Lantz.'

'Yes?'

'Nice work at the shelter this morning. That was a gutsy thing to do.'

Gutsy? No, he had to agree with the cop at the scene. It had been stupid. What would have happened to Miriam if he'd been shot?

Never mind, he knew what would happen. A.M. or Pam—or both— would adopt her.

He decided to stop by A.M.'s shop and tell her she had almost become a mommy. But when he got there and pulled on the door, it was locked. It was Saturday, wasn't it? He peered through the glass door—and noticed a small hand-lettered sign in front of his nose.

> *We're moving!*
> *Please stop by*
> *our new location*
> *236 Oak St.*
> *when it opens August 14*

Moving? New location? What the—

Pam. She and A.M., and Sylvia, no doubt, must have been planning this since Miriam's birthday party, or possibly before. And no one had mentioned it to him!

He nearly ran the three blocks to the new shop. It was a hot day, and he was dripping sweat when he got there. There was no sign on the door, but in the dim interior Richard could make out a solitary man measuring and sawing studs. He rapped on the glass. The carpenter opened the door three inches and said, 'Yep?'

'I'm looking for the shop owner. Is she here?'

'Nope.'

'Are you expecting her?'

'Nope.'

'Can I come in and look around?'

'Nope.'

'I'm a good friend of hers.' The man shut and locked the door. 'Thanks a lot,' Richard said. 'You've been a big help.'

Through the glass, he could hear the man say, 'Yep,' and then the saw started up again.

He walked briskly back home, too hot and tired to run, and jumped in his car.

* * *

A.M. answered the door wearing nothing but black panties and a pink tank top.

'You're moving the shop?' Richard said.

She laughed. 'Come on in.'

It was warm inside, even with the shades drawn, which perhaps explained A.M.'s clothing, or lack of it. Before Richard could settle himself into a chair, she was walking away, toward the kitchen. Her black hair was down and unbraided, swaying from side to side as she walked, brushing her buttocks. She came back a moment later with a tall glass of lemonade, which she handed to him without a word.

They sat and looked at each other for a long moment. He glared at her and she smiled placidly back.

215

He took his first sip of lemonade. It was too tart. 'You're moving?'

'Yes.'

'That's it—yes?'

She laughed lightly. 'Okay, okay. Pam and I have been talking for a while about how to make my shop actually pay for itself. Pam had some good ideas, and once I started listening, I found that Sylvia had a bunch of insights that I'd been brushing off for a long time. I took a hard look at what I've been trying to do and came up with a new business plan.'

'All right, that's cool. Why didn't you tell me about it?'

'Why didn't you tell me about Mrs. Bambi?' He started to answer and she put up her hand to cut him off. 'Never mind. You had your reasons. I had mine. At first it was just brainstorming, and when things actually started happening... Look, Richard, I know you hate my designs.'

'That's not—'

'It's okay. Everybody hates my designs. Everybody around here, anyway.'

'What's that mean?'

She looked at him silently. He took another sip from the glass and set it down on the table at his elbow. It was too sour to drink.

'Okay,' A.M. said, 'here it is. The old location sucked; I never got any tourist traffic at all. You know the tourists think Oak Street is the entire town. So when Pam told me a storefront on Oak would be opening up soon, I went to the bank with a proposal to move my shop there, and they gave me a loan.'

'Why would they give you a loan? There hasn't been a single month in the last four years that you've made a profit.'

'Because last month I sold my entire inventory, with a contract for future shipments.'

'What?' he said. 'To who?'

'A couple of years ago, Pam sold a little bungalow to a big shot windsurfer from Germany. It turns out that she's a buyer for a clothing chain in Europe. You saw her—that gal with the purple streak in her hair and the cute butt. Pam brought her back to the shop and after half an hour she bought my entire stock. She says she can sell everything I can make in Germany, Japan, and Mexico. Apparently, those countries are full of wackos—I mean sophisticated shoppers—that love weird fashions. Who knew?'

216

Richard shook his head in disbelief.

She said, 'It looks like I'm going to have to hire people to keep up with the demand.'

'So what do you need a shop for?'

'I like having a shop. But I obviously can't sell my old stuff here in the land of the timid twits, so I created an entirely new line. Nice, boring, conventional, stodgy sportswear. I think it's dumb, but Sylvia and Pam think I can sell about seventy thousand a year of the stuff.'

'Can I see it?'

'Not yet. Wait for the grand opening. I'll give you a private showing.'

Richard couldn't think of anything to say. He was a little angry and... something else he couldn't identify. He forgot himself and took another sip of lemonade. Yuck. 'It's...'

'What?'

'It's not going to be the same.'

'You're right. I'm not just going to be the hottest chick in town any more. I'm also going to make money.'

'Not that, dummy. I like coming into your shop and sitting in the back and drinking coffee.'

'Well, you can still do that.'

'Not if you're busy with customers all the time,' he said.

'You want me to stay poor so you can keep getting a free cup of coffee?'

'No... No, I'm happy things are going well for you. But...'

'Richard. Things change. You think our relationship's going to stay the same now that you're with Pam? And the shop had to change too, my silly linear friend. You know Sylvia was unhappy about supporting my hobby. I've been losing money since I first opened Mayatek. If this hadn't happened, I'd have had to close by the end of the year. This way, at least I have a shop where you can hang out.'

'Well... okay. But you should have told me.'

'Ditto.'

They glared at each other for a moment, and then he laughed. 'This is the worst lemonade I've ever had.'

'Well, to hell with you. You need practice puckering up.'

'I get plenty of puckering, thanks.'

'I meant so you can kiss my butt.'

'Okay.'

She stood up and shoved her nearly naked rear at him. He spanked it sharply. She spun around, yanked him out of his chair into a dancing pose, dipped him, gave him a big kiss on the cheek, and dropped him on the floor.

* * *

'You did what?' Pam said.

'I sat down.'

'Why the hell would you do that?'

'I couldn't think of anything else. He was going to keep shooting the door until the lock gave out, and maybe someone inside would have been hurt.'

She gaped at him. Then she set down the skillet she'd been holding. They were just starting to cook dinner, and she'd been about to sauté some onions. He was glad she'd put the thing down instead of beaning him with it.

'When's Miriam getting home?'

'What?'

'When will Miriam get home?'

'I don't know, maybe half an hour.'

She grabbed his hand, pulled him upstairs to the bedroom, and slammed the door.

'What are we doing?' Richard said.

While she kissed him she unbuckled his belt. 'I love you, you idiot,' she said, and tore his shirt off.

* * *

'We have to have some rules about this stupid box,' Richard said.

'Why does there have to be rules?' Miriam said.

'Because otherwise everything would fall apart and we'd find ourselves floating in the middle of the river without a boat or a paddle to push it with.'

'Also,' Pam said, 'your dad likes to be in charge.'

'No, I don't,' he said.

'Yes, you do.'

He tossed some popcorn at her. They were sitting on Miriam's bed, with Richard in the middle, Pam on his right. Since he was in the middle, he held the popcorn. So he was in charge.

'Are you ready for the rules?'

'Okay.'

'Okay,' Pam echoed.

'During the school year, no TV before your homework is done. You have to spend more time reading than watching TV, like Clarence said.'

'But you don't have a baseball bat.'

'I'll buy one. Third, I have veto power on any videos that we rent. Fourth, when you're watching TV, I'll...' He shook his head ruefully. 'I'll watch with you. I want to know what you're seeing. Okay?'

'Okay, Dad.'

'Any questions?'

'Can we get cable?'

'Absolutely not,' he said.

'How about a satellite dish? Please?'

'No. But you can rent one or two movies a week.'

'Okay.' She was pouting, but he knew that she thought she had won.

'All right. Hit Play.' The TV began showing previews; it would probably take ten minutes before they got to the opening credits for Aladdin. 'I talked to A.M. today,' he said to Pam.

'Really? About what?'

'I stopped by her shop.'

'Oops.'

'She says you've been helping her out since, what, May? And you never said a word.'

'Well,' Pam said, 'she told me she'd prefer that I didn't discuss it with anyone. Then she said she meant especially you.'

'Why?'

'I think she wanted to surprise you. She knows what you think of her clothes.'

'Everyone thinks I hate her clothes.'

'Well, don't you?'

He thought about that for a second. 'I don't particularly like them. But I like watching her wear them.'

She dug her elbow into his ribs, scattering popcorn.

'Hey!' Miriam said in alarm. 'Oh, look, the movie's starting.'

Richard put one arm around each of his girls. The silly music started and the titles rolled by. Maybe this wasn't so bad after all.

* * *

The following Friday, Richard picked up the Examiner and instantly felt light-headed. Side by side on the front page were two headlines over Frank's by-line: 'Mrs. Bambi no's gunman' and 'Mrs. Bambi knows charity,' with a picture of him in between them.

The first was a no-frills account of his derring-do at the shelter. It named him as the author of the long-running Mrs. Bambi column.

So did the second article, which was a detailed and astonishingly accurate account of his years of quiet philanthropy. The three major endowments to the hospital, including the latest one on Clarence's behalf. His donations to the children's hospital in Portland and to the theater group in Hood River. The gifts he'd made to the schools. Buying the shelter a new house, how much he'd paid for it, and a long list of the money and sweat equity he'd contributed since its founding.

It described the out-placement program the shelter used for women who were being stalked, when it was too dangerous for them to stay at the shelter house, and mentioned that Richard was the only man who had ever hosted one of these women. Every major contribution he could remember was listed, including the exact amounts.

Richard sat down on his couch and leaned his head back. How had Frank got all this information that was supposed to be confidential and anonymous? He'd have had to contact half a dozen people and convince them to cough up secrets that they'd sworn to keep.

What was this going to do to his position in the community?

The phone began to ring.

Chapter 19: Good Night, Mrs. Bambi

Mrs. Bambi Knows (Archive)

Scars are the price of love

Dear Mrs. Bambi:

I'm in love with a girl whose house is overrun by pets. I like animals as much as the next guy, but her parrot bites me, her cat claws me, her dog loves me so much he won't leave me alone, and her fish stare at me funny.

Is any girl worth this much aggravation?

—*Feathered and Furred*

Dear Clawed and Chawed:

Don't be a dunce. Any woman with so much love in her heart that it spills over onto that many pets is worth a few scars.

Stay away from her bird and it won't bite you. Pet the kitty and feed it treats, and it will accept you as a loving slave. Play with the dog at appropriate times and order it to lie down when you're busy.

Eat the fish.

Dear Mrs. Bambi:

My parents used to yell at me for playing video games, but now I'm a naval aviator, flying jet fighters all over the world. How do I tell them 'I told you so' without sounding petty?

—*Tip Top Gun*

Dear Space Cadet:

Shut up. Didn't the Navy teach you not to arm your weapons unless you intend to use them? When you next see your parents, thank them for the loving guidance they gave you. That's all any adult child should ever say to his parents about his upbringing.

What you say to your therapist is completely up to you.

* * *

A few days after the articles appeared, Richard stood in his kitchen watching Kobi roll around on the grass in the back yard. She lay on her back, writhing as if mortally wounded. Then she stopped and looked from one side to another, tongue hanging into the blades of grass, as if waiting for applause. When none came, she resumed wriggling.

She was growing so rapidly he thought he could see it happening. When he'd picked her out of a litter of squirming black puppies in a barn in Odell, the orchardist had said that she'd probably be a good-sized mutt, maybe fifty pounds. The vet's latest guess was that she'd be over a hundred pounds when full-grown. He hadn't bargained for that. At this rate the dog would outweigh his daughter in a month or two.

The phone rang for perhaps the tenth time that morning. Richard turned from the window and waited for the machine to take the call.

'Uh, Richard, this is Sam. Carrie and I wanted to let you know that we're available to take Miriam on Friday if you're interested. We've been... uh, pretty busy lately, and I know Tiffannee's missed their Friday sleep-overs. So, um, give us a call.'

Busy? Sure they were, busy spreading the news that he was Mrs. Bambi. Sam and Carrie were, as far as Richard could tell, the primary source of the revelation, but he still couldn't figure out how they had known.

When Miriam returned that afternoon from playing in the park with her friends, Richard asked if she wanted to spend Friday night at Tiff's.

'Unh unh.'

'Oh. Why not?'

'She's not my friend any more.'

'What? I thought Tiff was your best friend.'

'Not since she told on me.' Miriam snapped a banana off the bunch in the fruit bowl, sat down at the kitchen table, and started peeling it slowly and carefully.

'What do you mean, honey? What did she tell?'

'I told her a secret and she promised not to tell anybody, but she did.'

'Well, that's a bad thing to do, but maybe you could forgive her.'

'Unh unh.'

'Why not?' Richard said.

'Because she got you in trouble.'

Richard's stomach did a somersault. 'What do you mean, Miriam? What secret did you tell her?'

'I told her that you were Mrs. Bambi, and she told her mom and dad, and they told everybody else.' Now that the banana was completely peeled and all the little strings pulled off, Miriam began eating it in dainty bites.

Richard leaned back against the counter behind him. He felt dazed. 'You knew that I'm—that I wrote Mrs. Bambi?'

'Sure, Dad.'

'How did you know?'

'I don't know. I just knew.'

He hadn't told her because he'd thought it would be too confusing— your daddy is pretending to be Dear Abby—and he wasn't sure she could keep the secret. Given his own confusion about his role as Mrs. Bambi, how could he explain it to her? And what could a ten year-old understand about it, anyway?

More than he thought, apparently. Richard watched her methodically eat her banana. When she was done, she ran outside and tried to play catch with Kobi. She threw a chewed-up rubber ball and the puppy caught it in her jaws—and refused to give it back.

*   *   *

The two young women behind the long desk, apparently intended to be receptionists but busy filing their nails and gossiping about someone named Bill, ignored Richard as he walked purposefully past them into the offices of the Examiner. He threaded through the maze of cubicles, opened the door to Frank's office, and closed it behind him.

Frank didn't look up from his computer monitor. 'Sit down. I'll be done in a second.'

Richard remained standing. It took two minutes' worth of seconds before Frank turned to face him.

'Traitor,' Richard said.

'Oh, shut up. Sit down. You want some coffee?'

'Everything in that article was confidential.'

'Really? The people I talked to didn't tell me that.'

'Who? Who did you talk to?'

'What, you want names?' Frank said. 'I can't reveal confidential sources.'

'It was Gail, right? And that doctor, what's his name, Monrad. Who else?'

'What are you going to do, sue them? Bite them on the nose? Call them really bad names? Give me a break.'

'Why did you do it, Frank?'

'Why? To save your ass, you stupid idiot. And mine, now that you mention it. And I'm not expecting a fruit basket or anything, but I wouldn't mind if you admitted that it's working. Had any beers thrown in your face lately?'

Richard sat down. They stared at each other for several minutes, during which the phone rang twice but Frank ignored it.

'Those contributions were a private thing,' Richard said. 'I just wanted to help, and I didn't want to get famous doing it. You've ruined everything.'

'I think you're confusing me with the moron you see in the mirror. Who wrote the Mrs. Bambi columns, your grandmother? Who made large anonymous contributions by hand-delivering checks with his name, address, and phone number on them?'

'Okay, so I didn't try very hard to cover my tracks. I didn't expect a buzz-cut thick-neck semi-illiterate newspaper editor to pry into my life and drag all my secrets into broad daylight.'

'You want to stay private, stop doing public acts. Like distracting a gunman from shooting up the women's shelter. Or like buying the shelter in the first place. Or dragging other people's secrets into your column. You know what's really bothering you?'

'I can't wait to find out.'

'You've been Bambied, my friend. You can dish it out, but you can't take it.'

He was right. There was only one thing to say. 'Fuck you.'

'Give me a call sometime,' Frank said as Richard got up to leave. 'I'd like to buy you a beer.'

* * *

The next several weeks were perhaps the strangest time of Richard's life since he'd moved to Hood River with an infant girl he'd no idea how to raise. One by one, without fanfare or comments, the lawsuits against him and the Examiner were dropped. When he stopped in the coffee shop, timidly wondering whether he would drink coffee or wear it, people would argue for the right to buy him a coffee instead of lining up to throw it in his face. When he went across the bridge, the toll booth guard would say that the person in front of him had paid his toll, and eventually they simply refused to take his money.

A.M. and Nadine both went out of their way to apologize for how they'd treated him when his identity was revealed.

The phone rang dozens of times every day, but he never answered it. Strangers called to apologize, or to say how much they admired him, or to ask him to speak to some group or another, or to ask for money. He rarely called anyone back. He considered changing his phone number, perhaps getting an unlisted number, but decided that the new number would get out somehow, and then he'd have memorized the new one for nothing.

Pam sold Clarence's rental property and was talking to a couple from Spokane who were very interested in starting a B&B at the farm. Clarence's lawyer concluded negotiations with the company that was going to buy the mail order business. The movers were expected to come and haul away the inventory and files any day now.

The garage grew steadily more complete, the construction crew working more rapidly than Richard would have believed possible, until it lacked nothing but paint and the new bike that he had promised to buy Miriam.

And one rainy day, when they were headed to Portland for shopping and a movie, Richard pulled the car off the Interstate five miles west of Hood River.

'Do you see that?' he said.

'Wow!' Miriam said.

Although it was raining lightly, the sun shone through a rift in the clouds behind them. Ahead of them, a brilliant rainbow spanned the Columbia River Gorge, with one leg in Oregon and the other in Washington. They watched as the arc of light shimmered, fading and growing stronger as thin, low clouds wafted over the breach in the overcast and passed on. It was a fairy highway, sparkling and glimmering, standing astride the Gorge like a bridge to paradise.

'It's an omen,' Miriam said. They sat on the berm for ten minutes, the unheeding cars zipping past them and rocking their car with their wakes, until the coruscating flow of light faded and died.

* * *

Despite what A.M. had said, Richard didn't expect more than a minor change in style and a face-lift from her new shop. He and Pam walked together to the new location, in the heart of the busiest stretch of downtown, around nine on the morning of the grand opening. In an hour the public would be admitted, but they had been promised a private tour.

A hand-carved, brightly painted wooden sign hung over the entrance, proclaiming the same name as the old place: Mayatek. Richard leaned in to try to peer through the glass door, but Pam yanked him back and knocked on it. Sylvia opened the door, grinning, and stood aside to let them in.

The difference from A.M.'s old store was so enormous that Richard wasn't sure he was in the right place. It seemed so... normal.

The bizarre can't-be-seen-in-public styles were gone. The weird animal hats, the high-strapped sandals, the breastplates and breechcloths and Christmas ornament jewelry and lamp shades and exposed groins and bare breasts and vests that couldn't be buttoned.

In their place was a shop of rich colors, spot lighting, and neat racks filled with practical, stylish sportswear. Ethereal music played softly in the background. Richard wandered from one display to the next. A.M.'s new fashions were easily recognizable—this is a vest, a sweater, a dress—unlike her old styles, which no woman in North America would have known how to put on even if she could have got past the immodest cut and the strange colors.

There was, of course, an abundance of fleece—this was the Northwest—but the patterns were different than any he'd ever seen: chevrons, bold stripes, helixes, a repeated blur that looked like one of the Mayan numeral gods, and a jaguar skin pattern. She must have had one of the mills create custom patterns for her. How could she possibly afford that?

There were heavy cotton shirts with a cut reminiscent both of her old Mayan styles and also of medieval tunics. Hiking shorts, long dresses, swimsuits, overalls, and rompers and undersized vests for children. At first glance everything looked conventional, but a second look showed glimpses of A.M.'s humor in the sloping angle of a hemline, the lush drape of a blouse, a startling splash of fuchsia.

At the checkout counter a glass case displayed gold and silver jewelry, handsome pieces with a subtle Mayan flavor. Richard looked up and saw A.M. leaning against the wall, watching him. She wore black leggings and a tight, deeply cut, red sleeveless blouse.

'What do you think?' she said.

'You're going to make a fortune! I love this stuff!'

A.M. laughed. 'Richard, you are my new target customer. Conservative, boring, American, Hood River.' Richard looked behind him to see Pam and Sylvia with their arms around each other, laughing. 'Meanwhile, I sell the good stuff to the Europeans and Japanese, and everybody's happy.'

'And you get rich.'

'Not rich. Very comfortable, maybe.'

Richard went through the store again, picking out a yellow-and-black bumblebee vest for Miriam and a blue cotton shirt for himself, becoming A.M.'s first customer at her new location. Then he helped her carry a mannequin, one of her old space-insect dolls, out to the street. It was dressed in a high-cut one piece bathing suit, a jaguar vest, sandals, and mirrored sunglasses. A.M. chained it to a pole outside the shop and was officially open for business.

Pam kissed him and left for work, but Richard hung around for a while. He saw three women actually buy clothes in the very first hour; that would have been a banner month in the old shop. In a lull between customers, A.M. took him into the back room. The coffee machine was there, and the old, beat-up table, piled high with books and patterns—and pulled up to the table was a director's chair with his name across the back.

227

'You'll always have a place to sit here,' A.M. said.

He felt himself tearing up. 'I'm really happy for you,' he said as they hugged.

When he left a little while later, he stepped out into the sunshine, feeling really happy. When he closed his eyes, he could feel the light on his face, a gentle breeze knocking the bag with his new clothes against his leg. He turned to head home and found his way blocked by Connie, his sometime stalker.

'Richard!' she shrieked. 'You never had cancer, did you? You just had an advice column!'

'Connie, I can't talk right now.'

She grabbed his arm with a grip like a glove full of hex nuts. 'I've tried to be subtle, Richard—' A velociraptor would be more subtle. '—but I can't wait any longer. Why don't you want to go out with me?' Why didn't he like to sleep on shards of glass? 'Is it my hair? I can change it.'

Richard couldn't take any more. 'Connie, I'm gay.'

She dropped his arm and stepped back. 'Gay? But your daughter...'

'She's adopted.'

She took another half step back. 'But your girlfriend, Pam...'

'We're just friends, really.'

Her hands fluttered up and fell back. 'But I thought...'

'Look, Connie—would you consider getting a sex change operation? Because I think I could really go for you if you were a guy.'

She moaned and took another step back, then whipped around and clopped off on her high pumps, her shrill voice keening unintelligibly, her bony arms flailing as she almost lost her balance.

Richard tried not to laugh, but all he could manage was to keep it from becoming a guffaw.

*   *   *

Karen had declined Richard's offer of a going-away party. The least he could do was bring coffee and doughnuts on her last morning in Hood River, a few days after A.M. opened her new shop. When he arrived with Pam, there was a small group of people in her tiny apartment above the hardware store, trying to decide what to do and where to stand since there was no furniture at all. Karen had donated almost the entire contents of her place to the

Salvation Army. She was in the bathroom, ignoring the milling herd, packing a few last toiletries into a small bag.

He stuck his head into the tiny room. 'I brought some doughnuts,' he said.

'I would have expected croissants from you.'

'The closest croissants worth eating are in Portland. I figured you could grab some on your way through. Meanwhile, have a Safeway chocolate-frosted cream-filled doughnut.'

'Thanks, I'll pass. Where's Pam?'

'Right here,' Pam called from the kitchen. 'There isn't room in there for three people.'

Karen looked great. Her long brown hair was pulled back with combs. She was wearing torn jeans and a deep green blouse that matched her eyes. She looked well-rested and impatient to get going.

'San Francisco,' a woman said longingly. Richard looked at her—pointed face, short blonde hair, a dozen earrings—and decided he had never met her before. How could he have lived in such a small town for ten years and not know everyone? Maybe it was time to start meeting some new people. Perhaps Pam could help him...

'Just for a while,' Karen said. 'I think I'd like to end up in Taos, but I have some friends in Frisco that I haven't seen in years.'

'Maybe you'll decide to stay,' Pam said. 'For a big city, it's pretty nice.'

'Maybe.' Karen glanced around the room. Everyone was looking at her. 'Well, I guess I'm ready.'

She followed the crowd down the narrow stairs. Her new Explorer was parked at the curb. Karen beeped it and opened the back door, leaning in to search for something on the seat. While several people walked around the new car, checking it out, Richard looked over Karen's shoulder. Everything she owned was in this car, and the storage area behind the seats was only half full.

'This is your influence, right?' he said to Pam, nodding at the car.

'Nope. I told her to get a black one.' Karen's was bright red. 'She won't listen to anybody.'

Karen said her goodbyes to everyone, saving Richard and Pam for last.

'I think we'll close on the farm next month,' Pam said. 'I'll have Leo send you the money.'

'But give us your address when you get settled,' Richard said. 'I'd like to know how you're doing.'

'Thanks, both of you, for all your help,' Karen said. 'You two take care of each other. And Richard—don't screw up.'

'What? Me?'

'And no more advice columns. Keep your big nose at home, where it belongs.'

Pam laughed, but he didn't have a big nose. Karen gave him a hug and climbed up into the Explorer. He watched her drive away.

Wherever she ended up, she was going to have a nice little nest egg to start over with. Leo had been too conservative in his estimate of Clarence's net worth: it was going to be closer to four hundred thousand than three.

A new town, a new life. No idea where she'll end up or what she'll do when she gets there. Karen was a few years older than Richard had been when he'd taken that same journey and ended up in Hood River. As he put his arm around Pam and they walked back to her office, he felt sure that Karen would flourish in her new life, just as he had.

*   *   *

'You know the mayor wants to put a statue of you in the park,' Pam said. They were lying in bed in the dark with their arms around each other. Every now and then the light from a passing car would shine across the wall, climb up to the ceiling, and fade out.

'Yeah, well the mayor's an idiot. The city doesn't have enough money to build a skate park, let alone put up a statue.'

'He wants you to pay for it.'

'Ah ha,' he said, 'you're making that up.' He reached down and tickled her naked ribs with both hands. In a moment she had won the battle and was sitting on him, holding his arms down. 'Okay, you win. But I can still reach a certain pendulous part of your anatomy with my tongue.'

'Lick away, slave boy. But while I have your attention, let me ask you something.'

'Sure.'

'Where do you think we're headed—you and I?'

'Right now? I think I'm headed down.'

'I'm serious, Richard.'

He dropped his head back to the pillows and looked up at her. Her curly hair was hanging down in a droopy cloud, obscuring most of her face.

'I can be serious,' he said. 'To tell you the truth, when Rosalind died, I never thought I'd fall in love again. And that was okay, because I had Miriam. I thought part of my wife lived on in my daughter, and I dedicated myself to loving her.

'But since I met you, I've come to realize that Miriam is the center of my life, but she's not all of my life. She can't be, and she shouldn't be. And that leaves room for me to love someone else. And I do.'

'You do?'

'Yes, I do.'

'I would love to hear you say it,' she said.

'Oh, you would, would you?'

'Yes, please.'

'Let go of my arms.' She did. He sat up so she was kneeling over his lap and wrapped his arms around her. They were pressed tightly together, face to face. 'I love you, Pam.'

'And I love you, too, Richard,' she said.

And that was the last talking they did for a long while.

* * *

The next evening, Pam, Richard, and Miriam ate bowls of strawberry ice cream as they watched a movie on Miriam's narrow bed. Kobi lay against the wall, waiting patiently for them to finish so she could climb in bed with her mistress.

Miriam was wearing her new vest; she had hardly taken it off for a week, despite the hot days. When both she and Pam were starting to fall asleep, Richard stopped the movie and shooed her off to the bathroom to brush her teeth. Pam left to go do the same.

'Dad,' Miriam said as he tucked her in, 'how did you and Mom meet?'

He thought for a moment. 'I was on a raft in the Pacific—'

'No, Dad. I mean really.'

'Oh. Well.' He sat down beside her on the bed. 'I tripped over her feet in a movie theater.'

231

'Were you clumsy back then, too?'

'What do you mean? I'm not clumsy. But anyway, no, I don't know how it happened. She had these dainty little feet. But I tripped over them all the same, and spilled my popcorn and Coke all over the floor. I felt like a dope. She was there with a girlfriend, and her friend was laughing her head off, but your mom was very nice to me. She apologized, and asked if I was okay, and she offered to let me share her popcorn. So I sat beside her and we ate a big tub of popcorn together, and every now and then we'd reach at the same time and our hands would touch. When the movie was over I asked her if we could have dinner some time, and she said yes.'

Miriam looked at him steadily. 'And then you fell in love and got married?'

'That's right.'

'And she had me, and then she died.'

'Yes.' He patted her arm, trying to hold back the tears that suddenly welled up.

'Dad?' Miriam said.

'Uh huh?'

'Is Pam going to come live with us?'

He snorted in surprise. But after a moment, he realized that she was serious, and she deserved a real answer. 'I don't know, honey. We haven't talked about it yet. But I think she might. Would that bother you?'

'No, I'd love it. Would she be my mommy?'

'I think she'd love that more than anything else in the world.'

'Could you ask her? Please?'

He laughed. 'All right, but give me a little time, okay?'

'Okay.'

He kissed her and reached over to turn out the bedside light. 'Good night, munchkin.'

Miriam's soft voice floated up from the darkness. 'Good night, Mrs. Bambi.'

Chapter 20: Scrapbook

Dear Mrs. Bambi:

Why is the sky blue?

—*Curious*

Dear George:

It's depressed by all the nasty goings-on down here.

Dear Mrs. Bambi:

My husband and I separated recently after twelve years of marriage. I tried to be a good wife, but I just couldn't take his running around any more. I found out almost as soon as it started, in our first year of marriage, because he really didn't try very hard to hide it. When I confronted him, he said it was his right as the man and the breadwinner to do whatever he wanted, and anyway he was just obeying a biological imperative, whatever that means.

After I moved out, one of my coworkers asked me to dinner. He's a very charming man, extremely handsome, and a great windsurfer. I've known him for many years and always admired him, but he never paid any attention to me, which was proper, I suppose, because I was married.

To make a long story short, we had sex on our first date. I didn't really want to, but he was so charming and I was so, you know, lonely. He insisted and so I said okay. And it was great!

I want to slow down a bit now, but I don't know how, because I gave in that first night, so how can I say no at this point? We get together for dinner once or twice a week, and it seems like we rush through the food to get to bed. The sex is always fabulous, but something's missing. I'd like to actually talk to him, get to know him a little better. He's so charming!

My friends tell me I'm being a naive fool. I think maybe they're jealous. They say he sleeps with every bimbo in the Gorge, and everyone knows it, and now I've joined the club. We never promised to be faithful to each other, but I guess I did hope, a little, that he would, I don't know, maybe fall in love with me?

I don't have any evidence that he sleeps around. It's hard to believe he would do that to me. What do you think?

—*Confused But Happy*

Dear Stupid:

Are you a baboon? Is your rump bright red?

Listen to your friends and dump the worthless weasel right now. Can't you tell when you're being used? He doesn't care about you, he never did, and he never will. Maybe he's charming, but so is a Venus flytrap. You're the fly, you silly insect.

Didn't you learn anything from your scumbag husband? This is the age of lethal sex, my dear, and this playboy may end up killing you.

Dear Mrs. Bambi:

We have two cars and I can't afford the insurance on both of them any more, not to mention the license fees. I have to sell one of them, and I can't decide which one it should be.

I drive my pickup all the time. I use it at work and my dogs love to ride in the back, too. We also have a little import sedan that my wife uses. It's not practical for hauling stuff, it's not very sexy, it doesn't handle winter roads very well, but it gets good gas mileage.

I think it's obvious I should keep the truck, but my wife disagrees. What do you think?

—*Practical Guy*

Dear Mr. Boring:

I think life is short. Sell them both and buy a little red convertible sports car. Grab your wife and go for a long drive in the country. Stop and pick flowers. Go parking and do the beasty thing under the stars.

Tell your boss to buy a company truck instead of using yours. Stay home when the roads are bad. Take your dogs for a walk instead of a drive.

Believe me, you'll live longer and you'll have more fun doing it.

Dear Mrs. Bambi:

I'm a Taurus. What's your sign?

—*Little Bull*

Dear Star-struck:

My sign is DO NOT DISTURB.

Dear Mrs. Bambi:

My little sister is sleeping with her boyfriend. I don't want to be a snitch, but I really don't think it's a good idea, and she won't listen when I tell her to cut it out. She's a junior in high school—what happens if she gets pregnant, or catches some yucky disease? Her life would be ruined.

Mom and Dad would have two cows and fall over dead if they knew their precious little baby was doing THAT. She's been doing THAT for over a year, and I'm really worried for her. What should I do?

—*Big Sis*

Dear Sissy:

Lock her up in the basement until she's twenty-five. While you're at it, lock yourself in there, too.

Okay, that probably won't work. Sit down with her and have a calm, quiet, big-sister chat. Just treating her as an equal will probably shock her socks off. Tell her you know what she's doing, and while it's her own business what she does with her body, it's not a survival trait to get sexually involved with peckerwood high school boys.

Find out what she's doing to protect herself. Educate her if you have to. Some people still think that if they don't French kiss they won't get AIDs or a surprise little bundle of joy.

235

Dear Mrs. Bambi:

I understand hadrons and leptons, but what the heck is a boson? Does it have anything to do with Bozo the Clown?

—*Particular*

Dear Geek:

I love particle physics guys; they're so elementary.

A boson is a particle that has even spin, like a photon or many of the mesons. You can easily tell one of these from other particles—like electrons and protons, both of which have odd spin—by the wild hair and the red, bulbous nose.

Dear Mrs. Bambi:

Why are men so obsessed with long hair? Every man I've ever dated has told me the thing they love most about me is my hair. Great for him: it takes at least two hours a day to keep it in shape. I want to cut it off, but I know I'd never have sex again.

You can always spot a woman who is securely married. She has short hair.

—*Rapunzel*

Dear Goldilocks:

Men like long hair BECAUSE it takes you two hours a day to care for it. That's two hours during which you're not competing with them in business or gossiping about them to your friends or spending their money.

Also, every man has a secret fantasy of having his naked body rubbed down with his woman's flowing hair. Think of Jesus and Mary Magdalene.

Keep your hair. Dump your loser boyfriend. Find a Son of God to go out with.

236

Dear Mrs. Bambi:

School starts next week, and my son refuses to go to fifth grade. He hated fourth grade and he claims that if the teachers don't kill him, the playground bullies will. He won't go shopping for supplies or clothes; he says that's not necessary because he's not going, and I should just save my money for a rainy day.

I've tried to reason with him, but he is the most stubborn kid I've ever known. He insists I'll have to drag him into class every day and chain him to his chair. I don't think I can do that: I can't even get him to eat his green beans.

His father is no help, either. The lazy lug just sits in front of the TV and says that our so-and-so son will go to school if he knows what's good for him.

Help me, Mrs. Bambi, you're my only hope.

—*L*

Dear Leia:

You and Han might have been happier if you'd decided not to have kids. Ruling the Galaxy is a whole lot easier without them.

I assume you've been sending him to public school. Maybe home schooling would be better for your son, or maybe he really needs a private school. If neither of those is possible, have a talk with your school's principal and psychologist; they can probably help.

Or you could just sell the little Lego lizard to a band of cut-throat pirates and be done with it.

Dear Mrs. Bambi:

A new table of recommended body weights just came out. All the weights were revised down—again. Who dreams up these numbers, the American Sisterhood of Anorexics? To meet my ideal weight I'd have to lose twenty pounds, then lop off a few limbs.

Why is our society so obsessed with gauntness? Where did anybody get the idea that these sunken-cheeked skeleton models are glamorous or beautiful?

—*Pleasingly Plump*

Dear Chubby:

When most people worked outdoors, the ideal was pale skin. When food was scarce, plumpness was the sign of health and wealth. Now that many people work under fluorescent lights and food is abundant—and every prepared food is loaded with fat, salt, and sugar—our idea of perfection is a woman who is thin and tan.

The doctors who make the weight charts are idiots. Buck the trend. Live your own life. Ignore society's warped, disfiguring standards. Find your own ideal weight and stop obsessing over your figure, you fat cow.

Dear Mrs. Bambi:

What's the best thing in life?

—*Searching*

Dear Lost and Found:

Love, of course. And pasta. Love and pasta. And chocolate. Love, pasta, and chocolate. And a great car. And world peace. And Mozart.

Okay, it's this: listening to Mozart while driving your Ferrari as your lover hand-feeds you chocolate-covered pasta and tells you that peace has just broken out all over the world.

Also from Chris Mason...

Welcome to Marmot
Population 32

Chris Mason

Part One

* * *

Mayor Material

Bad Directions

There was a wide shoulder ahead. Kevin Calenda pulled his Subaru wagon over onto it and switched off the engine. He rubbed his eyes; he could feel a massive headache coming on.

Stepping out of the car was like walking into an oven. Despite the shade of the Douglas Firs that crowded the narrow road, it was hot and so dry he could feel his skin threatening to crack. It was early afternoon in mid-August, but this was ridiculous. When he'd left Portland this morning the projected high had been 72; this felt like 90.

Kevin did a few stretches before reaching back into the car to grab his notebook. It hadn't sounded that hard when the young woman at the Inn of the White Salmon—more of a girl, really—had given him the directions. He had tried not to let the religious tattoos, nose and eyebrow piercings, and spiky violet-and-black hair sway him, but on reflection he believed he had made a mistake to trust someone who looked like a devout myna bird.

His notes were clear; his handwriting had always been excellent, and his speedwriting was just as legible, to him at least. He was accustomed to transcribing quotes perfectly, word for word. He read, "You've gone the wrong way if you see Bethel Congregational on the left, New Beginnings on the right, and Our Savior on the left. Turn right from our parking lot. You'll see the Mormons on the right, then Grace Baptist on the left. The road will merge with 141A, then after a while you'll pass Husum Church of God on the left, and Mt. Adams Baptist on the right. Bear left in Trout Lake, then pass the Presbyterian Church on the right. After that it's easy, just look for Forest Road 88 then 8810 and it will lead you right to it."

He'd just wanted to do one last hike before leaving the Northwest, and a friend had recommended Sleeping Beauty. All of his hiking books had gone to friends or the Goodwill, so he had to rely on vague—or precise but wrong—directions from strangers. As a result he had made several bad turns and found himself on the outskirts of nowhere three times. He checked his watch: 12:45. He'd hoped to be on the trail almost an hour ago.

There was no traffic at all on this road. He was pretty sure he was back on 141, but he hadn't seen a sign for a while. He did a few more stretches and got back in his car, deciding to give it fifteen more minutes before giving up.

But it didn't take that long. The view suddenly opened up, revealing Mt. Adams in all its glory, the snow pack completely melted but a few glaciers still clinging to the slopes. A few minutes later he entered the town of Trout Lake, which was more like a crossroads than any real town he'd ever seen. The road curved to the left, then he passed the Presbyterian Church, just as the myna bird had said he would.

"Thank you, Jesus," he shouted at the top of his lungs. He felt safe doing that only because his windows were rolled up and the AC was on max. Otherwise, given the rundown rustic look of things around here, he might have been in danger from a random blasphemy-avenging shotgun blast.

Because he was so late, and the myna had turned out to be right in the end, he didn't even consider pulling in to the Forest Service ranger station and asking for real directions. He was just looking for road 88, that should be simple enough.

An hour later Kevin pulled off the road again. The threatening headache had receded with the echoes of his blasphemy, but it was coming back full force now. There was no Road 88. There had probably never *been* a Road 88. He'd be willing to bet that they'd stopped at Road 66. After realizing that he was lost again, he'd turned back and driven more slowly. He hadn't reached the ranger station yet—if it was even still there—but he'd seen plenty of Forest Service road signs, just not an 8810, an 88, or even a lowly 8.

He closed his eyes and rested his forehead on the steering wheel. It was getting too late to safely start a hike. He was going to have to give up.

That's when he heard a car pass him, going away from Trout Lake, in the direction he'd been searching before he turned around. He opened his eyes and looked in the rearview mirror. It was a mail truck. *If anyone could find a way out of this maze,* he thought, *it would be a mail carrier.* So he did a quick U-turn and followed the truck.

He'd thought perhaps the carrier would stop at a roadside mailbox, and he could pull up beside him and ask for directions, but there *were* no roadside mailboxes on this stretch. So he kept following. After a short while they turned onto what looked like a two-lane gravel driveway, but it had a sign proclaiming it to be Trout Lake Creek Road. He hadn't noticed this before, he'd been so intent on finding fictitious numbered roads. But then a new sign said they were *on* Road 88. The myna had neglected to mention that the road had a name as well as a number.

Then—it took his breath away—they passed Road 8810, which was the route to Sleeping Beauty, but after a slight hesitation Kevin kept following the mail truck. He wasn't sure why, except that he knew it was too late to start out. And he was hungry. They crossed the Pacific Crest Trail, which he thought was cool; he'd never hiked that one but he'd often thought he would like to. The truck turned left onto 8871, so Kevin followed it.

This road looked like a *one*-lane gravel driveway. He stayed far enough back so that he wouldn't be blinded by the dust. After another mile or so the truck turned left again. When Kevin reached that spot, he saw a handmade but handsome sign proclaiming Jack Rd. He was feeling a tingling in his fingers, as though he were in a horror movie and had just walked down— alone—into an unlighted basement looking for a weapon to fight the zombies. But he took the turn.

Then he suddenly realized that, unlike the Forest Service roads, Jack Road, while narrow, was paved.

Another left, another handmade sign, this one saying Fish Lk. St., which was also paved. He drove past a small lake on his left, evidently Fish Lake, and glanced back to the right just in time to see a roadside welcome sign, but all he had time to read was "Population 32." After a few more curves he found himself in another town, even smaller than Trout Lake.

"What is a town doing out here in the middle of the woods?" he said aloud.

There were a dozen or so decrepit houses, most of them collapsed in on themselves, but another dozen that were in good repair, with small gardens, freshly-painted siding, and lawn decorations. At the first intersection in town he saw a small cafe and some kind of shop on catty-corners, then he passed another that was surrounded by tidy little cottages, and then the mail truck stopped in front of a modern stone civic building, with Town Hall carved into the marble above the portico and clearly-marked straight-in parking spaces

4

in front. There were some beautiful, tall firs across the street from the hall that looked like overgrown Christmas trees.

Kevin parked his car and got out—and felt his mouth flop open. On a tall stone plinth in front of the handsome Town Hall building was a six-foot high bronze statue of an animal. Maybe a beaver. Kevin walked up and read the plaque on the base. It said simply, "The Marmot."

Available from 186publishing.co.uk and Amazon.com (US) / Amazon.co.uk (UK)

Other books from 186publishing.co.uk:

A Distant Voice in the Darkness
Leela Dutt

A chance meeting at university leads to a relationship that spans marriages, the world and the decades in this sweeping novel from acclaimed author Leela Dutt.
'Echoes of Powell's Dance to the Music of Time'

The Testing of Rose Alleyn
Vivien Freeman

Vivien Freeman's atmospheric novel brings late Victorian England hauntingly to life in the mind of the reader. In this beautifully written romance, we explore the choices facing an independent-minded woman at a time when women struggled for self-determination.
'Beautiful writing'
'A Book to Savor'
'Captivating'
...Amazon reviews

Printed in Great Britain
by Amazon